Spilled Milk
A Novel

Spilled Milk

A Novel

Paul Dale Anderson

2
五
5 Publications

Rockford, Illinois USA

2AM Publications
3211 Broadway
Rockford, Illinois 61108-5941
www.2AMpublications.net

Publisher's Note: This is a work of fiction. Names, characters, places, and incidents are
a product of the author's imagination. Locales and public names are sometimes used
for atmospheric purposes. Any resemblance to actual people, living or dead, or to businesses, companies, events, institutions, or locales is completely coincidental.

Book Layout © 2015 BookDesignTemplates.com

Spilled Milk/ Paul Dale Anderson. -- 1st ed. November 2015
ISBN 13: 978-0-937491-17-1 Trade Paperback
ISBN 10: 0-937491-17-9

E-book ISBN 13: 978-0-937491-18-8
E-book ISBN 10: 0937491-18-7

WARNING!

This novel contains graphic scenes of rape, mutilation, and murder. If such scenes offend you or might possibly trigger unwanted physical or emotional responses, please read no further.

For Ed Rooney, Pulitzer Prize winning reporter for the Chicago Daily News and my journalism professor at Loyola University

For Mike Royko, Roger Ebert, and Nelson Algren, friends long gone

And for Lizza, who urged me to kill again

"The young man or woman writing today has forgotten the problems of the human heart in conflict with itself which alone can make good writing because only that is worth writing about, worth the agony and the sweat. He must learn them again. He must teach himself that the basest of all things is to be afraid; and teaching himself that, forget it forever, leaving no room in his workshop for anything but the old verities and truths of the heart, the old universal truths, lacking which any story is ephemeral and doomed: love and honor and pity and pride and compassion and sacrifice. Until he does so, he labors under a curse. He writes not of love but of lust, of defeats in which nobody loses anything of value, of victories without hope and, worst of all, without pity or compassion. His griefs grieve on no universal bones, leaving no scars. He writes not of the heart but of the glands."
--William Faulkner, *Nobel Prize Acceptance Speech*, December 10, 1950.

"Quoth the Raven 'Nevermore.'"

--Edgar Allan Poe, *The Raven*

I was eighteen when four men abducted me, raped me, and attempted to murder me. I was nineteen when I came out of my year-long coma. No one pulled the plug on me during that time to let me die naturally. It might have been more merciful if they had simply pulled the plug.

I wasn't totally brain dead, but I wasn't conscious, either; for all intents and purposes I was a vegetable. My heart beat, my lungs pumped air into and out of my injured body. But I wasn't consciously aware of my surroundings. I couldn't move. I couldn't do anything for myself. My brain had essentially shut down from the unbelievable horror of what those four men did to me. For more than a year, my body worked at repairing itself while my unconscious mind replayed over and over again what those men did.

Do you know what it's like to be completely helpless? Not just to *feel* completely helpless, but to actually *be* completely helpless? I do.

And then, as if to add insult to injury, I learned my long-overdue hospital bills had been sent out for collection and I couldn't get credit anywhere—would never be able to get credit anywhere—because I had no job and might never be able to work again. I became a ward of the state, and Medicare and state medical supplements kept me alive while I was hospitalized. Otherwise, the hospital would have had no choice but to pull the plug on me and they never would have provided any type of reconstructive surgery or rehabilitation after I came out of my coma.

You may have heard about what happened to me on television news or briefly read about me in the morning papers. I'm Megan Williams, the girl who miraculously recovered after being raped and beaten and physically mutilated and left for dead, then barely surviving in a vegetable-like coma for more than a year. I guess it was a miracle that I did survive. But what those men did to me was far from miraculous, the scars they left will never completely heal, and those men still haven't been caught and punished. Although some wounds have healed, others have not. I need closure. I have been stitched up like Frankenstein's Monster, but many of the holes in my mutilated body still bleed like the stigmata of a martyred saint.

Do you want to see? Go ahead and look because heaven only knows how often others have stared at or had to look at my naked body during the past three and a half years, beginning with those men who cut me and took off all of my clothes and tied me up and did all those terrible things to me. Not only did those four men do unspeakable things to me, but they made me do things to them, too: things I never would have done if my life hadn't been threatened and they hadn't first cut me a little to show me they meant business, proving to me they would certainly cut me a lot more or maybe even kill me if I didn't do whatever they asked. I should have let them kill me. When they were finished with me, they did try to kill me. First, they cut off my nipples and sliced open both breasts. What you see now are only surgical reconstructions. They shoved sharp things inside of me, too, both front and rear, top and bottom. And when they left they surely thought I was dead, and I thought I was dead, too. But I wasn't dead, and I didn't die physically. I should have died. Why didn't I die? It would have been much better for everyone if I had died. You, of all people, must agree it would have been better if I had died.

For one thing, cops take murder a lot more seriously than rape. If I had died, police might have hunted down those men and shot them or locked them up and put them away where they couldn't do bad things to good people anymore. But police never found my four rapists. I don't think police really tried.

My sister Susan found me not long after the rapists had left me for dead. Susan and I shared an apartment and Susan came home from work in time to discover my naked body bleeding out on the floor. Susan worked three to midnight as a waitress at Terri's Restaurant over on Third Street. It was after two AM when Susan finally got home. Susan was twenty-one, and she had taken care of me since Mom and Dad had filed for divorce and life at home had become one unbearable fight after the other. As soon as I turned eighteen, I moved out of my parents' house and moved in with big sister Susan. I'm sorry Susan was the one who found me.

And I guess I'm glad she didn't come home much sooner. If she had, those men would have still been inside the apartment or inside me and they would have done to her what they did to me. But Susan had waited around for late-night diners to finish their desserts and their coffee so she could collect all her tips from the tables.

Police speculated that Susan, not me, had been the planned target of those men. But, when they didn't find Susan at home, they decided to rape me instead. Susan always was an exceptional beauty, good looking and super smart. She still is, despite all that's happened since she found me so badly cut up and barely breathing. I wasn't the only victim of those men, you know. Susan, and even Mom and Dad, were victims, too. Dad blamed Mom and Mom blamed Dad because if I were still living at home those men wouldn't have found me alone in that cheap apartment late at night. You'd think what happened to me would have brought Mom and Dad closer together rather than driving them farther apart. Not so. When I regained consciousness, Mom and Dad's divorce had become final and somehow they both blamed me for making their differences irreconcilable.

I spent another year in and out of the hospital, undergoing a series of reconstructive surgeries to my face, my chest, and my lower body. I can't have children, and I can never have normal relations with any man, even though I look fairly normal if you don't look closely enough to see the ugly scars. The plumbing doesn't work right anymore; some of it doesn't work at all. It still hurts horribly when I use the bathroom. Some parts of my body are completely numb, and others are rife with phantom sensations that recall excruciating pain as though I'm reliving the torture all over again. I'm not normal, and I'll never be normal again.

But I survived. I now have my own apartment that I pay for with my paltry Social Security Disability check. I don't own a car, but I can walk wherever I want to go or take public transportation.

And I own a gun.

The gun is a nine-millimeter Beretta 92-FS. It's very heavy. I can barely lift it to aim. I bought the used Beretta at a pawn shop for five hundred dollars. It's been fired a lot, but not by me. Not yet, anyway.

I keep the gun loaded. Do you want to see my Beretta? I can show it to you. I carry it in my purse. Don't ever try to visit me uninvited. You may discover I know how to shoot the damned thing. I do, you know. I do know how to shoot the damned thing.

It's been almost four years since I was raped and left for dead. The first year I don't remember at all because I was comatose. I remember the second year only too well because I was in constant pain. The third year was filled with what ifs and why mes and feeling very sorry for myself. You're probably feeling sorry for yourself right now, aren't you? You're probably asking yourself: Why me? What if I hadn't gone out tonight? Was there anything I could have done differently?

This year is different than the previous years. This year I don't feel sorry for myself. This year I feel sorry for them, for the four men who raped me and left me for dead. You should feel sorry for them, too.

I don't remember exactly when the change came over me. It wasn't because of the psychiatrists or counselors or clergy who tried so hard to get into my messed-up head. It wasn't because of the prescribed pain-killers or anti-depressants I finally had the fortitude to discard, to throw away in the trash as those four men had trashed my innocence and trashed my life. It wasn't because I had learned to forgive and to forget, because I could never forgive nor forget what those men did to me. I changed because something inside of me—something that had been cut up and left for dead—had changed.

Perhaps it was scar tissue that had grown inside my mind. Perhaps it was remembering hearing in church when I was a child that God demanded "life for life, eye for eye, tooth for tooth, hand for hand, foot for foot, burning for burning, wound for wound, stripe for stipe." Perhaps it was the Devil whispering in my ear the way those men had whispered in my ear while they were doing terrible things to me. For whatever reasons, I've changed. I'm not the same woman I once was.

Have you heard of that heroic woman who hefted a car with her two bare hands to rescue her trapped child from beneath the wheels of a

Volkswagen? Women—even normal women—possess incredible strength. I've lost any children I could possibly have. I don't expect I need to save my strength in order to save a child I'll never have. Do you?

I've lost my parents because of what those men did. My sister no longer looks at me with love but with pity. I no longer see myself as the woman I once was but as the monster I have become. I have lost everything that once mattered to me.

I am no longer normal. I can never be normal.

I still hear voices whispering inside my head. Some of the voices I hear belong to those four men.

But the voice I hear most now is either the voice of God or the voice of the Devil—I don't know which, and I don't care—demanding life for life, eye for eye, tooth for tooth, hand for hand, foot for foot, burning for burning, wound for wound, stripe for stipe.

Because I have lost everything that once mattered to me, the only thing that matters at all to me now is saving the girl-child I'll never have—and saving women everywhere, especially my sister Susan—from going through what I went through.

How, I see you want to ask, will I be able to do that? How? Watch, and I'll demonstrate.

Why me? you have a right to ask before I begin. It's quite simple, really. I chose you because I saw you look at me the way those men looked at me when they raped me. Don't try to deny it. I saw craven lust in your eyes, and eyes are windows to the soul. You wanted to do to me what those men did to me. Didn't you? Don't lie! I know you did.

Are those tears I see glistening in your eyes now? I know you can't answer because I duct-taped your mouth shut so no one will hear your screams. You want to tell me you're sorry? I don't believe you. You can't be sorry yet. I haven't done anything to you yet.

Yes, I came home with you to your own apartment when you asked. Yes, I drugged your drink. Yes, I bound your hands and ankles with duct tape. Yes, I cut your clothes off with this pair of pinking shears. Pinking shears are much stronger than scissors. They cut through anything.

You know what comes next, don't you? This is all I could think about while one of those men held a knife to my throat and made me take the others, then him, into my mouth. I thought about biting it off, actually, but I knew they would kill me if I did. I should have. I should have bit the first guy's cock off. But I was afraid. I was afraid they would cut me worse than they already had. So I didn't bite. I didn't scream when I had the chance. I did what they told me. And they cut me anyway.

So now I'm cutting you. I know you weren't one of the ones who cut me. I haven't found them yet, but I will. And when I do, I will do to them what I'm going to do to you.

You're innocent, you say? You didn't do anything to me? Don't make me laugh. No man is innocent.

But I'm going to show you mercy those men didn't show me. I'm going to make certain you die. How? you ask. I'm going to tease you so your cock fills up with blood before I cut it off. That way I'll make sure you bleed out and die because your heart will be pumping like mad, all the blood in your body will rush into your genitals, and when I cut your dick off the blood will gush out like a fountain.

What's the matter? You don't like the feel of my hands on your body? Isn't there anything I can do to arouse you? How about if I take you in my mouth? Would you like that?

Oh, poor boy! You're too scared to get aroused, aren't you? It's all shrunken and shriveled up like it's trying to hide. I guess I'll just have to cut it off anyway. You'll eventually bleed out, but it may take a long time. Don't try to struggle. It won't do any good.

There. Snip snip. All gone.

Now how should I amuse myself while you're busy bleeding? I know. I'll snip off your nipples. There goes the left one. There goes the right one. Men don't need nipples anyway.

Still not enough blood. Do you have any knives in the kitchen? Don't go away. I'll be right back.

Look what I found. A butcher knife. Hello? Can you hear me? Open your damned eyes! Don't die on me yet. I want you to see what I'm doing to you.

You weren't cooperative when I wanted to show you mercy, so no mercy for you, my pet. Let me roll you over so I can get to your back-side. I want you to feel this. First, we'll cut off that useless bag between your legs. There, that's gone. Next we'll open you up down there just like a woman. I'll insert the blade into your rectum like so. Then I'll cut downwards. Now that's what I call bleeding. You're bleeding a lot. It won't be long now. Still conscious? No? Too bad.

I wonder who will find you like this. Will it be a lover? A friend? Your parents? Your landlord? It doesn't matter. Whoever finds you will be horrified. They will remember what they saw for the rest of their lives.

Don't worry. I won't leave until I'm sure you're dead. I can be patient. I learned to be patient in the hospital. In fact, I was a patient patient in a hospital for more than a year. I was the most patient patient any hospital has ever seen. Then, for another year, I was an impatient patient as an outpatient. You don't appreciate my sick sense of humor? Too bad. I thought it was a funny play on words.

Your heart must be slowing down because your blood stopped gushing and now it's only oozing out slowly, little more than intermittent trickles and dribbles. You know you're about to die, don't you? You feel your life draining slowly away. You can't stop it. It's already too late. Nobody can save you. There's nothing you can do, nothing anybody can do. But you don't want to live now anyway, do you? You don't want to live without your precious penis.

Die, goddamn you! Die, you motherfucker! Die! Die! Die!

CHAPTER TWO

Rodney Engleworth was a writer.

Rodney was an old-school newspaperman who had once worked as an investigative reporter for the *Chicago Daily News* before that venerable rag got swallowed up by the *Chicago Sun-Times* and afternoon circulation and corresponding ad revenues drastically declined back in the mid-seventies. People preferred to consume newspapers in the mornings. either at breakfast tables with morning coffee or riding the El to work downtown in the Loop. Nights were for relaxation, and people watched nightly television news instead of reading. Like so many other old-time newsmen who lost their jobs to mergers and technical innovations, Rodney had deserted the big city to work for a variety of small-town rags until, at age seventy, Rodney Engleworth was relegated to writing a weekly column for a tiny suburban free newspaper that contained mostly ads, obituaries, legal notices, and canned news-releases. Investigative journalism was dead, and Rodney Engleworth lamented the fact that he was still alive.

From age thirty-something until his mid-sixties, Rodney had been, like many great newspapermen, a closet alcoholic. It began with stopping for a drink or two after work to share news tips with other reporters, including rival wordsmiths from the *Chicago Tribune* and *Chicago Today* (the former *Herald-American* of Ben Hecht's *Front Page* fame) located directly across Michigan Avenue from the Sun-Times building. The north loop had plenty of watering holes where reporters gathered, and Rodney Engleworth became a regular at several of them. When Rod lost his job at the *Daily News*, he drank even more, but he did it alone at home in the suburbs. As the years went on, he drank more and more. Rod was still an alcoholic, but he hadn't touched a drop since three months after Helen, his wife of forty-some years and the love of Rod's entire life, died of the insidious cancer that slowly ate up her insides and finally stopped her heart. Rodney woke up very late one afternoon, hungover as hell, and realized there was so much he didn't remember about his last days with Helen and the months after her passing because he had been passed-out drunk. Rod searched in vain for written records and photographs that might remind him of the last ten years of his life, but there were none he could find. Oh, sure, he had piles of weekly newspapers with his by-lined coverage of city council meetings and local sporting events, but they didn't matter. For some strange reason, he felt it was important to recount all that had happened to him personally and exactly when and how it had happened. He racked his brain and began to write down what little he could remember clearly—both the good times and the bad—and he kept writing, and when he wrote he didn't drink. Instead of his usual feel-good column about the best restaurants in town (all of whom advertised in the paper and gave him free drinks when he visited), he began relating his personal story in print. He didn't care if anyone wanted to read about the day Helen's doctor delivered the dreaded diagnosis that Helen—only fifty-seven at the time—definitely had cancer because the biopsy had come back from the pathology lab to prove the tumors were malignant. He didn't care if anybody ever read what he wrote, but Rodney wrote about it anyway. He wrote about the dreaded spectre of death that had hung over his head and Helen's like a shroud, the many operations that carved up his wife the way a cook carved a turkey at Thanksgiving, about the gut-wrenching radiation and the nauseating chemo that made all of Helen's beautiful hair fall out, even her eyelashes and pubic hair. He wrote about the cancer briefly going into remission and then coming back more malignant than ever. He wrote about the fear and frustration, about the pain and the dread. He wrote about the afternoon the oncologist told Helen new tumors had metastasized and spread to her spinal cord. And he wrote about the day the doctors gave Helen less than six more weeks to live because the tumors were spreading now into her vital organs and there was nothing left the surgeons could carve. And he wrote about the day Helen had died, what he could remember of it. Everything after that was a blur, an alcoholic stupor that he couldn't remember no matter how hard he tried. He knew there had been a wake and a funeral and an interment for Helen, but he couldn't even remember where Helen was buried. That was the final straw. Now he was an alcoholic who didn't drink, and as long as he was writing he didn't feel a need to drink. So he wrote his heart out and remained sober.

At first, his editor was angry. "This isn't the type of shit I'm paying you to write," ranted Timothy Goodman, owner, publisher, managing editor, and chief cook and bottle-washer of the *Twin Rivers Gazette* when Rod turned in the first weekly column about Helen. Tim was half Rod's age, a desktop publishing guru who made money selling advertising and not news. People picked up free copies of the *Gazette* at grocery stores and retail merchants more to read about who in town had filed for divorce or bankruptcy than to read news about local events. Rod's weekly column and the stories he wrote about council meetings and sporting events were filler for the display ads and classifieds and obits that kept the *Gazette* in business. But Tim agreed to run a new personal-reminiscences column by Rodney Engleworth on the condition that Rod continue to write all the other stuff the *Gazette* needed to call itself a newspaper. Tim wasn't a writer, though he wasn't too bad at turning out advertising copy, and Tim needed someone to write the filler so he could devote all his precious time to selling advertising and formatting the paper on his desktop computer. Tim spent more time chasing ad dollars and playing with his computer than most men spent chasing women and playing with their hard dicks.

Something about Helen's story struck a chord in the hearts of readers, and circulation doubled after Rod's new column began appearing. Tim was able to charge a lot more for advertising with audited increased circulation, and Tim even added eight additional pages to each weekly edition to accommodate the ads and provide Rod more room for his reminiscences.

Rod and Tim delivered weekly editions of *The Twin Rivers Gazette* themselves, dropping off stacks of free papers at advertisers and local restaurants every Wednesday. Since it was already after six PM when Rod delivered papers to Terri's Restaurant on South Third Street, Rod decided to eat dinner at Terri's, his favorite place to chow down in Twin Rivers. It wasn't merely because Terri's Restaurant was open twenty-four hours, served great-tasting food, and kept one's coffee cup refilled without charging extra no matter how long one stayed that made this Rod's favorite sit-down restaurant. Nor was it because Terri's reminded Rod of the old Billy Goat Tavern in the Emerald City beneath Michigan Avenue where, during his bygone days at the *Daily News*, Rod had devoured cheeseburgers ("cheeps, no fries") and beer alongside Mike Royko, Roger Ebert, and Nelson Algren. It was solely because Susan Williams worked nights at Terri's that Rod ate there at least once a week after Helen passed away and Rod finally sobered up. Susan was tall, slim, blonde, blue-eyed, rosy-cheeked, vivacious, and looked a whole lot like Helen had looked when Rod first met the love of his life more than forty years ago. Helen had been in her mid-twenties back then, and the resemblance of Susan to Helen was remarkable. Rod knew he was too old to be in love with Susan Williams, but he couldn't help himself. Just being in the same room with her made him happy.

Lots of other people loved Susan, too. Rod could tell by the size of cash tips they left on the counter or tables. People who came in and ordered a two-dollar coffee would often leave a dollar tip. Rod always gave Susan at least twenty percent of the bill, plus an extra buck or two for keeping his coffee hot and the cup refilled. Rod didn't have a lot of money, and he didn't want to appear extravagant, but Susan was always friendly and provided excellent prompt service. She deserved the extra bucks.

Susan was one of four waitresses that worked the early evening shift. Rod had never been in Terri's in the mornings when the place was allegedly packed solid with breakfast and luncheon crowds. Since Terri's Restaurant was one of the *Gazette*'s regular advertisers, however, Rod had twice written glowing reviews about his evening dinners at Terri's. All of Terri's waitresses knew his name and treated him with respect. Terri's was one of the few places in town where people still appreciated the power of the press.

And Terri's didn't serve alcohol.

Twin Rivers had been a relatively-new residential community on the Metra line west of Chicago when Rod and Helen bought their single-story bungalow a few years after they married. Houses in Chicago and immediately surrounding suburbs were far too expensive for the newly-weds, so they had looked farther and farther west until they found a house they could afford. Rod could easily hop an express train and be downtown in thirty minutes. Helen worked in an office in nearby Oak Brook, and Twin Rivers seemed like a reasonable commute by car. Helen also thought Twin Rivers was the perfect place to raise a family. The family they had planned when they bought a house, however, never came to fruition. Rod eventually appropriated the spare bedroom that would have been a baby's nursery into a workroom where Rod once kept his Royal manual typewriter and now kept his HP computer and printer. He had three four-drawer Steelcase filing cabinets for his notes and notebooks, a wooden bookshelf for reference books and dictionaries, and piles of faded newspapers stacked on the floor containing stories he had written.

Forty years after moving into the house out in the sticks, the countryside around Twin Rivers had filled in with thousands of other houses and businesses that made the once-small town part of the greater Chicagoland community. It was impossible now to tell where one suburb ended and another began. Hundreds of thousands of people lived near Twin Rivers and the Metra line. Not everyone who lived in the area was nice. Where once local residents were unafraid to leave their houses and cars unlocked, they now added deadbolts to their doors and installed Lojacks in their automobiles.

Rod dropped off the stack of newspapers at the cashier's counter and took a booth in Susan's section near the coffee counter in the back of the restaurant. Susan immediately brought him a cup of black coffee and a menu. Rod already knew what he wanted, and he ordered an open-faced hot beef sandwich with mashed potatoes and gravy. Susan took his order and submitted the order to the kitchen.

"I was so sorry to read that your wife died," Susan said when she returned with a plate piled high with food. "I read your columns each week, and I should have said something to you before now. I know how terrible it feels to lose someone you love."

"Have you lost someone close to you?" asked Rod.

"My sister. She didn't die, but she may as well be dead. It's been almost four years since the tragedy, and Megan and I never talk about what happened. In fact, Megan doesn't talk to me about much of anything anymore."

"Was your sister in an automobile accident?" asked Rod.

"No. She was raped and her body badly cut up with sharp knives. She might have died if I hadn't found her and called 911."

"*You* found her?"

"Yes."

"I'm sorry. It must have been terrible."

"It was. Terrible for Megan, and terrible for me."

"Where did this happen?"

"Right here in Twin Rivers. At the apartment Megan and I shared on Fifth Street."

Rod didn't remember hearing about an assault here in town, but four years ago Helen was undergoing treatment for a recurrence of the cancer that eventually killed her. Rod wasn't paying attention to anything but his wife four years ago. When Rod wasn't at the hospital, he was home drunk or drinking to get drunk.

"Did the police catch the men who raped your sister?"

"Not yet," replied Susan.

Rod knew that the window of opportunity to apprehend criminals began to close after seventy-two hours. If the cops hadn't caught Susan's sister's rapists in four years, that meant police had no viable suspects and the window, though not completely closed, might as well be. Twin Rivers had a very small police force, and they had no time to work cold cases.

Not only had the population of Twin Rivers increased dramatically in recent years, the populations of surrounding suburbs had also increased and so had violent crime. A quarter of a million people lived within a fifteen-minute commute of here, and more than five million people lived within an hour's drive. Looking for those rapists without a solid lead was like looking for a needle in a haystack.

"I'm sure the police are doing all they can," said Rod. "Was your sister able to identify any of the perpetrators?"

"She saw their faces. She described them to the police when she came out of her coma."

"I'm so sorry," said Rod again.

"When you described how helpless you felt when you saw your wife lying in bed after the doctors had cut on her, you described exactly how I felt when I discovered my sister. You put into words what I couldn't. Thank you. I think you helped a lot of people with what you wrote. I know you helped me."

"You want to do something," said Rod, quoting verbatim from memory what he had penned in last week's column, "but there's nothing that you *can* do. You pray that it's only a dream, but you know it's not a dream. This isn't some horrible nightmare you can wake up from and everything will be the way it always was before. This is real, and you know nothing can nor will be the same ever again. Not ever. You feel powerless, like being caught in the turbulent current of some onrushing river cascading through rough rapids prior to plunging over the cliff at the top of a waterfall. Everything moves too fast to comprehend.

Your body and mind are reeling. You can't stop what's happening and you can't escape. You feel like you're drowning, and you are."

"That's what I felt when I found my sister," said Susan.

"She survived?"

"She was in a coma for more than a year. Then she had to have extensive plastic surgery. But, like Humpty Dumpty, doctors couldn't put her back together again the way she was. She's horribly scarred, inside and out."

"And you?" Rod asked. "What about your scars? Have your scars healed?"

"I still have nightmares about finding Megan cut up. Only, in some of my nightmares, it's me I find like that."

"They say time heals all wounds," offered Rod. "Give it time."

"Do you believe that?" asked Susan.

"I want to," said Rod. "They also say what doesn't kill you makes you stronger. I'm not sure I believe that, either."

"I have to go take care of other customers," said Susan. "I just wanted to thank you for writing. It helps to know I wasn't the only one to feel that way."

When Susan came back to refill Rod's coffee cup, she smiled but said nothing more. She seemed embarrassed at already having said much more than she had intended.

Rod decided he would stop by the local police station tomorrow or the next day and talk with some of the cops. Although he hadn't covered a police beat in nearly forty years, he did know one or two men on the Twin Rivers force. If nothing more, he could get a copy of the official police report which should be public record. Maybe he could even talk someone into taking a fresh look at the case.

Meanwhile, Rod still had papers to deliver. Here he was, seventy years old, and still a paperboy like he had been at fourteen. Only now, instead of peddling a bicycle and throwing individual papers at front porches of neighborhood houses, he drove a car and dropped bundles of papers at commercial establishments. The more some things changed, the more other things remained the same.

Rod left a hefty tip on the table and paid his bill at the cashier's counter. He still had work to do, and Rod had miles to go before he could sleep.

CHAPTER THREE

You thought I would be easy, didn't you? You thought because I had scars all over my face and my body that I'd be grateful when a good-looking guy like you paid attention to me. I am grateful. I am grateful to have this opportunity to see your body naked. Do you want to see my naked body? You showed me yours, now I'll show you mine. My body isn't pretty anymore. It used to be pretty, real pretty. That was before I was raped and cut almost to shreds.

Look closely at the scars. Notice how my breasts are stitched to-gether. The nipples aren't real, you know. They were made by a plastic surgeon, and they only look real. But I can't feel my nipples or my breasts. Most of the nerves in my body were severed by those men or by the surgeons trying to save my life. I don't feel much of anything anymore. Oh, I still feel pain. Most of my pain isn't real, either, merely recurring memories of the same pain I felt when those men raped me and cut me.

Let me show you my ruined vagina. You can't touch it because your hands are tied, but you can look. Touching my pussy wouldn't do you any good anyway. I don't feel anything down there now but pain.

You don't know about pain, do you? You've never felt like your skin was on fire because your skin had been peeled away from nerve endings, have you? Surgeons took skin from my inner thighs to patch my face. This scar on my neck is where the men started to cut on me. They held a knife to my throat and made me do terrible things and then they made me swallow. When I tried to spit out what they deposited in my mouth, they cut my throat and made me swallow blood along with semen. They made me take each of them into my mouth. Each time I hesitated or didn't do exactly what they wanted, they cut me.

And then they shoved themselves inside my vagina and my anus and they nearly ripped me apart. I was a virgin, you know. I was only eighteen and I was a good girl. I was saving myself for marriage. I had never done more than heavy petting before they raped me.

Who would want to marry me now? You? I can't have children, you know. Nothing down there works anymore. I can't have children and I can't have normal sex. All I can have now—all I want now—is revenge.

I know you weren't one of the men who raped me. Someday I'll find them and do to them what I'm about to do to you. But they aren't here now, and you are. So I'll practice on you what I intend to do to them.

Where shall I start cutting? You have a pretty face. I'm sure most girls find you attractive. Let's see how you look with patches of skin peeled away from your forehead. Should I use a butcher knife? How about a box-cutter? Yes, a box-cutter has a sharp blade. Don't worry if the blade is a little rusty or dirty. You won't live long enough to get an infection.

Let's see if I can make a straight line. Oh, don't move around like that. Look what you made me do! I cut too deep. I only wanted to peel away the top layer of skin. Now I'll have to make the other cuts deep like the first one. There. Lots of blood. Want me to wipe the blood out of your eyes so you can see what I'm going to do next?

Let's take some skin off your inner thighs. I'll insert the blade north of the knee, draw it slowly up the thigh, and stop before I reach your scrotum. Now a parallel line up the same thigh. Then cross-cuts on top and bottom. There. I'll peel the skin off.

How about the other leg? No? Then let's start on the stomach. I'll insert the blade just below your navel. Let's cut downwards toward your penis. Should I stop? Oh, this is so much fun! I can't stop now.

I see you haven't been circumcised. I think it's time someone took care of that for you. I need something to hold your penis when I cut the foreskin. Let's see what I have in my purse. Oh, look! I found a pair of pliers. What can I do with these? Let's start with your scrotum. I'll open up the jaws of the pliers real wide so your left testicle fits between them. Then I'll squeeze on the handles of the pliers until the jaws squeeze tight on your left testicle. Does that hurt? I hope so.

Oh, I felt the testicle go crunch. Something broke inside. Let's do the other one so you have a matching pair. There. All done.

Now let's take the end of your penis in the jaws of the pliers like those men forced my jaws to accept their cocks. I'll pull the head all the way out of the sheath. Stop moving around like that or I'll cut off more than I plan. We'll slice off all of the skin, not just the foreskin. If I don't cut evenly all around, I'll just have to cut deeper and take off another layer. So much blood! Did you ever see so much blood before?

Now you know pain. That's what I felt like when those men cut me.

I want you to feel the pain for a long time. I've felt my pain for four years. Don't worry. You won't have to endure your pain as long as me. But I'm not going to kill you quite yet. I want to enjoy your pain while it lasts.

Are you still conscious? I lost consciousness after they shoved a knife up my ass. Let's roll you over so I can do the same to you.

This is a butcher knife with a nine-inch blade. The blade is about an inch wide. See how it feels as I insert it into your rectum. If I were to insert the blade all the way inside, you would surely die. So I'll only insert it part-way. Feel that? Or have you passed out from the pain already?

You have a nice house. I noticed framed pictures of your family on the mantle in the living room when you brought me into your home earlier tonight, hurriedly ushering me through the living room toward the bedroom. Where are your wife and children? Are they away for the entire weekend? Visiting grandparents perhaps? Why aren't you with them? Don't you wish now you had gone with them?

When the cat's away, the mouse will play. That's what you thought, wasn't it? How long was it after they left the house that you went out to bars to pick up women? An hour? Two? I bet you couldn't wait.

What did you think when you saw me sitting alone in that dingy bar over on Third Street? Did you think I was a prostitute? No, the way I look I couldn't be a prostitute. Did you think I would be easy, or were you simply curious about my scars? You picked me up, I didn't pick you up. Oh, sure, I smiled at you when you sat down. You saw me looking at you out of the corners of my eyes. I was wondering when you'd make a move on me. I knew you would. I could tell what you wanted when you walked in.

You probably couldn't see all my facial scars from a distance in the dim light, but you saw them clearly when you moved closer. You didn't have to buy me a drink, but you did. You didn't have to invite me to go home with you, but you did. You didn't see me slip the sedative into your drink. It clearly warns on the prescription bottle not to drink alcohol when taking this drug or you'll experience extreme drowsiness. You could barely keep your eyes open as you drove me to your house. You got out of your clothes while I was getting out of mine, and as soon as you put your head on the pillow, you passed out.

That's how I managed to put duct tape on your wrists and ankles and cover your mouth with tape. An itsy-bitsy teeny girl like me couldn't manipulate a big man like you without a little help from the pharmacy. I waited patiently for you to wake up before I did anything else to you. I'm nothing if not patient.

Notice how patient I am now? I'm in no hurry to see you die. I want you to know what real pain is like. What else can I do to cause pain while I'm waiting for you to bleed out?

Do you wonder what your wife and children will say when they come home and find you like this? Do you think they'll know what you tried to do to me? Do you think they'll know that their husband and father went out to a sleazy bar where he picked up a scarred woman and brought her into their home and tried to fuck her on the same bed your wife sleeps on? Do you think they'll care what happened to me that made me do this to you?

No. They don't care about me. No one cares about me. It's as if I died when those men raped me and cut me. Maybe I did die. Maybe I'm a ghost.

No, I don't think I'm a ghost. Ghosts have no material substance that can hold a knife or a box-cutter. Ghosts can't do to you what I'm doing to you.

Let's see what else I can do. Your upper back is still intact. Let's take all of the skin off your back, peel it like peeling a potato. We'll use the butcher blade instead of a paring knife. I'll cut your skin into long strips. Then I'll pull on it as I work the knife between the layers of dermis. How does that feel? Cat got your tongue? Ugh. This is getting messy.

Please excuse the latex gloves I'm wearing. These are the same kind of gloves plastic surgeons wore when they worked on me. I buy the gloves at the drug store in a big box of one hundred. Not only do latex gloves keep my hands from getting bloody, they don't leave finger-prints. I put the gloves on before I touched anything. The men who raped me wore gloves exactly like these. Those men were prepared when they broke into the apartment. I came prepared, too. I brought gloves, pliers, knives, and the box-cutter in my purse.

When I've finished with you, I'll use your shower to wash blood from the gloves, knives, and box cutter. I may even take a shower my-self to get your spattered blood off my naked body. Then I'll dress and go home all sparkly clean.

Of course, I'll never feel really clean after what those men did to me. How can I? How can I ever be clean again?

Are you still with me? No? Passed out from the pain? You still have a little blood left. I can tell because as I strip your back, blood wells up. It doesn't pour out like it did before so you're probably getting close to taking your last breath.

I can't tell you how much I've enjoyed our time together. Being with you tonight was more therapeutic than years of talking with psychia-trists. I'm almost finished with your back. Shall I turn you over and do the same to your front?

Oh, poor boy! You're so limp. Moving you is like moving a sack of potatoes.

I know what I'll do next. I'll draw a big smiley-face on your neck. We'll use the big butcher knife and cut your throat from ear to ear. Now you look like you're grinning, like you're happy. I feel like the comedian who always leaves his audiences smiling. Or did that comedian always leave them laughing? I forget which.

I can take off the duct tape now. First, your lips. Then your wrists. Finally, your ankles. I'll simply ball it up and put all the used duct tape into a zip-lock baggie I brought along in my purse. You look so peaceful. All the pain is gone now, isn't it? Opening your throat took all of the pain away.

They—the men who raped me—thought they had done that to me, too. When those men had finished with me they cut me all over and thought I would bleed out before anyone could find me. They didn't expect my sister Susan would find me. I hadn't bled out all the way when paramedics arrived and pumped plasma back into my veins. Susan should have let me die. It would have been better for everyone if I had died.

A part of me did die that day, the good part of me. When I lost my innocence, I heard dark whispers in my mind that made me want to do terrible things to the men who raped me. I was too scared to do any of those things to them then. But I'm no longer scared. What do I have to be scared about? The worst things that could happen to me have already happened. I lost my virginity, my ability to have children, the feeling in most of my body, and the unblemished looks I once had. I've lost my ability to earn a living and to get credit. I've lost my family—my mother and my father and my sister Sue avoid me like the pariah I've become— all because some men thought it would be fun to take a woman against her will. Those men had their fun. Now I'm having mine.

Wasn't that fun? No? You're smiling like you had fun. It wasn't the kind of fun you expected when you picked me up, was it?

I'll leave you now. I want whoever finds you to know we had fun together. Your poor penis looks raw. Isn't that what happens after you have fun? Your penis gets raw and practically disappears? I didn't cut it off completely, you know. I just whittled it down a little.

Do you think the men who raped me will know I'm going to do that to them when I find them? I hope so. I will find them, you know. I saw their faces when they raped me, and I'll never forget what each of them looks like. They wore gloves, but they didn't bother to hide their faces because they planned to kill me when they finished. All were white men. The leader was tall, maybe 23 or 24 years old, clean-shaven, black hair and hazel eyes, and he had a scar on his abdomen that might have been from a knife wound. Another was a year or two younger, medium height, skinny, real long greasy-red hair, and bright blue eyes. A third man was good-looking like you, except he had a beard. He was medium build, and he had blond hair and blue eyes. The fourth was still a teen-ager, maybe sixteen or seventeen. He had acne all over his face and back. His hair was long and his eyes were brown. I'll recognize all of them when I see them again. I'll keep looking until I find them.

The police speculated the four men saw my sister Susan in the res-taurant where Sue still works and followed her home a time or two just to learn where Susan lived. Susan usually leaves work around midnight, and the four men thought they could simply enter the apartment before midnight and wait for her to arrive home. They easily picked the lock on the back door because I had left the deadbolt unlocked for Susan and the key lock in the doorknob was real flimsy. They didn't expect to find anyone else in the apartment when they entered, but when they saw me they decided to rape me instead of Susan.

They could have quickly killed me and sat around and waited for Susan to come home, but they didn't want to just kill me. They put a knife to my throat and told me not to scream. They slapped duct tape over my mouth and bound my wrists behind my back with more duct tape. They cut off all my clothes and pawed me inside and out. Then the leader put the big knife to my throat and made a small cut to show me he meant business before he pulled the duct tape from my mouth. He made me do each of the men, and then he took his own turn. Finally, he put more duct tape over my mouth so no one could hear me scream as they raped me and cut me up.

They must have tired of waiting for Susan, or maybe they felt they had enough fun for one night. They left before Susan got home, thank God. Otherwise, they would have killed Susan, too.

Someday those four men will come back to do Susan. She's the one they really wanted to rape, and they'll try again when they think it's safe. My sister moved from that apartment on Fifth Street, and she's no longer listed in the telephone directory. But she still works at Terri's Restaurant. Eventually, those men will visit the restaurant and follow Susan to her new apartment on Eleventh Street. This time they'll make sure Susan lives alone before they try to rape her.

I live in an apartment directly behind Susan's building. Susan doesn't know I moved again, doesn't know I live close enough to observe the back stairs leading up to the back door of her apartment through a pair of binoculars. I make certain I'm home every night before midnight so I can see Susan park her Toyota in the alley behind her building, climb the stairs, and enter her apartment. I wait for those men to come. I know they will come.

I can be patient. I'm nothing if not patient. I learned to be patient in the hospital.

When those men come, I will be ready for them. I know how to use a gun, and as you discovered tonight, I know how to use knives. I can get from the back door of my apartment to the back door of Susan's in less than three minutes if I hurry. I've practiced, and I've timed myself. I should be able to reach those men before they have time to pick Susan's door lock.

I don't care what happens to me after that. If I have to shoot those men, I will. But I won't shoot to kill. I'll only wound them. I want them to be alive when I start cutting. I'll do them right there on the back steps where everyone can see. I want people to see me get my revenge. I'll cut the cocks off each of those four men and stuff their own bloody dicks in their mouths. What happens to me after that is totally irrelevant. I don't give a flying fuck.

It's time for me to go home now and watch for Susan to get home from work. Being here with you tonight has been tons of fun, hasn't it? In fact, you'd have to say it's been a real scream.

CHAPTER FOUR

Rod spent Thursday and Friday researching Megan Williams. He searched first through the online files of the *Gazette* on one of the two desktop computers in the *Gazette* front office. Tim rented a small storefront on Third Street for the *Gazette*, and Tim—still a bachelor at thirty-four—lived in a two-room apartment in the back part of the office. The *Gazette*'s front office was less of a working newsroom anyway than it was a convenient place for people to drop off advertisements and news releases. Tim had provided, on one side of the room, a beat-up old wooden desk and a not-so-new Dell computer for Rod to use. Tim's own desk was more modern. It had an attached credenza where Tim's two computers—a desktop HP running windows and a Macintosh with a complete desktop publishing system—were networked to a color laser printer and a scanner. Tim plugged ad copy, Rod's text, and photographs into something called Adobe Creative Suite and InDesign. He fiddled and tweaked copy and pictures so perfectly-laid out page-proofs emerged from the oversized laser printer. Tim e-mailed a .pdf of each issue to the company that actually printed the newspaper each week.

Rod searched through all of the .pdfs saved on the hard drive. Tim had set up a wi-fied local area network that allowed Rod to access the stored files going back six years. Anything earlier than that, Rod would have to page through hard copies of the newspaper. Although the *Gazette* didn't run regular news stories, it did carry police blotter listings of crimes committed within the Twin Rivers geographical boundaries, copied from the city's web site. Only the category of crime (aggravated assault, aggravated battery with firearm, armed robbery, home invasion, homicide investigation) and the date and location of occurrence were listed. Rod went back four years and searched through issues until he found an aggravated assault to an unnamed woman living on Fifth Street. He wrote the date down in his notebook.

Rod checked the online issues of the *Daily Harold* and the *Chicago Tribune* for an entire week after the date of the assault. Neither newspaper had bothered to run a story on Megan Williams' rape and attempted murder. Rod did find a small article in the *Suburban Trib* about a Megan Williams coming out of a coma after a year in a suburban hospital, but nothing was mentioned about Megan being a rape victim. It was Friday afternoon when Rod finally found time to go to the police department and ask to speak with officer Joel Giffords. Rod had interviewed Giffords for the *Gazette* after Giffords made detective and was appointed to the county-wide major crimes task force. A dozen local communities had organized the regional task force to combat the increase in major felony crimes, especially violent crimes, across jurisdictional boundaries. If anyone knew what was being done to solve the assault on Megan Williams, it would be Joel Giffords.

Criminals often committed crimes in different cities, and the task force's main task was to connect the scattered dots on similar crimes and spearhead a coordinated effort to apprehend violent criminals. Besides collecting case files and gathering intelligence, the task force provided a cohesive unit with the authority to cross jurisdictional boundaries.

It had been nearly six years since Rod had done the puff-piece on Giffords, but the man still remembered Rod and the nice things Rod had said about him in print. Joel Giffords was a big guy, six-two and two hundred pounds. Rod felt tiny at just six-feet and weighing in at less than 170 the last time he checked. Giffords was in his early forties now, his brown hair still cut in a crew-cut the way he had worn it when he was an MP in the Army. Rod considered Giffords a good cop, probably too good to be wasted on a small town like Twin Rivers.

"Sorry to hear about your wife," Giffords offered as he shook hands with Rod.

"You read about it in the *Gazette*?" asked Rod.

"Sure did. I read your stuff every week. What can I help you with?"

"I understand there was an assault and attempted murder in town about four years ago. I thought I'd do a follow-up piece on how efficiently our Twin Rivers Police solve crimes."

"You won't be able to use that case as an example of a solved crime," said Giffords. "We have a pretty good clearance rate, but the Williams case is still open."

"Why?" asked Rod. "I understand the victim gave a complete description of her assailants. Plus, they must have left DNA all over the crime scene."

"We collected DNA samples on all four assailants in the Megan Williams case. We've also matched our samples to DNA recovered at other rape scenes in nearby locales. Problem is, Mr. Engleworth, we can't match the DNA to any known perpetrators in the national databases. None of the four have been arrested previously for a felony, and none of the men served in the armed forces. Their DNA isn't linked to a name, and the perps didn't leave fingerprints. Plus," added Giffords, "Megan Williams remained in a coma for a year following the assault. She wasn't able to provide descriptions of her assailants for an entire year after the crime, and none of the other rape victims lived to provide descriptions at all."

"So you haven't caught the four men?"

"Not yet. Why are you so interested in that case? I can give you a dozen recent cases we've solved. Burglaries, home invasions, hit-and-runs, even a homicide. But the Williams case is still unsolved."

"How many other major crimes remain unsolved?"

"Only two that occurred in Twin Rivers. The Megan Williams case from four years ago, and a local homicide from two weeks ago."

"A homicide? I didn't hear about a homicide in town."

"We haven't released any information about it yet. A young guy, late twenties, lived alone. His landlord only found the body yesterday when the smell became so bad everyone in the building noticed and complained. I just got the autopsy report back an hour ago."

"You're working homicide now? I thought you were still on the task force."

"I'm still on the task force. But this homicide has some similarities to other homicides in nearby towns so the task force got called in on it."

"What kind of similarities?"

"I'm sorry. I can't talk to the press about an on-going investigation."

"How about off the record? The *Gazette* never runs any hard news anyway, so you don't have to worry. I'll do a puff-piece on the wonderful work the Twin Rivers Police Department did clearing the other cases. I won't mention anything about the Williams assault or the recent homicide."

"Why are you so interested in the Megan Williams case and the recent homicide?"

"I'm an old newspaperman, and my nose for news is twitching."

"Just curiosity?"

"Yes. And in the interests of full-disclosure, I should tell you I learned of the Williams case from Megan's sister. She's a waitress at Terri's Restaurant. I don't know Susan well, but I do know her."

"Did she tell you we think she was the intended victim and not Megan?"

"No, she didn't."

"We had Susan staked out for a month or two after the assault on Megan. We thought maybe the four guys would make another try on her. They didn't."

"Do you think they still might?"

"Hard to tell. Those bad boys have been busy elsewhere. We're sure they're responsible for the rapes and murders of at least three other women and probably a dozen more we can't be certain about. Megan Williams was the only one they left alive to identify them, though I'm certain they didn't intend for her to survive. They may try to kill Megan again if they discover she's still alive. And they might go after Susan to get to Megan or simply go after Susan because Susan is a looker."

"What are my chances of seeing the complete case file?"

"Slim and none. I can get you a copy of the four-year-old case report, but that's the best I can do."

"I'd appreciate that. And then we can talk about the cases the department has solved."

"I'll turn you over to Elsie Dorr. She's the department's public information officer. You can pick up the Williams case report at the desk on your way out."

"Thanks."

"Don't mention it. I appreciate the piece you wrote about me when I made detective. You're a good writer, Engleworth. I looked you up.

You worked the crime beat on the *Daily News* way back when, didn't you?"

"A long time ago."

"I read some of the stories you did on Sam Giancana and the Chicago Outfit. You've got a knack for tying things together, don't you?"

"I used to have a knack," said Rod. "That was a long time ago, Detective."

"Did you really see that guy the mob allegedly hung on meathooks in Cicero and shoved an icepick up his ass?"

"Aiuppa and Accardo allegedly ordered that hit. I witnessed the crime scene and wrote about what I saw and whom informed sources said did the job for the Chicago mob. Supposedly, Angelo "The Hook" LaPietra did the wet work in that Cicero warehouse. He used a blow torch and an icepick. He took a blowtorch to the victim's private parts and used an icepick on the eyes and rectum."

"So if I showed you autopsy pictures, you wouldn't be too squeamish to look at them?"

"I've seen lots of bodies in seventy years."

"This one is cut up pretty bad. And it's partly decomposed."

"The guy from Twin Rivers killed two weeks ago whose body was found only yesterday?"

"Yeah, that's the one. The only other person I've seen cut up like that was Megan Williams."

"Why would you show me the autopsy photos?"

"Just a hunch. You were real good at putting two and two together and coming up with the right answer. Think you could do it again?"

"I could try. You think there's a connection between the two cases?"

"We don't have a motive yet for the killing. I've got my own theories, but I could use a second opinion. You game for taking a look? Off the record, of course."

"Show me the pics."

Giffords open a locked filing cabinet and removed a manila envelope. There were twenty-some color thirty-five millimeter glossies in the envelope.

The victim had been male, but it was difficult to tell from the photographs. His penis and scrotum had been removed, and there was a deep gash between the anus and where the genitals had once been. In another photo, the man's nipples had been severed from his chest. There were ragged holes where the nipples and surrounding flesh had once been. Dried blood looked black in the photos. The man looked like a pinto pony. His flesh was pale white, the blood black.

His face was frozen in agony, indicating he'd been alive, awake, and aware when his genitals were cut off and his nipples removed. He died of exsanguination when at least five pints of blood escaped from gaping wounds.

Black blood was everywhere. The corpse was displayed on the floor of his living room, the carpet stained black. His clothes were piled on the floor near a couch. There were two empty cocktail glasses lying on the floor next to the body.

"The glasses had been washed clean," said Giffords. "No prints nor DNA on either of them. They were put back in place by the assailant after the fact."

"Did you find a murder weapon?"

"No. The medical examiner said the cuts were made by a butcher knife and a pair of pinking shears. Notice the saw-toothed marks on the base of the penis."

"She cut the guy's dick off with pinking shears?"

"That's what it looks like. Why do you say she instead of he?"

"It's obvious to me a woman did this. Women use knives and pinking shears all the time, and most men don't. Plus, a woman would feel more comfortable than any man doing this to another man. A man might feel comfortable using a gun and a razor blade to kill another man, but he wouldn't cut a guy's dick off unless he was a deranged sicko like Angelo "The Hook" Pietra sending a message from the mob. Then he might do something this extreme. But those kinds of mob hits have gone out of style these days. And the victim doesn't look like he's connected to the mob. Who was he? Do you have a name and occupation?"

"Benjamin Willard, age twenty-nine. Divorced. His landlord said he was quite a ladies' man. Neighbors said Willard regularly picked up women and prostitutes and brought them to his apartment. He worked construction during the summer and did odd-jobs and snow-plowing during the winter. He drank a lot when he wasn't working."

"Any police record?"

"Minor traffic violations. Some unpaid parking tickets."

"So it's definitely not a mob hit. Could be a revenge killing of some sort. He was divorced? Did you check out the ex-wife?"

"She's happily remarried. She was at home with her new hubby at the time this killing took place. She seemed genuinely broken up when I told her Willard was dead. She shed real tears."

"Perp could be a prostitute Willard picked up somewhere. Maybe he brought a prostitute home and beat her. Maybe he refused to pay her."

"Possible."

"You said there were similarities between this murder and the assault on Megan Williams? What kind of similarities?"

"Nipples cut off. Blade inserted into the rectum. Left to bleed out. Duct tape placed over mouth and around wrists."

"Do you think the four men who raped Megan Williams killed Willard?"

"Do you?"

"No. I don't think Willard was killed by a man. I think Willard was killed by a woman."

"So do I."

"Whoever did it must have really hated Willard. No one cuts off a guy's dick unless she hated the guy."

"Or hated dicks."

"So what are you saying, Detective? Killing Willard wasn't personal but symbolic?"

"What do you think, Mr. Newspaperman?" asked Giffords.

Rod studied all of the pictures again before he answered. "Yes," he said. "She was sending a message. It's obvious."

"Who was the message meant for?"

"Men? All men? A particular man? I don't know."

"You haven't lost your knack, Engleworth. You just confirmed what I thought when I saw the body at the scene." Giffords scooped up the photographs and put them back into the manila envelope and locked the envelope up in the filing cabinet. "You would have made a good cop."

"I've known a few cops in my time. Some good, some bad. All I ever wanted to do was be a newspaperman. I grew up with papers, reading them, delivering them, writing for them. In my day, reporters wanted to work for newspapers, not radio or television. My day is gone, and it's too late for me to change. I'll always be a newspaperman."

"You still have an audience. Everyone in town reads your column."

"That's nice to know."

"Come on, I'll introduce you to Elsie Dorr. She can get you the info on our solved cases. I'll have a case report waiting for you when you finish."

"Thanks, Detective."

"Call me Joel."

"My friends call me Rod."

Elsie Dorr was a petite redhead whose official title, displayed on her business cards and on a name plate screwed to the front of her desk, was Twin Rivers Police Department Community Relations and Public Information Officer. She was a uniformed police officer in her early thirties who wore a big gun in a leather holster on her hip, and she talked real fast like a native-born New Yorker. She had a firm grip when she shook hands, and her hazel eyes were friendly and open like she genuinely enjoyed meeting people. Rod liked her the moment he met her.

"We have the best case clearance rate in the county," she said, handing Rod a printout of the same police blotter Rod had viewed online. "We've solved all major crimes in our jurisdiction during the last five years, except the two cases Sergeant Giffords says you already know about. I've crossed those two off this printout. During the past five years, we've had a total of 647 felony cases. Six-hundred and thirty-three have been successfully prosecuted in county court. Twelve are awaiting trial dates. Two cases remain open."

Rod glanced at the printout. There were only nineteen homicides listed, less than four murders a year. Six of those homicides, Dorr explained, had been committed during armed robberies of businesses or home invasions. Eleven killings were attributed to a spouse, close family member, or neighbor of the victim. Two were bar brawls that escalated into murder when one or both parties produced a weapon. In seventeen of the nineteen homicides, one or more eyewitnesses identified the assailant.

The other six-hundred and fourteen felonies included home invasions, physical assaults either with or without a weapon, sexual assaults, armed robberies, burglaries, motor vehicle theft, and a half-dozen other categories of major crimes. Again witnesses helped solve many of those crimes by identifying suspects. Twin Rivers had a relatively low incidence of violent crimes for a city of nearly one-hundred thousand inhabitants and a relatively high case clearance rate.

In fact, despite a small police force of fewer than two hundred sworn officers, Twin Rivers' clearance rate was phenomenal. "Nationally," Dorr said, "less than half of all violent crimes and less than twenty percent of property crimes are cleared by arrest or exceptional means within a year of the occurrence of the crime. We've managed to clear almost all of the crimes committed within our jurisdiction. We're very proud of our record."

"You should be," said Rod.

"We work cooperatively with other law enforcement agencies, and we run regular patrols of businesses and residential areas. We maintain a high visibility police presence on the street, and that keeps crime rates low. Plus, you may have noticed the new video cameras installed at most intersections. We have found high-definition video cameras are an effective deterrent to crime."

"What can you see from those cameras?" asked Rod.

"Follow me and I'll show you our communications and command center. Our dispatchers can monitor crimes in progress and route officers accordingly." Dorr took Rod to the second floor, then down a long hallway to a locked room marked "Admittance Restricted." Dorr waved her electronically-encoded ID tag over the sensor adjacent to the door and the door popped open.

There were a dozen men and women in civilian clothes with headsets seated at computer terminals. Ten flat-screen color monitors were mounted on two of the walls. Each monitor displayed separate camera views divided into four quadrants. Two uniformed officers, one a Captain, supervised the entire operation from a platform near the back of the room.

"We can zoom in on faces or license plates," said Dorr, "or follow suspicious persons or vehicles by redirecting the cameras."

"Isn't this an invasion of privacy?" asked Rod.

"Not at all," said Dorr. "Monitoring what people do in public is no different than putting additional officers on the street to observe suspects or suspicious activities. We don't peek into windows of houses. We can see through windshields and windows of some vehicles, however. We can often tell how many people are in the vehicle and even if some of them are armed. But we don't invade the personal privacy of residences without a court order. This is no different than what cops have always done. Except now we record activities and we can review those files at a later date to obtain accurate descriptions of persons and vehicles, dates and locations, and other data the human eye often misses."

"Fascinating," said Rod. "I didn't know you had this. How long have the cameras been in operation?"

"Two years," said Dorr.

"And you record everything the cameras see?"

"We digitally record images to a hard drive. We can go back and search by date and location."

"Can you access the records for locations closest to where that homicide occurred two weeks ago? The medical examiner estimated Willard's time of death was between ten PM and two AM on the night of the twenty-first or morning of the twenty-second."

"We can."

"May I see those recordings, please?"

"I'll have to ask the Captain," said Dorr. She walked to the back of the room and talked with the tall uniformed man on the raised platform. When she returned, she said, "Watch the monitor on the far left."

The monitor's screen went blank, then a menu popped up. The Captain plugged time, date, and location into a search field. The screen showed the intersection nearest Benjamin Willard's apartment.

"What are we watching for?" asked Dorr.

"A woman."

"A woman? Any woman?"

"Any woman riding in a car with Willard. I think a woman killed Willard when he brought her to his apartment. Would they have to pass that particular intersection to get to Willard's apartment?"

"Not necessarily. They might have come from the opposite direction where we have no cameras. You asked for the closest intersection. Unfortunately, we can't afford to have cameras everywhere. Do you see Willard's apartment building on the left near the far end of the block? It's the four-story brick building."

"You're familiar with the case? Did you view Willard's body at the crime scene?"

"I'm familiar with the case, but I didn't go to the scene. I must have driven past that apartment building thousands of times when I was a patrol officer, though, and I answered a domestic disturbance call there once. So I know the building."

"It there a back entrance?"

"Sure. The place has to have a back entrance to meet fire codes."

Rod watched the date and time stamp at the bottom of the screen scroll away the minutes. Street traffic was relatively light at that time of the night, and Rod scrutinized every car that passed the apartment. None stopped nor parked. One car came from the other direction and turned into an alley around 10:30 PM, and Rod requested Dorr stop the replay. "Can we get an enhancement of that car?" he asked.

Dorr signaled the Captain to take the images back a few frames and blow them up. "Zoom in on the car, please," she said. "Let's get a make on the plates and see the faces of the driver and any passengers."

It was too dark to see faces clearly, but it was obvious the driver was male and the passenger female. It was impossible to tell if anyone rode in the back seat.

"Freeze frame there," Dorr told the Captain. "Can I get a printout, please?"

Dorr walked to a networked inkjet printer behind the Captain's desk on the raised platform. When she returned, she asked Rod to follow her back to her office so she could run the plates.

Rod studied the printed picture while Dorr entered the license number in the DMV database. "That's Willard's car," she confirmed. "It's a black two-year-old Dodge Challenger registered to Benjamin Willard."

"Got a magnifying glass?" Rod asked.

Dorr rummaged inside a desk drawer and brought out a large magnifying glass. Rod tried to make out facial features, but the faces were in shadow and weren't recognizable even when magnified.

"Definitely a woman passenger," said Rod. "The driver is probably Willard."

"There's a large parking lot behind the building," said Dorr. "They used the alley to get to the parking lot. Probably used the back stairs to get to Willard's apartment on the third floor."

"Pass that news on to Joel Giffords. He needs to see this."

"I'll do that. I'll make him a photocopy of the printed picture."

Rod found a copy of the case report on Megan Williams' assault waiting for him, as Giffords promised, at the information desk near the entrance and exit to the Police Department.

Megan had been sexually assaulted, physically mutilated, and left for dead. The case was classified as an aggravated assault, rather than a rape and an attempted homicide. That explained why few people in town knew what had happened, and why police hadn't launched an all-out manhunt for the assailants and why the major newspapers hadn't covered the story. Sexual assaults were delicate business. Police wanted to protect the privacy of the victim and the victim's family as much as, if not more than, police wanted to apprehend the assailants. There was a certain stigma about sexual assault that followed victims around for the rest of their lives, and neither the police nor the press wanted to irrevocably damage a victim's reputation. Names were often withheld and victims were usually described only as "a white female, aged eighteen." Sexual assault on a person under eighteen was always, at least in Illinois, statutory rape. Statutory rape was treated differently than the sexual assault of an adult.

The first officer on the scene had described Megan's injuries as "Significant." Megan had cuts on her face, torso, and lower body that were life-threatening. Her entire body was bathed in blood. No weapons were found at the scene. Megan was unconscious, and she was unable to describe her assailants or what had happened. She was rushed to the hospital by ambulance, and attempts to obtain semen samples proved impossible after Megan underwent emergency surgeries to her vaginal and rectum areas. No photographs had been taken of the victim at the scene of the crime because of the necessity to halt the bleeding and rush the victim to the hospital.

Follow-up investigations included an interview with Megan after she had regained consciousness. She described her assailants as four men in their late teens or early twenties. They wore gloves, but they didn't bother to hide their faces. All were described as white. The leader was tall, maybe 23 or 24 years old, clean-shaven, black hair and hazel eyes, and he had a scar on his abdomen that might have been from a knife wound. Another was a year or two younger, medium height, skinny, long greasy-red hair, and bright blue eyes. A third man was good-looking, medium build, and he had blond hair, blue eyes, and a beard. The fourth was still a teenager, maybe sixteen or seventeen. He had acne all over his face and back. His hair was long and both his hair and eyes were brown.

Megan Williams told the investigating officer who interviewed her when she revived after being in a coma that she was certain she could recognize all four men if she saw them again, even after a year. Perpetrator DNA had been recovered from skin and hair samples found at the scene, but no fingerprints. Assailants were classified at this time as "Unknown." The case remained open and investigation was listed as "Ongoing."

If Megan Williams were eighteen when the assault occurred, Rod calculated she would be twenty-two now. Her four assailants were now, respectively, twenty-seven or twenty-eight, twenty-six, twenty-five, and twenty.

Where were those men now? Would they try again to kill Megan Williams? Would they try to rape Megan's sister Susan? How many other rapes and murders had they committed in the past four years?

Rod was determined to find answers to those questions and others. Who had killed Benjamin Willard? Why was Willard tortured to death? Was there a relationship between the attempted murder of Megan Williams and the actual murder of Benjamin Willard four years later? Inquiring minds wanted to know, and Rodney Engleworth had an inquiring mind. Rod's nose for news was twitching like mad. Rod smelled a story bigger than anything he had written for decades.

Unfortunately, if he did find answers to all of his questions, he had no way to break the story. The *Twin Rivers Gazette* never printed hard news.

CHAPTER FIVE

Rod was surprised to receive a telephone call from Joel Giffords shortly after seven PM on Sunday evening. Rod usually spent Sundays reading newspapers, a very old habit left over from his newshound days. He didn't know how—and didn't really want—to break his weekly newspaper reading habit. He began with devouring delivered copies of the *Chicago Tribune* and the *Sun-Times* in the morning with coffee, feasted on the *New York Times, LA Times,* and *Washington Post* online in the afternoon, dined on the *Boston Globe, Miami Herald, Saint Louis Post-Dispatch* mid-afternoon, and snacked on local and network television news, including *60 Minutes,* in the evening. *60 Minutes* had been delayed tonight because of some sporting event that went overtime. Rod didn't feel like getting up from the couch to answer the telephone call when the phone rang because no one ever called him at home on Sunday nights except telemarketers. Tim preferred to use e-mail to communicate, so it couldn't be Tim Goodman on the phone. But the phone kept ringing, and Rod finally got out of his chair and went into the other room to answer the land-line.

"We've got another one," Giffords' recognizable voice sounded in the receiver. "Wife and kids just got home from visiting the wife's parents and found the body."

"Where?" Rod asked.

"Logan and Eighth. You'll see the roadblock and crime scene tape. Tell the patrolmen I called you and they'll let you through. It's another bad one, Rod. If you've just eaten, don't come. I don't want anyone upchucking on the evidence."

Rod was at Logan and Eighth Street in ten minutes. This quiet residential section of Twin Rivers had been invaded with sirens and flashing red and blue lights from a half-dozen squad cars, an ambulance, the county Medical Examiner's Meat Wagon, and the Sheriff's Department's forensic van. Residents and spectators were kept from the scene by barricades and yellow crime scene "Police Line—Do Not Cross" plastic tape. Similar barricades and yellow tape blocked off both Logan and Eighth Streets and traffic was being rerouted to McKinley and Ninth.

Rod found a parking place for his ten-year-old blue Ford Focus on McKinley and walked around the block to Logan where he flashed his press pass at two uniformed patrolmen who redirected traffic and made sure spectators stayed behind the lines. "Sergeant Giffords invited me inside," Rod said. One of the patrolmen nodded, then lifted the tape to shoulder height and let Rod scootch beneath the yellow plastic.

"Second house on the right," said the patrolman, pointing at a modern ranch-style with two-car attached garage. The yard was lit up with high-intensity halogens and forensic people were prowling the grounds with their fine-toothed combs searching for evidence.

Rod showed his press pass and mentioned Giffords' name again to the young patrolman at the front door. "Sergeant Giffords is in the master bedroom on the right," said the patrolman, handing Rod a pair of latex gloves and plastic booties to tie on over his shoes. "Are you familiar with crime scene protocol?"

Rod said he was. He stepped into the booties, tied them around his ankles; he slipped his hands inside the latex gloves and snapped the elastic to his wrists. There were a dozen police officers and crime scene technicians searching the house for clues, and Rod did his best not to disturb anything as he made his way through the living room to the back bedroom. He noticed framed photos of a happy family—husband, wife, and three children—on the fireplace mantle and placed around the room on various end tables and knick-knack shelves. Two of the children were little girls and the boy looked about six or seven. Rod wondered if the pictures were recent or if the kids had grown.

Giffords greeted him at the door to the master bedroom. There were three smaller bedrooms, one for each of the kids, on the other side of a hallway, but the master bedroom was as large as the other three combined and had a private bathroom. It also had a California King-sized bed in the center of the room with a man's naked body spread-eagled on top of bloody sheets.

"Someone peeled patches of skin off the body before slitting the guy's throat," said Giffords. "Didn't cut his cock completely off, but might as well have."

"He was skinned alive?"

"Looks like it."

Rod moved into the room and took a closer look at the body. The man was positioned on his back. Chunks of skin were missing from his forehead, his chest, his abdomen, and his thighs. His penis was a bloody mess. His neck sported a gash from one ear to the other, and the top of the head had been pushed back to open the flesh as wide as possible so sinews and cut arteries protruded from the opening.

"Looks like she used four separate instruments to torture the guy," said Giffords. "Box-cutter on the wounds on the forehead, back, and thighs, pliers on the testicles, paring knife to peel away the skin, and a butcher knife on the neck."

"She?"

"Or he. We don't know yet. Forensics found long blond hair in the shower drain, and we should be able to determine the perp's sex once the hairs are analyzed. But I'm betting it was a she."

"The perpetrator took time to shower?"

"She had all the time in the world. M.E. says the guy died on Friday night before midnight, and the wife and kids were out of town all week-end. They got back tonight between five and six. One of the kids found her father and screamed bloody murder. The wife took a quick look and called 911. We had to transport the hysterical wife and kids to the hos-pital. They've been sedated, and we can't question them further until the sedation wears off. Terrible thing for kids to see. They'll never be the same."

"The perpetrator wanted the wife to find him and see him like this. Probably wanted the kids to see, too. We're dealing with one sick puppy here, Joel."

"Still think she was trying to send a message?"

"It's obvious, isn't it?" said Rod.

"So who's the message for? Just the wife and kids?"

"No," said Rod. "She wants every man who sees what she did or hears about it to fear she'll do the same to them if she gets her hands on them."

"You think she seeks publicity?"

"Yeah. She wants the message to reach someone in particular."

"Why did she pick this guy to kill?" asked Giffords.

"I think he was a target of opportunity, someone who came on to her in a way that made her want to kill him."

"So, you're saying Willard and this guy—his name's Bill Murphy, by the way—were random targets? She didn't personally know the vics before she killed them?"

"They're substitutes for someone she does know. That someone is whom she wants to get the message loud and clear."

"Any idea who that someone might be?"

"No clue yet."

"Must be someone she hates real bad."

"I agree," said Rod.

"We can't let this get out, you know," said Giffords. "It would panic the city to know there's a madman—or madwoman—castrating men and cutting them to shreds. I've been ordered to keep this under wraps. I called you tonight because you promised to keep this off the record. I'm going to hold you to your promise."

"I think that's a big mistake," said Rod. "She'll keep on killing. You should warn people so they can take precautions. Send out news releases to all the media. Hold a news conference. Let people know what they can do to protect themselves."

"No can do," said Giffords. "The Chief and the Captain want to keep this completely under wraps. You said yourself you think she wants publicity. I don't like withholding this kind of thing, either. But I don't want to play into her hands by panicking people."

"Thanks for calling me tonight," said Rod. "I appreciate your trust."

"Thanks for your input, Rod. You still have the knack."

"What I have is a nose for news. I was trained by some of the very best in the business, worked with some of the best every day for years. Old-time newspapermen—and maybe one or two newspaperwomen—could smell out a story a hundred miles away. We saw connections where others saw none. We nosed around until we got lucky. Not only did we see connections, we *had* connections. We had connections in all the rival papers—to reporters and rewrite men and compositors and even delivery drivers—and we had connections to politicians and policemen and to the man in the street. We were plugged into taxi drivers and bus drivers. Everyone knew our bylines and everyone wanted to do us favors because we could do favors in return. The press had power in those days. People fed us information all the time. And we sniffed through that information and came up with leads that we followed up on, fitting those leads together like pieces of a giant jigsaw puzzle, until we could see the big picture and had an entire story that made perfect sense. And when we broke a story, we named names. None of that namby-pamby "informed sources tell us" bullshit. We attributed facts to named sources and we quoted those sources verbatim. We didn't rely on voice recorders or video recorders. We relied on our own memories and written notes. All of us old-time newspapermen knew shorthand, and all of us could type at least ninety words per minute. We pounded out our stories on upright manual typewriters with names like Royal or Underwood or Allen or Corona. We dropped dimes into payphones and dictated our breaking stories over the wire to rewrite men who worked the rewrite desk in newsrooms. And when our stories broke, when they appeared in print, those stories had to be correct, complete, current, and 100% accurate. People relied on us to tell them true. When our stories

broke, heads usually rolled. Sometimes those heads belonged to politicians, sometimes to mob bosses, sometimes to crooked cops, and
sometimes to murderers, embezzlers, and even common criminals. We
didn't dare get it wrong. If we didn't have the facts straight or didn't
make the right connections, it was our own necks on the chopping block
because our by-lined names were on the story. So we always got it right
before we filed the story. You can call that a knack, if you want. I call
it professional journalism. And all professional journalists develop a
nose for news."

"Whatever you want to call it, you've still got it."

"I haven't used it for years, Joel. I'm a little rusty. But it's starting
to come back. I can feel it."

"It was sure working when you came up with the picture of Willard's
car with a woman in the passenger seat. I might eventually have thought
about checking those recordings, but you saved me the time and effort.
I'm glad I cued you in about Willard."

"Keep me cued in, Joel. And I promise I'll keep you cued in. The
killer will kill again, you know. She has to. She won't be finished until
the message reaches the right men and she does to them what she did to
Willard and Murphy. She wants them to know what's in store for them.
That's the message she's sending."

"Why is she doing this in Twin Rivers? Why not suburbs like Ev-
anston or Arlington Heights or Elgin or Barrington or Lombard? Why
here and not someplace else?"

"Because she lives here. She doesn't care about any of those other
places. She only cares about sending messages to men right here in
Twin Rivers. Besides, I don't think she owns an automobile."

"What makes you say that?"

"We know she rode in Willard's car to the first crime scene. She probably rode in Murphy's car, too. Did you check both cars for prints? DNA? You might find something in the cars that will help identify the killer."

"We didn't think to do Willard's car. I'll make certain we do Murphy's."

"You might also want to check video recordings for a lone woman on foot. Check the bus stops near both homicide locations. Willard and Murphy lived two miles apart. The killer probably lives somewhere in between."

"You amaze me, Rod. You really do."

"You boys done gawkin' and talkin'?" asked a morgue assistant from the medical examiner's office. "Can I bag him and tag him?"

"Take him away," said Giffords. "We're done taking pictures."

Two coroner's assistants wheeled a gurney into the bedroom. They lowered the gurney to the height of the bed. One of the men opened a black plastic body bag and a white body sheet. They wrapped the body in the clean shroud, then rolled the stiff onto the body bag and zipped the corpse inside the bag before rolling the bag onto the gurney. They wrote the victim's name, address, and today's date on a cardboard tag and tied the tag to the zipper slider.

"We'll keep him on ice after the autopsy" said the morgue attendant as he wheeled Murphy from the room.

"When can I expect the autopsy report?" Giffords asked.

"When you get it. The docs are backed up right now. Lots of people dyin'."

"Tell the doctors to put a rush on this one, will you?"

"Yeah, sure," said the attendant. Rod knew every job was a rush job in forensic medicine.

"Did you get a toxicology report on Willard?" Rod asked Giffords.

"Not yet. I was lucky to get a preliminary autopsy report. Tox screenings always take two or three weeks after the autopsy."

"I'm wondering what the killer used to drug her victims."

"You think the victims were drugged?"

"How else would a woman manipulate a man into letting her cut him up?"

"Sex? Maybe the guy let her tie him up because he was into kinky sex?"

"She used the promise of sex to get the guy to take his clothes off and get him into bed. But you saw the marks on Murphy's lips, wrists, and ankles where she removed duct tape after Murphy died. Did Willard have the same marks? I bet he did. What are the chances two men would allow themselves to be bound and gagged by a woman because both men were into kinky sex? Slim and none. I think she drugged them, rendered them unconscious while she bound them, and cut on them after they regained consciousness. Would you let a woman tie you up when you were naked? I sure wouldn't. I don't think the victims would, either."

"So you're saying she knocked them out with a drug? Must have been orally administered. She didn't give them an injection. There were no needle marks on either body."

"She drugged their drinks with a fast-acting sedative. Remember the two clean glasses in the crime scene photographs of Willard's living room? The killer washed those two glasses after Willard drank from one of them."

"We thought she washed the glasses only to remove fingerprints."

"No. she washed those glasses to remove traces of the drug. If it's a controlled substance, it's traceable."

"We didn't find any drinking glasses here in Murphy's bedroom nor in the living room."

"She must have drugged Murphy's drink elsewhere. Perhaps in a bar where they met earlier on Friday night. Circulate Murphy's photograph to all of the bars in the area. Maybe you'll get lucky and find a bartender who remembers Murphy and the woman he was drinking with. Bartenders can usually recall the faces of customers. Sometimes they even remember what the customer likes to drink."

"It's a long-shot."

"True. But what else do you have to go on?"

"Not much."

"Then get going on it. People's memories fade with time. It might already be too late if the bars are busy on weekends. Your two best leads right now are the cameras on the street and the bartenders in local drinking establishments. You'll know more when you get the autopsy and toxicology reports. But you can't wait. The window of opportunity for catching the killer is already closing."

"I'll get right on it. What are you going to do?"

"I'm going to stop at Terri's for a cup of coffee on my way home. I think I've had enough excitement for one night. I hate to admit it, but I'm not as young as I used to be."

Giffords smiled. "How old are you, Rod?"

"Seventy going on eighty," said Rod. "In the old days, I could keep going until I pieced the puzzle together and had answers to all my questions. Now I have to do things a little at a time."

"You've been a big help. Thanks for coming out on a Sunday night. I wasn't sure if the R. Engleworth in the phone book was you or if it were still even a good number."

"I've had the same number for forty years. The only thing that's changed is the area code. It used to be 312. Now it's 708."

"You don't have a cell number?"

"I only have a land line. I know how to use a cell phone, but I don't need the added expense. I'm living off Social Security and the pittance the *Gazette* pays. So, no, I don't have a cell number."

"What do you do if you need to call someone in an emergency?"

"I borrow a phone from somebody—practically everyone carries a cell phone these days—or I look for a pay phone. There are still a few pay phones around, but not very many."

Rod drove his Focus to Terri's Restaurant on Third Street, five blocks west and twenty-two blocks north of Murphy's ranch-style house on Logan Avenue. None of the nearby businesses appeared open at ten PM on Sunday. Most people were at home watching the ten o'clock news or already in bed because tomorrow was the beginning of a new work week.

Rod didn't know any of the three waitresses on duty tonight. "Sunday and Monday nights are Susan's nights off," explained the frumpy middle-aged sour-faced woman who worked the counter when Rod inquired about Susan. Rod ordered coffee and noted the restaurant was practically empty. Terri's stayed open twenty-four hours a day, seven days a week. But it could have closed on Sunday nights and few people would have noticed.

Downtown Chicago wasn't like most of the suburbs. Chicago had a viable nightlife. The city by the lake remained brightly lit up and full of traffic at all hours of the day and night. If one sought excitement on Sunday night, one went downtown to the north loop where there were theaters and restaurants and bars and tourist traps and tons of people. Few people from the city came out to the far-west burbs on Sunday or Monday nights.

But a constant flow of traffic between the city and the western suburbs generated decent revenue for Terri's Tuesdays through Saturdays. The Metra station was less than a block away, and people taking the train stopped in for coffee or a quick meal. Terri's was also on the main drag between Bumfuck, Iowa, and the big city. People who wanted to avoid construction delays or tolls on Interstate 88 or Interstate 90 often used the old east-west federal highway that ran through Twin Rivers.

Tonight, however, Terri's was as dead as Bill Murphy. What was missing more than anything, Rod decided, was Susan Williams. Susan's smile could light up the restaurant like a thousand neons. Without Susan, the place seemed desolate and dark.

Rod was certain there was some connection between what happened to Megan Williams four years ago and what had happened today to Bill Murphy. He didn't suspect Susan directly. Susan had been working both the night of Willard's murder and this past Friday night when Murphy was killed. Rod didn't know Megan Williams, but he didn't suspect her, either. Megan had been horribly hurt, and neither her mind nor her body had completely healed, at least according to Susan. He couldn't imagine anyone in Megan's condition physically capable of those murders. No, the killer was likely a woman who knew second-hand what had happened to Megan Williams. But who could that be?

The police department had never released complete details of Megan's assault. No newspaper had printed the story of Megan's rape, only

the story of her miraculous recovery from coma. First responders, doctors, nurses, and others who treated Megan Williams knew many of the
details, including the extent of her physical injuries. So did Susan and
Susan's parents. People often talk about tragedies, and any one of those
people could have told other people about what happened. The killer
could have learned what happed to Megan and mimicked, like a copy-
cat killer, the rapists' MO. Rod had hoped Susan would be at work tonight so he could ask her who—besides Rod—she may have told about
Megan's assault during the past four years.

Rod finished his coffee. When no one came to refill his empty cup,
he dropped $2.50 on the counter—all the frumpy woman deserved for
a tip was fifty cents—and left.

He drove by Susan's old apartment on Fifth Street, the place where
Megan was assaulted, and looked at the physical layout of the building.
Like most apartment buildings in Twin Rivers and nearby suburbs, the
front of the building had a brick façade, but the back was made of
painted wood with wooden stairs leading up to balcony-style landings
on each of the floors. An alleyway ran the length of the entire block,
and there were garages and parking spaces along both sides of the alley.
The rapists had followed Susan home from Terri's Restaurant and noted
where Susan parked her car and which stairs she took to her apartment.
When they returned to rape Susan and raped Megan instead, they probably parked back here, took the back stairs up to the third floor, and
jimmied the lock until the door opened.

The alley was dark except for the faint glow coming from a single
streetlight at the other end of the block. Lights from apartment windows
afforded very little illumination and only cast gray shadows over the
alley floor. No one would have noticed a strange car parked in that alley.

Nor would anyone have noticed four men climbing the stairs to the third floor.

Susan had moved from the apartment on Fifth Street to an apartment on Eleventh Street. Rod drove by Susan's new apartment and noted that it looked essentially like the old one. This building was slightly newer, however, and the back side was solid brick like the front side. But the back stairs were made of painted wood and ran up the outside of the building, exposing anyone climbing those stairs to view.

This alleyway was much better lit than the previous one. Flood-lights, strategically positioned on various apartment buildings, illuminated the alley itself without intruding into apartment windows to keep residents awake. As Rod drove the length of the alley, he felt eyes studying him from those apartment windows. He had the odd feeling that the killer was among those watching him.

Now, more than ever, Rod was certain Susan was the key to solving not only the recent murders of two men, but the attempted murder of Megan Williams.

It was after eleven when Rod returned to his own home. He felt to-tally exhausted. Sundays were supposed to be a day to recharge batteries. Today had been busier than usual. His batteries felt drained, and his arthritis was beginning to act up.

"I'm getting old," Rod told himself as he looked at his reflection in the mirror after brushing his teeth. His once-brown hair, what was left of it, had turned mostly silver. His hairline had already receded a good inch or more and would soon meet up with the growing bald spot on the back of his head. His nose looked much larger than he remembered, and his earlobes looked longer, too. His once-muscular neckline now sported loose skin like a turkey's neck, and there were dark bags of wrinkled skin beneath his brown eyes.

Rod turned out the lights, and he wondered where time had gone and how much life he had left. Had he really drank so much of his life away? Yes, he admitted. He had. That time was gone, and he'd never get it back.

Helen, too, was gone. And he'd never get her back, either. All he had left of her were the memories.

But his nose for news was still as sensitive as ever. He still remembered how to sniff out a story. And, even if he didn't have a real newspaper to write for, he intended to keep sniffing until he uncovered the killers and exposed them in print.

Rod fell asleep thinking of Susan Williams and her sister Megan.

CHAPTER SIX

I see you driving through the alley in your powder-blue Ford. I see you looking up at Susan's apartment. I know what you're thinking.

You're a dirty old man who should be ashamed of yourself. If I get my hands on you, I'll make you feel ashamed. You're more than twice Susan's age. You're old enough to be her grandfather.

Susan's my sister. She's innocent and gullible. I protect her.

Susan doesn't know I'm watching her. Susan doesn't even know where I live. I left no forwarding address when I moved. I'm not listed in the telephone directory. I've changed my looks since the last time Susan saw me. Rather, plastic surgeons have changed my looks so not even my sister recognizes me. I don't even recognize myself.

My face and my body have been reconstructed, not from memory nor from photographs of the way I once looked but mostly from the imaginations of the male sculptors who pieced me back together. Surgeons used what little they had to work with to create an entirely new me. Those four men beat me mercilessly as they raped me and cut me. They broke my nose, shattered my cheekbones, knocked half my teeth loose. I have a new nose now, shallow cheeks, and a reconfigured mouth. I have capped teeth, dental implants, and a partial bridge. My smile, when I do smile, looks lots different than before. My breasts, which were sliced and diced, are both larger and fuller than the tiny nubs that had barely sprouted at eighteen. They're augmented with silicone and they look like large scoops of ice cream topped with cherries. They feel as cold as ice cream, too.

I visit Terri's restaurant every day to look for the men who raped me. I know they will someday show up, either individually or all four together. I'll recognize them because I can never forget them. I think of them all the time.

I think about what I will do to them when I find them. I'll recognize them for sure, but they won't recognize me. Susan didn't recognize me the dozen or so times she saw me in the restaurant. I try not to sit at her tables or at the counter. I don't want her to get too close. Why take chances?

Susan and I were very close once, as close as sisters could be. She took care of me when our parents split up. Now I take care of her, only she doesn't know I'm around. I know those men will come for her. They told me what they wanted to do to her, and then they showed me exactly what they would do to Susan the next time they saw her. Because they couldn't do it to Susan, they did it to me instead. I can't do it to them, not yet. So I do it to other men instead. But when they come for Susan, I will be waiting. I'll know those four men as soon as I see them. I will stop them before they reach Susan. I love my sister. I will protect her.

Remember that, old man. I know the color and make of the car you drive. I memorized the license plate. If I see you stalking my sister, even talking to my sister, I'll cut you up. I'll follow you until I learn where you live. I'll enter your house late at night and do to you what you'd like to do to Susan.

All men are the same. I can see that now. Men only want one thing. Even my father is the same. I thought he was different. But he's not.

What men really want is to hurt women. Men say they love women, but that's a lie. Men hate women. It begins with hating their mothers when their mothers won't give them all they want on demand. They don't want their mothers to live a life of their own. They want their mothers to dote on them, to be at their beck and call constantly, and when that's not possible they hate their mothers and find ways to hurt them.

It continues on through adolescence when boys expect girls to worship their sexual organs, to burn up with desire at the very thought, and if women don't give them what they want when they want it, they take it by force.

And when men marry, they want their wives to be completely devoted to them while they have their little flings and affairs, and to give them sex when *they* want it, never when the wife wants it. And they want their wives to endure the pain of childbearing so the men can say, "I made this child and my wife had nothing to do with it."

And even when men are too old to get it up anymore, they lust after women and want women to worship their limp organs.

And if women refuse to do any of these things on demand, men punish women by beating them or cutting them and forcing them to do things women don't want to do but men don't care what women want or how badly they hurt women to get what *they* want.

And when the women are all used up, the men leave them as if those women were already dead and go out and find other women to hurt. Younger women. Prettier women.

That's what my father did. He left my mother after hurting her terribly. Maybe he didn't beat on her physically, but he beat on her emotionally.

Is that what you want to do to Susan, old man? Do you want to hurt my sister?

I'm watching you, old man. I know what you look like. I know the car you drive. Stay away from my sister. If you get near her, I'll make you sorry.

Sundays and Mondays are difficult days for me. Susan doesn't go to work, so I stay home and watch her apartment. I stay awake all night, every night. I sleep a little in the mornings after the sun comes up, and I only leave my apartment when Susan is at work. That's when I shop for groceries or stop by Terri's for dinner and a slice of pie. But Sundays and Mondays I stay home and watch.

I have no life. Those four men took my life away from me. I might as well be dead. I would be dead except for Susan. She saved me.

So now I'll save Susan. I'll protect her from men, all men. I won't let any man hurt her.

Sometimes I get lonely. Sometimes I want to walk across the alleyway and knock on my big sister's door and talk with her the way we used to talk. Susan and I could cry together over all the terrible things that happened to us: mom and dad separating; the break-in at Susan's old apartment; my rape and mutilation; Susan finding me near death; mom and dad's divorce; dad's new wife; the monster I have become.

But I can't do that, can I? My sister doesn't know me anymore. I'm not the same person I once was. I don't look the same; I don't think the same; I don't act the same.

Besides, there's no use crying over spilled milk. Life must go on, the psychiatrists in the hospital insisted again and again until I believed them. I need to pull myself together. I need to face the future and forget the past.

How can I forget what happened to me? The drugs those doctors forced on me didn't make me forget. Drugs only make a person drowsy. Besides, I found much better uses for those drugs. I realized I made a mistake when I threw all those drugs away. I fished them out of the trash.

"Take only at bedtime," instruct the labels on the pill bottles. "Warning! May cause extreme drowsiness. Do not attempt to operate machinery." Don't drive. Don't think. Just sleep.

I don't sleep much. When I do sleep, I dream about what those men did to me. I wake up screaming. When I'm awake, I daydream about what I'll do to those men when I find them.

I wait patiently by my window watching for them. I learned patience in the hospital. I patiently endured each of the successive reconstructive procedures when doctors cut me open once again and then sewed me back together. I had to wait for each procedure to heal before doctors could cut my flesh again. How many painful procedures did I endure? How many years did it take?

They will come. I know they will come. It's only a matter of time. I have all the time in the world.

When they come, I will be ready. I wait for them to come. I pray for them to come.

There was a time, when I first came out of my coma, that I never wanted to see those men again. I didn't want to think about them, about what they had done, and I couldn't recall their faces. Something inside me blurred their features and their words and their actions. When the police visited me in the hospital and asked what the four men looked like, I didn't remember. Were they young or old? I didn't remember. Were they black or white? I didn't remember. All I could remember was they were men. They had these things that stuck straight out from their middles and they put those hard things into my mouth until I wanted to puke and they rammed those things inside me until I wanted to scream but they made me swallow my puke and they stifled my screams. All I could remember was they were men. Men had hurt me. They hurt me bad. They ripped me open and tore me apart and they pounded me the way hammers pound nails and they cut me all over and made me bleed and finally I went away to someplace where they couldn't hurt me anymore. I went away, and I stayed away for a long time. I didn't want to come back, but when I did come back I still hurt. It took me a long time to remember exactly what happened. It took me a long time to remember their faces. I had all the time in the world, and gradually I remembered. I told the police what I remembered, but by then the police had given up looking for the men who had raped me. The cop who interviewed me filled out a report, but I could tell he didn't think it did much good after more than a year.

But I'm patient. I have all of the time in the world. I know those men will come for Susan again.

I remember exactly what each of them looks like. I remember their faces, their bodies, their voices. I remember the smell of their sweat and the taste of their semen. I remember what they did to me. I want them to remember, too, what they did as I cut off those things they rammed inside me. I want them to remember what they did as I cut off their nipples, their noses, their ears. I want them to remember, because I can never forget.

I want them to know what it feels like to be helpless. I want them to know fear and feel pain.

I want the last thing they remember is me.

CHAPTER SEVEN

Rod awoke to the sound of birds. It was a beautiful fall morning. The air was crisp and clean, and tiny dust motes danced in sunbeams that streamed between slats in the venetian blinds. Rod had once been a night person and he had missed the miracle of mornings. But, as he aged, he gradually became a day person and finally, when he stopped drinking, morphed into a morning person.

After using the bathroom, he scooped coffee into a twelve-cup coffeemaker, added water, and left the coffee to perk while he showered and shaved. He seldom sang in the shower, but today he did sing because today he felt like singing. It was a great day to be alive.

During the months and years of Helen's protracted illness, Rod felt not only helpless but entirely useless. There was absolutely nothing he could do to save her. Once Rod had delivered his wife into the hands of doctors, he had to defer to their judgment. After all, they were supposed to be the experts.

But, as Helen's condition worsened, Rod began to question her doctors and discovered they knew little more than he did about this particular illness. Cancer was the great unknown, and no two tumors behaved alike. Doctors heroically tried to defeat death by trying new things to see if any of those things would work. Doctors were like dumb automobile mechanics who first replaced the spark plugs, then replaced the distributor cap, then overhauled the engine and still couldn't get the car to start. When one treatment didn't work, they tried the next step outlined in the AMA repair manual. When that didn't work, they tried something else, something different. Eventually they tore the entire car apart and tried to put it back together without all the necessary parts. When the rebuilt car still didn't start, they simply left it to rust while they worked on other cars. They always had plenty of broken-down cars waiting to be fixed. Some they got running again, even if only for a little while. Some were eventually salvaged for parts. Most, especially the older models, wound up on the junk heap called the autopsy table.

Rod watched as the expert mechanics called oncologists hooked Helen up to expensive computers and ran sophisticated diagnostics. He watched as they ground valves, replaced wires, and changed oil and hydraulic fluids. They got Helen up and running, and they called her back in and performed periodic maintenance, but she kept breaking down until they shook their bewildered heads and said they had done all they could do because they didn't know what else to do.

Rod learned that doctors were just as helpless when it came to fighting cancer as he was. And, in the end, just as useless.

But today Rod felt like he knew what he was doing and he felt far from helpless. Rod had cut his eye-teeth doing investigative journalism. He had run down more leads and tracked down more killers than most homicide detectives. Rodney Engleworth was a born reporter who was hot on the trail of a big story.

Today Rod felt reborn. He felt alive for the first time in years. Joel Giffords had treated Rod with respect and had actually seemed grateful for Rod's input. Susan Williams regularly read Rod's column and had thanked Rod for writing. For the first time in a very long time, Rodney Engleworth felt useful, and maybe even necessary.

Next on Rod's to-do list was to talk again with Susan about her sister. Rod wanted to personally interview Megan and hear from Megan first-hand what happened four years ago. He wanted Megan to describe each of the men who had raped her.

Today was Tuesday. Rod had spent most of Monday writing his promised puff piece about the police department's commendable clearance rate. He accessed FBI crime statistics from the Justice Department's websites, compared case clearance rates with other cities of the same size, and concluded that Twin Rivers had indeed done a commendable job. Rod had interviewed Police Chief Darrel James and Captain Edward Gross, the tall uniformed captain Rod had seen supervising the communications room. He took digital photos with Tim Goodman's Nikon D610, a 24.3 mega-pixel DSLR camera. This would be the lead story in Wednesday's *Gazette*, the kind of thing the Chamber of Commerce loved and so did advertisers and local readers. He ran the story past Elsie Dorr and got her approval. Rod had e-mailed Tim the entire story as a Word file and attached a dozen digital photos for Tim to choose from late last night. Tim had likely stayed up all night editing and formatting the 64-page issue in InDesign.

Rod's "Reminiscences" column about life with Helen had already been written and edited. Tim's deadline for e-mailing a .pdf of the entire 64 pages was ten AM Tuesday. The printer had plates running on the presses before noon, and bundles of the printed newspaper were delivered to the *Gazette* office no later than noon on Wednesday.

But today was technically Rod's day off. Tim, on the other hand, never took a day off. He spent Tuesdays updating the *Gazette*'s subscriber database and distribution drop-off addresses. Although the *Twin Rivers Gazette* was primarily a local newspaper, subscribers included libraries throughout the state, plus former residents who had moved as far away as Arizona or Florida and who wanted to stay in touch with happenings in their old home town. Audited circulation had exceeded 65,000 copies, and the average copy was now read by four people before becoming fish wrappers or winding up in the bottoms of bird cages. Lots of people were reading Rod's words every week. He felt far from useless.

Rod sat at the kitchen table and read the *Tribune* and the *Sun-Times* while sipping coffee. The house was empty without Helen, and Rod missed hearing her bustling about the kitchen while he read the morning papers. The whole place was much too quiet. He could hear the grandfather clock tick-tocking in the living room.

Rod had thought once or twice about getting a dog or a cat to keep him company, but he never took the time to visit the animal shelter. Having a pet was a nice idea. Someday he'd get around to it. He didn't have time to think about that now.

"DNA hit leads to charges in 6 rapes," read the head on the left-hand lead column of Tuesday's *Trib*. Rod carefully read every word of the article, including the continuation on page 14. A serial rapist was arrested in Chicago when a state lab returned results from vaginal swabs taken as long ago as nine years. The article reported that labs were seriously backed-up, and police were frustrated by long delays in obtaining results. Giffords had mentioned that the men who had raped Megan Williams were linked by DNA to rapes in other suburbs. Rod wondered how many serial rapists there were active at any one time. A hundred in the Chicagoland area? Two hundred? More? Statewide, approximately six thousand DNA cases were submitted to the state labs annually, and approximately twenty-five hundred of those were sexual assault cases. Priority case analyses were usually completed within thirty days. Routine cases often took six months or longer to be processed. The Illinois statute of limitations on rape was currently ten years from the date of the assault. There were still six years remaining before Megan's rapists went scot-free. Could police find the men before the statute of limitations ran out? Were those four men still raping other women? Would they try again to rape Susan Williams?

Rod was acutely aware that serial rapists, like serial killers, often continued to commit the same kind of crimes until they were caught. Did any or all of the four reside in Twin Rivers? Did they live in a nearby suburb? Or were they Chicago natives who went out to the suburbs only for their kicks?

How would he ever find them?

Rod decided to let the police continue to search for the rapists while he concentrated on protecting Susan Williams. He could keep an eye on Susan easily enough. She worked three to midnight at Terri's, and Rod could stop in at the restaurant every night for dinner and stay as long as Susan refilled his coffee cup. After she left work, he could follow her home to make certain no one else was following her. If he spotted any of the four men who had raped Megan watching Susan, he could call Giffords or even follow the men until he discovered their identities. Just to be sure he had an accurate description of the men, he'd also interview Megan Williams later today. He'd wait until Susan began her shift at the restaurant and drop by for a cup or two of coffee. He would ask Susan for Megan's address and go talk with her. Then he would return to Terri's for supper and a slice of pecan pie.

Rod dressed in a white shirt, a blue blazer, and tan slacks. He hated to wear a tie, but he decided a tie was important when he spoke with

Megan Williams. He found a red-and-blue striped tie that wasn't too wrinkled or soiled and tied it under his collar. Now he looked like an old-time newspaperman. All that was missing was a Walter Winchell style hat.

Rod sat at the counter, nursing a bottomless cup of coffee, when Susan Williams arrived at work. She smiled as soon as she saw him, and he smiled back.

When she refilled his cup, he said, "I want to talk with your sister."

"Why?" she asked.

"I want her to describe her assailants. I read the police report, but I want to hear if she has anything to add. Will you give me her address and phone number?"

"I can't."

"Why not? You know who I am. I don't want to hurt Megan. I just want to help."

"I can't because I don't know where she lives, and I don't have her current phone number."

"What do you mean?"

"I mean, Megan has disappeared. She moved from her apartment and disconnected her telephone."

"When?" asked Rod.

"At least two months ago. I hadn't heard from her for a while, so I stopped by the apartment she got after leaving the hospital. Someone else was living there. I tried to call Megan's phone number, but it was no longer a working number."

"How long since you saw her last?"

"Maybe six months or longer. I don't remember," said Susan. She was being evasive.

"You didn't go to see her for at least four months? I thought you said you and your sister were close?"

"We were close. But that was before...before...."

"Before she was raped?"

"Before she was cut up."

Rod understood what Susan was saying. Or, rather, what she wasn't saying. She wasn't about to admit, not even to herself, that she simply couldn't bear to see the way her sister looked now. Rod understood that because he couldn't bear to see the way Helen had looked, either, toward the last when Helen wasn't the same woman, the woman he had married. She was merely a ghost of that woman he had loved. Cancer, and the multitude of surgeries, had taken a drastic toll. Helen's hair had grown out barely enough to appear scraggly and bristly and patchy. Her flesh had shrunk so she looked more like a living skeleton, a survivor of Auschwitz, than a human being. She had wasted away almost to nothing. She was so drugged up with pain medications that she didn't recognize Rod, either, though he came to visit her every day. She looked at him with a blank stare like he was a complete stranger.

Rod couldn't bear to stay at the hospice with Helen very long each time. He visited for only an hour each day, sitting silently by her bedside. Then he kissed her on the forehead and left to get drunk. Rod had promised to stay with Helen through sickness and health, until death they did part, and he had kept his promise. But each visit took its toll on him, too, and he only made those final visits out of obligation. Susan had made no such promises to her sister. She had no obligation to visit Megan every day. She visited as seldom as possible because she couldn't stand to look at what had happened to her once-beautiful sister.

"Didn't Megan have reconstructive surgery?" Rod asked softly.

"Yes. The last time I saw her, her face was all bandaged up. All I could see were her eyes."

"Her face must have healed by now."

"Probably."

"I'm sorry, Susan."

"I am, too," said Susan. Her eyes suddenly filled with tears, and Susan turned away and ran for the kitchen.

Rod wanted to follow her into the kitchen. He wanted to put his arms around her and tell her it was all right, tell her he knew how she felt. But he didn't do that. Instead, he sat at the counter and felt like a heel for making Susan cry.

Rod finished his coffee. He dropped a five dollar bill on the counter and left the restaurant before Susan came back.

Outside, the sky had clouded over and the sun was nowhere in sight. As Rod walked to his car he noticed flocks of birds flying southward in V formations. The afternoon had suddenly turned cold. A brisk wind blew in from the northwest, and dark storm clouds were gathering off to the west.

Summer was over. Fall had fled and winter was coming early this year.

CHAPTER EIGHT

I saw you make my sister cry. I told you what would happen to you if you hurt my sister. Don't you believe me? You should believe me.

I've got your number, Mister. I've got your license plate number, and I'll soon get your phone number and your house number, too. I'm watching you. If I see you anywhere near my sister again, you'll be a dead man. Hear me, Mister?

Of course not. Even I know I'm speaking only inside my head. You can't hear me. Nobody but me ever listens to me anyway. Why should I say anything aloud?

Can you read minds? I can read minds. I can read *your* mind. I know what you want to do to my sister. I won't let you.

Sometimes I get so angry I could spit.

You men are all the same. You only want one thing. I'm sitting at the opposite end of the restaurant from the counter, as far away from Susan's section of tables as I can get. I couldn't hear exactly what you and Susan were saying, but I can guess. Did you tell her what you wanted to do to her? Is that why she's crying? Did you whisper all those naughty things in Susan's ear the way those four men whispered naughty things in my ears when they raped me?

Susan has dried her eyes and she's back working the counter as if nothing happened, but I saw you make her cry. I know you hurt her. I'll get you for that.

I won't follow you now. I'll wait until I see you again. I can be patient. I'm nothing if not patient. I know you live in Twin Rivers. I'll find you. Sooner or later, I'll find you.

But now I must stay here to protect Susan. Those men will come for her. I know they will. It's only a matter of time. I'll recognize them when I see them. I have the sharpened butcher knife, the Beretta, and the box cutter in my purse. I'm ready for them when they come.

They won't recognize me. If my own sister doesn't recognize me, those men won't. Besides, they probably think I'm dead. I would be dead if Susan hadn't come home when she did and called 911.

They have to come here to Terri's and then follow Susan home to her new apartment on Eleventh Street. If they have been watching Susan's old apartment on Fifth Street, they'll know that Susan no longer lives there. An old guy lives there now with his dog. The dog's a big Doberman. I hope the dog bites them.

I walk by that old Fifth Street apartment practically every day, but I haven't seen them watching. I have to walk everywhere I go because I can't afford a car. Even if I could afford the down payment on an old junker, I have such bad credit I couldn't finance the remainder. Susan now lives on Eleventh Street, and I live on Tenth Street, right behind Susan. Terri's Restaurant is on Third Street. When I walk the seven blocks east to get home tonight, I'll pass by the old apartment on Fifth Street. I hope I see the four men there.

It takes me twenty minutes to walk to Terri's, and twenty minutes to walk back. Susan can drive that in half the time. But Susan will stay after her shift ends to take care of her customers and collect her tips. I'll be home before she is.

I want so badly to talk to Susan, to cry on my big sister's shoulder like I did as a little girl, for us to be as close as we once were. But I know that's impossible. I know she blames herself for what happened to me, for not being there, for coming home late. I don't blame her. In fact, I'm glad she wasn't there. If she had been there, they would have done the same to her that they did to me. And who would have called 911 in time to save either of us? Nobody. Both of us would have bled out and died. Neither of us would be alive to mete out equal punishment—biblical justice—to those four men.

They need to pay for what they did. And they will.

I don't see any of them in this restaurant. I've been coming here every day Susan has worked for the past two months, and I haven't seen them. But I know I will. I'm certain they will come. I will be patient. I'm nothing, if not patient.

But now I must leave. I don't want any of the waitresses to wonder why I'm here so often and stay so long. They already know I'm a regular customer, but Terri's has many regular customers. The food is good, the service is fast, and the prices are reasonable. But I don't dare overstay my welcome.

I leave a small tip and pay cash at the register. Outside the restaurant, only half a block away, is the bus stop. I sit there and see who enters and leaves the restaurant. Across the street is the Metra station. After an hour or two at the bus stop, I'll wander over to the Metra station and watch the front of the restaurant from there. No one bothers me. No one notices me. I'm the invisible woman.

I used to be pretty. People noticed me when I was pretty. Now everyone, my sister included, turn their heads away when they see me. They were taught as children, as was I, that it's not polite to stare at a person's scars. My scars aren't quite as visible at night in dark drinking establishments, but they're clearly visible inside the brightly lit Terri's Restaurant and outside during daylight hours.

I also walk with a pronounced limp. When those men rammed knives into my private parts, they severed important nerves from my spinal cord to my lower limbs that caused my left leg to be partially paralyzed. I have to drag my left leg behind me like Chester Goode in reruns of *Gunsmoke*. Both legs move, and I can stand and walk. But messages from my brain seem to take a little longer to reach muscles in my left leg than the right. Thus the slight drag.

Is it any wonder that my own sister doesn't recognize me? I'm not the same person she once knew. I've changed so much in the past four years that there are days even I don't recognize myself. I blame those four men. They did this to me.

I grew up believing fictions that all men were supposed to love and protect women and save women from predators. I dreamed of someday finding a Sir Galahad who would marry me and protect me always from all harm. I believed in fairy tales and dreams coming true and miracles. In fairy tales, it was usually the evil Queen or the wicked stepmother who wanted to harm little girls, never the Prince. I didn't realize as a child that most fairy tales were written by men. Why would men warn women about men?

Little Red Riding Hood must have been written by a woman. The Big Bad male Wolf wanted to devour the little girl in that memorable fairy tale. The wolf disguised himself as the girl's grandmother after killing and eating the grandmother. In some versions of the tale, the girl—and not the huntsman—kills the wolf. In some, the ones obviously rewritten by men, the wolf either ravishes the little girl or Red is saved at the last moment by the sudden appearance of a huntsman who slays the wolf with his axe.

No huntsman came to save me from the wolves. Only my sister rescued me. Oh, sure, there were men among the paramedics. There were male doctors who operated on me. But they were only doing what they were paid to do. My sister acted out of love.

Men don't understand love and family the way women do. Take my father, for instance. He left my mother, who loved him unconditionally despite his many affairs which took time away from her and the family, and he hurt her deeply. He left Susan and me. He abandoned us. He left love behind for cheap thrills with women who didn't know, or didn't care, that he was married.

You can't trust men. You can't trust any of them.

A police car drives by and pays absolutely no attention to me. Why haven't the police caught the rapists yet? Do they even care? Aren't they paid to care? Men are all the same. Even policemen.

When I was in the hospital for reconstructive surgeries, I heard on television that Illinois has the worst backlog of DNA rape kits in the country. Until a recent law passed that required police to submit Sexual Assault Forensic Evidence (SAFE) kits to state laboratories, rape kits sat on shelves in police storage rooms unprocessed. Thousands of rape cases went unsolved because the police put such low priorities on solving sexual assaults compared to other crimes that many rape kits were still unprocessed twenty years after the assault. Is it a joke that that rape kits are called SAFE kits? Apparently, some men must think so.

Sometimes I get so angry I could just spit.

Spitting is unladylike. Women aren't supposed to spit. Not even when men ejaculate in a woman's mouth.

It's time to move from my comfortable bench at the bus stop. The wind is cold and makes me shiver. It looks like it's going to rain.

The inside of the Metra terminal is out of the wind and feels much warmer than the bus stop. About a dozen people stand on the outside platform facing the train tracks. Twin Rivers isn't the end of the line for commuters, but almost. It's one of the final stops before the train reaches Elgin. Most express trains don't stop here. Locals arrive only once every two hours. It takes thirty-five minutes to reach downtown Chicago from the Twin Rivers terminal.

I find a seat on a hard wooden bench facing the windows on Third Street. I can see the entrance to Terri's restaurant half-a-block away. I can watch cars park near the front of the restaurant. If any of those four men show up, I'll get their license plate numbers. I'm not sure I'll be able to follow them on foot, but I intend to try.

I wish I had a car. It would be so much easier to follow those men if I had a car. My driver's license has expired, but I could renew it. Then I could rent a car when I really needed one. There is a car rental place directly across the street from the Metra station. I can see their sign from here. Can you rent a car without a credit card? I don't have a credit card.

I live frugally on my disability checks. Social Security deposits my monthly checks directly into a savings account. I access my savings account via an ATM at the local bank. I might have enough money saved up to rent a car. I don't want to spend any money unless I need to.

Half of my monthly check goes to pay the rent on my apartment on Tenth Street. The rest I spend on food. I buy my clothes at a resale shop on Fourth Street. All of my furniture and dishes came from that same resale shop. So what if nothing matches. No one but me ever visits my apartment.

The pawn shop where I purchased the used Beretta is three doors north of Terri's Restaurant. I had to pay extra for the gun because I have no valid identification and no state Firearms Owner Identification card. The pawn shop owner's wife took pity on me when I said I was a rape victim who lived alone. She sold me the gun under the counter with no paperwork. I also bought a box of nine-millimeter ammunition. I promised not to tell anyone where I got the gun.

I have never actually fired a gun in my entire life. I practice aiming and squeezing the trigger without a magazine inserted. I think I'll hit what I aim at. But I'm not certain.

The Beretta makes my purse heavy. I'm aware I have the gun with me. I go nowhere without it. My purse is a brown leather bag with a shoulder strap. I'm right handed, and I carry the purse on my right shoulder. I can reach into the bag and have the gun in my hand in less than a second and a half. There's already one bullet in the chamber. It takes another half second to snap the safety up and cock the hammer. I've practiced. I've timed myself. I'm ready for them when they come.

I know all about guns because I went to the public library and watched YouTube videos of the Beretta in action. I know all about a two-handed firing stance. I know a nine millimeter has some recoil, and I think I can handle the recoil even with my small hands. I'll know when I fire the first shot. I can fire fourteen more shots before the magazine is empty. I keep a spare magazine in my purse. I can depress the magazine catch, drop the magazine, and reload in two seconds. I know, because I've practiced and timed myself.

I've had plenty of time to practice. I sit alone in my apartment, staring out the window at the alley or the back of Susan's building, and I practice changing magazines. I also practice aiming out the window. I imagine having each of the four men, one after the other, in my sights. I squeeze the trigger. Someday, I'll do it for real. Maybe that someday will be today.

At nine PM, I return to Terri's for a cup of coffee and a piece of pie. Susan is hustling between tables, the counter, and the kitchen. I sit at my usual spot and observe her. She's very efficient. I'm proud of my big sister.

The restaurant is fairly full at this time of night with late diners who have finished their supper meals and ordered desserts. Terri's has the best home-baked pies. Most of the customers are locals who live in Twin Rivers or surrounding suburbs. A few are Chicagoans who drove all the way out here for a piece of pie and a bottomless cup of coffee. None of the customers are the men I'm looking for.

And then I see him enter the front entrance and take a seat at the counter. I'm sure he's the pimply-faced kid all grown up. He's maybe twenty or twenty-one. His hair is trimmed shorter than I remember. I strain my ears to hear him order. I'd recognize that voice anywhere. It's definitely him.

Susan, of course, doesn't know the guy from Adam. She smiles at him, takes his order, and a minute later she's back with a piece of hot apple pie covered with melting ice cream. She fills his coffee cup, and he dumps enough cream and sugar into the black liquid to turn it light brown. If the kid isn't already wired from drugs, he'll soon be flying on a sugar high.

I want to get up from my table and shoot the bastard right there and then, shoot him in the back and then pull his pants down and cut off his cock. But I don't want to kill just one. I want all four of them. I try to finish my pie, but the taste is bitter in my mouth. I've lost my appetite for sweet things. I watch the man look at Susan. He won't be satisfied with just coffee and pie. He wants her. I can tell. He wants to fuck her and cut off her tits.

Did he come here on his lonesome to make certain Susan still worked here? Or are the three other rapists waiting outside in a car? I dig in my purse for change to leave a tip. Then I get up and pay my bill at the register. I walk outside and look around before taking a seat at the bus stop. I try to see if there's a car parked on the street with three men inside. It's dark and starting to rain. I don't care if I get wet. I want to know what kind of car they drive and try to get the license plate numbers so I'll know it's them the next time I see their car. When the guy leaves the restaurant, I'll follow him to his car. I bet the other three are waiting in the car.

I'm getting more excited by the minute. I've waited four years for my revenge. Is tonight the night? I put my hand into my purse and finger the Beretta. The steel feels cold and comforting. I slip the safety to the off position.

It begins to pour. I see a dark-colored Dodge van pull up in front of the restaurant and the driver honks the horn. The pimply-faced kid comes out of the restaurant and climbs into the back seat of the van. I recognize the faces of the two men in the front seats as the van accelerates past me to splash water on me. I manage to catch only the last four digits of the rear license plate before the van disappears into the darkness.

But I'll recognize that van when I see it again.

I get up from the bench and trudge home through the rain.

CHAPTER NINE

Rod spent Wednesday afternoon delivering newspapers all over town. He made a special stop at the police station to drop off promised copies for the dozen or so Twin Rivers cops he mentioned in his lead article. Then he made the rounds of all the regular drop-off points, ending at Terri's Restaurant around 9:30.

When Susan brought him a menu and a cup of coffee, he apologized for upsetting her yesterday with so many questions. "I shouldn't have pressed you," he said. "I was being insensitive."

"You meant well," said Susan. "It's just...painful to talk about."

"I understand," said Rod.

"I'm really worried about my sister," admitted Susan. "Megan became more and more withdrawn each time she went back to the hospital for additional surgery. The last few times, she wouldn't even let me drive her. She doesn't own a car, so she had to call a cab. She said she didn't want to see anybody or be seen—she especially didn't want me to see her—until she was completely healed. I think she knew I blamed myself for the way she looked. I should have come home earlier. Maybe if I'd been there...."

"It's not your fault," said Rod. "Just as it's not my fault that Helen got cancer. You can't blame yourself. There was nothing you could have done to prevent what happened to Megan."

"But what if...?"

"No. You can't think that way. What's done is done. You have to accept that. I know it's tough without closure. Those men have never been caught. They're still out there. It'll help immensely once those men are caught and convicted. You'll see a huge difference."

"Do you think so?"

"I know so. I want to help police find those men. That's the only reason I asked to talk with Megan. Maybe she'll remember something important."

"I have no idea how to reach her. She simply moved out and left no forwarding address."

"Do you think she still lives in Twin Rivers?"

"She doesn't have a car. She doesn't have much money. So I don't think she went very far. She took her clothes, her twin–size mattress, some dishes and silverware. That's about all she owned. She didn't have any furniture to speak of. When her lease was up, she didn't renew the lease. She simply packed her bags and moved out."

"When was that?"

"End of March."

"That's more than six months ago."

"Yes."

"I thought you said she moved two months ago."

"Two months ago I learned that she was no longer living in the same place."

"When exactly was the last time you saw or spoke with your sister?"

"January or February. I don't remember exactly. I know I saw her around Christmas. I brought her a fruitcake and a card."

"And you haven't seen her since? Haven't heard from her?"

"No."

"Have you checked with the hospital?"

"She stopped seeing her doctors in April. She was supposed to come back for follow-up visits and additional counseling, but she didn't show up for her last appointments. She didn't refill any of her prescriptions, either."

"What drugs was she taking?"

"Pain medications. Sleeping pills. Anti-anxiety meds."

"She just stopped taking them?"

"She had to see the doctors every thirty days in order to get those prescriptions refilled."

"Jesus! You can't just stop taking anti-anxiety meds cold-turkey. Those are the kinds of controlled prescriptions that require gradual weaning or your mind can get all messed up. If you go completely off those meds, you'll get phobic or become paranoid. Some people go completely crazy. Do you think she's suicidal?"

"I don't know. She told me once I should have let her die. But the last time I saw her, she thanked me for saving her. She said she was getting better. She was looking forward to seeing her new face."

"She got a whole new face? The entire face?"

"Her face was badly injured. Her nose and cheekbones were broken. Her jaw was broken. She lost half her teeth. She had deep cuts on her neck and all over her face. It was a long and painful process to have reconstructive surgery, but she endured the pain. She said I wouldn't recognize her when the doctors finished with her."

"Did they finish?"

"I'm not sure. The state was paying the bills, and there were those big budget cuts to Medicaid and state subsidies last year."

"Do you have any idea what your sister looks like now?"

"No. The last time I saw her, most of her face was bandaged."

"How old is she?"

"She turned twenty-two in March. I sent her a birthday card."

"How tall is she?"

"I'm five-nine. Megan is an inch shorter than me."

"Heavy? Slim?"

"She put on weight in the hospital. But she lost most of it living alone in her apartment. I don't think she eats much at all. And she walks everywhere."

"Is she blonde like you?"

"Yes. Doctors shaved her head when they operated on her, but her hair grew out again."

"I'll try to find her. Is there anything else you can tell me that will help identify her?"

"Megan's vocal cords were damaged when those men cut her throat. Her voice sounds funny."

"How so?"

"Like maybe she chain-smokes cigarettes. She doesn't smoke, but her voice sounds raspy like she smokes a thousand cigarettes a day."

"Anything else?"

"Not that I can think of."

"That's not much to go on. I'll see if the hospital will give out any information."

"You don't have to do this."

"I want to help. You and your sister have gone through hell. The least I can do is put the two of you in touch again."

Susan left to take care of her other customers, and Rod looked around the restaurant for four men who might fit the description of the rapists. The supper crowd was thinning out, but the restaurant was still filled with people. Terri's did a good business on weeknights. Rod saw couples and families dining at tables, a half-dozen commuters fresh off the train sipping coffee at the counter, a few senior citizens enjoying slices of Terri's famous pies, and one lone woman sitting in a booth near the entrance nursing a cup of coffee. She looked relatively young—in her early twenties—and she wore a black hoodie that covered her hair and hid most of her face. She might have been a teenaged boy except for breasts tenting the front of the hoodie. She was intently watching a pimply-faced kid about the same age sitting at the far end of the counter.

Rod knew that many young people often frequented Terri's after school or early evenings, but few remained in the restaurant after ten PM on weeknights. Those two looked old enough to be college kids at the College of DuPage or maybe at one of the universities or technical schools in the area. Rod was looking for four men sitting together, but the only four men he saw gathered at the same table were older, wore business suits, and appeared too respectable to be anything other than executives or salesmen.

Rod ordered his usual, and Susan delivered a steaming plate of roast beef and mashed potatoes. She refilled Rod's coffee cup and made the rounds of her section with the pot of coffee.

The girl in the hoodie was still staring at the pimply-faced kid. Did she have a secret crush on him? Rod remembered staring at Helen the first time he saw her. He couldn't take his eyes off her.

The brown-haired boy seemed oblivious to the girl watching him. He, in turn, was watching Susan, his head and eyes following Susan around the room as she poured coffee and chatted with patrons. If Rod were too old to think of Susan romantically, the kid looked too young to have the same kind of thoughts. He should be thinking about the girl in the hoodie instead.

Why was it people always wanted what they couldn't have? Unrequited love made people miserable.

Rod had known true love for more than forty years. He had met and married his soul-mate, something most people only wish for. He considered himself lucky.

Sure, there had been rocky times in the marriage, especially near the end when Helen was more of a burden than a help-meet. Helen's job had supported them when Rod had lost his former job at the *Daily News*, and her income had made owning a house possible as Rod hustled low-paying free-lance assignments from suburban rags. They had lived together, loved together, and survived together despite all the bumps in the road. Losing Helen to cancer was part of the price Rod paid for forty-plus years of happiness. He'd do it all over again in a heartbeat if he got the chance.

The girl in the hoodie looked as lost as Rod had felt when he learned Helen was going to die. She was obviously lonely. Lots of lonely people came to Terri's not only for the coffee and a piece of home-made pie, but to be around other people. Terri's was a meeting place as much for travelers on the road of life as for travelers on the Metra and the federal highway. Rod hoped the lonely girl would get lucky.

Susan came by and topped off Rod's coffee cup. He finished his meal, dug in his pocket for a roll of dollar bills, and left four ones under his plate.

The girl in the hoodie dropped some coins on the table and paid her bill at the register. Rod watched her leave by the front door. She walked with a limp, dragging her left leg behind her.

Had she been in an automobile accident? Did she have a clubbed foot or an artificial limb? Had she been inflicted with some terrible childhood disease that left her partially paralyzed? Rod's heart went out to the poor girl. She was much too young to have to live with a disability. Sometimes life wasn't fair.

Tragedy struck young and old alike. Everyone had his or her cross to bear. Life was all about making lemonade from the lemons you were handed. Life could be sweet or it could be sour. The choice was really up to you which you wanted life to be.

Susan looked too busy to talk, and Rod decided it was time for him to go home and get some sleep. Tomorrow he could stop by the hospital and see if he could learn where Megan Williams currently resided.

He knew doctors wouldn't release medical information without a HIPPA form signed by the patient. When Rod had tried to learn certain details of Helen's condition to discover if all those surgeries were medically necessary, hospital administrators refused to divulge that information even to the patient's spouse of forty years. They claimed Rod needed Helen's signature before the hospital could talk to him about Helen's diagnosis and treatment.

Even after Helen had died, the hospital remained reluctant to release any information. Rod assured hospital administrators he didn't want to sue them for malpractice. He only wanted to know, after he stopped drinking, exactly what had happened and when. But they still wouldn't provide copies of her records without her signature on a HIPPA form.

Perhaps Joel Giffords had Megan's address. Rod would check with Joel after he talked with the hospital.

Rod paid his bill and walked out to the Ford Focus. It was still raining, a cold drizzle that was enough to require the use of windshield wipers. As Rod drove south on Third Street, he noticed the girl in the hoodie sitting at the corner bus stop. He almost stopped to offer her a ride.

But the girl would probably think he was only a dirty old man trying to pick her up instead of a kind-hearted and generous guy offering a helping hand in the rain. He drove slowly past her, and he didn't try to look at the face beneath the hoodie. He had been taught that it wasn't polite to stare, especially not at someone with a handicap.

Rod pulled into his own driveway ten minutes later. He parked his car on the drive because his attached garage was so filled with old newspapers there was no longer room for a car or even much else inside the garage. Why he still kept those moldy old copies of the *Chicago Daily News*, *Sun-Times*, and *Tribs* when they were such a fire hazard was beyond comprehension. He could access the *Sun-Times* and the *Chicago Tribune* online. And everything in the *Daily News* was old news that had absolutely no value except for by-lined stories he had written nearly half-a-century ago. He hadn't looked at them in years. But his ego wouldn't let him throw them away.

He used a remote to open the garage door, and he entered through the garage that connected with his relatively-small kitchen. His cookie-cutter house had been constructed in the early 1970s, and it was all laid-out on a single floor. Arthritis in his knees made Rod happy that he needn't climb stairs to reach his bed.

Rod's house was smaller than Bill Murphy's, though the layout was similar. Rod had an attached one-car garage, and Murphy's house had a two-car garage. Rod's house was constructed of white-painted wood, and Murphy's was all brick. Rod had three bedrooms and one bath, Murphy's home had four bedrooms and two baths. Rod lived in an older section of town, and Murphy lived in a newer sub-division. Murphy probably had an income ten times that of Rod's.

Rod would be up the proverbial creek without a paddle if Helen hadn't had health insurance through her employer. Nevertheless, Rod had depleted most of his savings after Helen became ill and no longer had an income. She had worked for the same employer for thirty years and they graciously kept her on the books for insurance purposes even after she was unable to work. But when her sick leave and saved-up vacation time was used up, they put her on unpaid leave until she died. Helen had borrowed against her 401 (k) to cover co-pays and medications when she was in hospice. There was precious little left of her savings after funeral expenses.

But the thirty-year mortgage on the house itself was completely paid. Rod's social security covered home-owner's insurance and annual real estate taxes. He had enough income from the *Gazette* to afford occasional meals at Terri's and put gas in the car. Monthly electricity, water, gas, and telephone bills ate up the rest.

Rod brushed his teeth. He was grateful to still have teeth to brush at his age, though many teeth were crowned and he had a partial bridge. He stripped down to underwear and crawled beneath the sheets.

From time to time, he heard raindrops hit the roof. Late fall in Illinois was dark and dreary. Most of the leaves had already turned brown and crisp, and fall rains sent the last of the leaves careening to the ground. The tall maple tree in Rod's front yard was beginning to look like a skeleton, its formerly-green flesh ripped off by harsh winds and pelting rains. When it finally stopped raining, Rod would need to rake the yard.

Tomorrow promised to be a busy day. Rod planned to begin with the hospital. Twin Rivers was home to a regional medical center that served several of the far-west suburbs. Rod hadn't been back to the hospital since he had tried to obtain Helen's medical records. The hospital had reluctantly released Helen's records only after Rod produced a copy of Rod's probate court appointment as executor of Helen's estate. He didn't hold out much hope of success at the hospital since he had no formal relationship with Megan Williams.

Rod's next stop would be the police station. If Joel Gibbons was in his office, Rod would ask Joel if he had a new address for Megan. If Joel were out of the office, Rod would ask Elsie Dorr.

If he couldn't get Megan's address anywhere else, Rod could check at the Twin Rivers Public Library. Not only did the library have a copy of the current city directory listing resident names and addresses, but the librarians might be able to do an online search or suggest other possibilities for obtaining Megan's location. Librarians had always been good friends to reporters.

And, if all else failed, Rod would place a classified ad in next week's *Gazette* asking Megan Williams to telephone her sister. If Megan still lived in Twin Rivers, the chances were good that she browsed the *Gazette*'s Personals and Classifieds. Nearly everyone in town did.

Rod fell asleep listening to the gentle pitter-patter of raindrops on the roof.

CHAPTER TEN

I know what *your* face looks like now, old man. This is your last warning. Stay away from my sister, or I'll make you sorry.

I saw you almost stop to try to pick me up. You wanted to, didn't you? I could tell by the way your car slowed as you drove past me. You pretended not to look at me, but I know you did look. You couldn't see my face under the sweatshirt's dark hood. Was it my breasts you looked at?

They're not real, you know. My breasts are only a facsimile, like the sculptured breasts on a marble statue of a Greek Goddess perched on a pedestal in a museum. But you couldn't tell that from a distance, could you? They're cold like marble, made of silicone gel and plastic, covered with skin stripped from my inner thighs. But you can't tell they're not real until you touch them.

I'm glad you didn't stop to pick me up tonight, old man. I'm waiting for Pimples to come out of the restaurant. This time, when Pimples gets into the Dodge van, I'll get the entire license number.

Seeing one of my rapists in the restaurant two nights in a row means the four are ready to follow Susan home. It's after eleven o'clock and Pimples is still inside Terri's. He'll come out when Susan's shift is over at midnight. He'll get into the van and wait for Susan to leave work. Then the van will follow her to her apartment.

Will they try to rape Susan tonight? Should I wait for the four at the apartment? Or should I walk up to the van as soon as I see Pimples get in and shoot the four men right here? Can I do what I want to do to all four bodies before the police arrive? I know police patrol this area. A squad car drives by every ten minutes or so. Do I dare chance the police will stop me before I can finish cutting all four?

Pimples comes out of the restaurant and waits for the van to drive up. I have no time left to decide. I finger the Beretta inside my purse. I see the Dodge van approach on the street. Pimples gets in. I get part of the license number as the van drives slowly past the bus stop and turns right at the corner. They're going around the block to wait for Susan to get off work. They intend to follow her home.

I get up from the bench and begin walking east toward Tenth Street. I want to be home and waiting for them when they follow Susan to her apartment. If they try to enter Susan's apartment, I'll shoot them on the back stairs. It will take police at least fifteen minutes to respond to shots fired. That will give me enough time to cut all four men and turn them into women.

I want all four of them to know what it feels like to be a helpless victim. I want them to feel the knife cut away their manhoods. I want to ram the knife inside each of them and hear them scream as the point penetrates their rectums. I want them to bleed out before the police reach them.

Then I can die happy.

I don't care what happens to me after I've finished all four.

I walk as rapidly as I can, dragging my left leg behind me. I pass the old apartment on Fifth Street where I was raped. I pass Sixth Street. Seventh. Three blocks left to go.

The night no longer feels cold. I pay no attention to the rain. I pass Eighth Street.

I'm almost home when I see headlights behind me. I duck behind the trunk of a large oak tree as Susan's Toyota drives past. I wait for the second set of headlights to approach. My right hand reaches into my purse and flips the safety off, and I have the Beretta in my hand when the Dodge van drives past.

I could have fired the gun at the van, but what if I missed? Isn't it better to wait until I have a clear shot at each of the men? I walk rapidly to the front entrance to my apartment building and climb the stairs to my floor. I rush through my apartment to the rear window and pick up my binoculars.

Susan has parked her Toyota and I see her ascending the back stairs of her building. The rapists are likely watching from the entrance to the alley. Now they know where Susan lives. They'll know which apartment is hers as soon as she enters. They intend to rape Susan in her apartment the way they raped me in our old apartment.

I'm a little out of breath, but I'm ready if they come for her now. I can get down my back stairs, race across the alley, and shoot all four men while they're climbing the stairs. The safety is off the Beretta. I have the butcher knife and box-cutter in my purse.

Will they wait until Susan is asleep? It's already after one AM. I'm sure they want to finish before sun-up. They want no one to see them in daylight.

I can be patient. I'll wait for them to be out in the open when I shoot them. I want to be certain to hit them and not kill them.

I've practiced day and night aiming the Beretta. I know how to align the sights. I know how to put the front post where I want the bullet to hit. I know how to squeeze the trigger.

My knife is sharp enough to split a human hair.

Tonight is the night I have waited for through four years of torture. True, I was unconscious during most of the first year, but the second year was pure hell and the third year wasn't much better. But this year I've acclimatized to pain. I own a gun. I've practiced aiming and firing the handgun.

And I've practiced cutting male members into small pieces like dicing frankfurters to add protein to baked mac and cheese.

Susan is inside her apartment now, and I see the Dodge van cruise slowly through the alley. The van stops directly across from Susan's apartment and parks in one of the empty spaces. The four men remain inside the dark van staring up at Susan's back door. Pimples looks like he can't wait to rape my sister. He's actually bouncing up and down in the back seat. The other three just sit there, silently waiting and watching.

As soon as the lights go out in Susan's apartment, all four men seem to perk up. The driver checks the LED time on his digital wrist watch. It's 3:10 AM according to my alarm clock. Now the rapists know what time Susan goes to bed. They'll give her a half hour to fall asleep. Then they'll make their move.

Now I'm the one who can't wait. I've waited for this moment for a long time. I have my gun, my knife, and my box-cutter. I've been patient, but my patience is wearing thin. If they don't make their move soon, I'll go down there and shoot them through the windows of the van.

And then they do make their move, but it's not the move I expect. The van's headlights come on as the engine starts up. My heart sinks as I watch the van pull out of its parking space and continue slowly up the alley to turn left onto Foster Avenue.

Are they only driving around the block? Why? Did they see a police car pass by on Foster Avenue? Did someone turn on a floodlight that wasn't on before? Did they see someone look out a window at them?

I wait for the van to return. When it doesn't, I wonder why the men left. Susan is in bed and probably sound asleep by now. The men could easily enter the apartment and Susan wouldn't know they were there until they grabbed her. Why didn't they do her while they had the chance?

I know they couldn't have seen me. I'm wearing all black, there are no lights on in the apartment behind me, and I'm half-hidden by window drapes. Besides, they would need to crane their necks at awkward angles to look up this way instead of across the alley.

And then it finally dawns on me. One or more of the men in that van needs to be at work tomorrow morning. When they raped me, they had entered the Fifth Street apartment shortly after midnight. Although it seems like it took an eternity, they raped me, cut me up, and left me for dead in the apartment within an hour and a half of entering. They were already gone before two AM when Susan came home and found me.

The reason those men didn't wait around to make certain I bled out was because they needed time to sleep a little and wash up before catching the train to downtown Chicago to arrive at a job before nine AM. They may live in the suburbs but they work downtown in the big city.

If they raped Susan tonight, it would be cutting things too close (no pun intended). It would be nearly six by the time they finished. They might not have enough time to make it home, wash up, and catch the train because of increased early morning traffic during rush hours.

One of them—probably the older guy who drove the van and seemed like the leader—has a good-paying respectable job in a downtown office. No one he works with suspects he's a rapist and serial-killer who gets his kicks by visiting the suburbs at night. He's the kind of guy who looks clean-cut and is always at work on time. There are millions of guys that look like him in Chicagoland. They work in offices, on the mercantile exchange, in the post office. They have nine to five jobs that pay well and provide cover for their other activities. He can't afford to show up late for work.

So the four men will be back, but not tonight. They will come back tomorrow or another night when they'll have plenty of time to enjoy what they're doing without worry about being late for work in the morning. They will come early, maybe even before midnight. They'll enter Susan's apartment, wait for her in the dark, and grab her when she comes through the door.

Tonight was only a scouting expedition. Last night they learned Susan still works at Terri's Restaurant. Tonight they learned where she lives. When they come back the next time, they intend to rape her and kill her.

This changes everything. Now I don't know when they'll return. It could be tomorrow, it could be the next night. It could be next week or next month. I'll need to stay at the window and watch for them constantly. If they make it up those stairs and into Susan's apartment before I reach them, I'll never have a chance to shoot all of them. Once they're inside they're practically home free.

I fall into a chair near the window and sob my eyes out. I cry and cry and cry. I had so many opportunities to shoot them when they were all together in their van, and I blew it. I should have listened to my intuition and shot them when I had the chance.

I stop crying and dry my eyes. There's no use crying over spilled milk. I'm a big girl now. I can be patient and wait for another opportunity.

I press the magazine release catch and drop the bullets from the Beretta into my purse. I rack the slide back and eject the single round in the chamber. I aim out the window and practice dry-firing. My heart is cold and I think about what I'm going to do to those men when I see them again. Next time I won't wait. Next time I'll kill them all as soon as I see them.

When next time comes, I'll be ready and waiting. Maybe I should also practice my knife skills, to keep them sharp. Ha ha. I can be a real cut-up when I want to be, can't I? Laugh, damn it! Laugh!

Who should I do if I can't do those four? Should I go out to bars and wait for some pervert to pick me up? Men like that deserve what they get and get what they deserve. I was so looking forward to cutting off a man's genitals tonight. I feel frustrated.

It's too late to do anyone tonight. Tomorrow is another day. Maybe I'll run into that old guy who made Susan cry. Maybe he'll try to pick me up and I'll do him. I'll go to Terri's early tomorrow, right after Susan begins her shift. I can hang around until eight or nine. I want to be back home before eleven, though. If those four rapists come back tomorrow to wait for Susan to get home from work, I want to be here. I can't let them get into her apartment. I'll recognize their van when I see it. I know the license number now. As soon as I see the van enter the alley, I'll head downstairs.

But if I see the old man in Terri's and he tries to pick me up, I'll do him first. I have plenty of time. I have all the time in the world.

CHAPTER ELEVEN

Twin Rivers Medical Center looked little different than it looked when Rod moved Helen from the hospital to hospice more than two years ago. Helen's organs were failing, and she required constant care. Her insurance, however, refused to pay for an extended hospital stay when there was no hope of recovery. Financial considerations forced Rod to move Helen into the nursing home across the street where hospice provided palliative care for end-of-life terminally-ill patients. Insurance covered fifty percent of Helen's hospice stay, and Rod was able to cover the rest from savings.

Rod began at the billing office. He told them he wanted to make sure they had the correct billing address for Megan Williams since Megan had recently moved. They asked Rod to confirm Megan's address, and he gave them the old address Susan had told him. The billing clerk said that was the same address they currently had on file for Ms. Williams.

Rod next went upstairs to speak with several nurses he knew in the long-term care wing where Helen had languished for 89 days before moving across the street to hospice. Those same nurses had cared for Megan Williams while she was in a coma and during two of her extended stays for reconstructive surgery. Rod hoped nurses would remember Megan and be able to fill him in on the extent of Megan's injuries and the work that was done to repair some of the damage to her face. Two of the nurses remembered Megan. They said that poor girl had suffered some of the most severe physical and psychological injuries they had ever seen. It was a miracle that the child had survived. No one ever expected Megan to recover. But she came out of the coma after a year, and most of her wounds had eventually healed, although she was left permanently scarred and partially paralyzed. Megan had to endure exhaustive physical therapy to learn to walk again. After Megan was released from the hospital, plastic surgeons had worked on her as an out-patient for nearly two years. No one had seen Megan since she had completed facial reconstruction. Only the doctor and his staff at the clinic knew what Megan looked like now.

Rod tried to speak with the plastic surgeons, but they refused to give Rod any information without the patient's express consent. They wouldn't even confirm Megan was a patient.

Rod tried Joel Giffords at the police station, but Giffords was working a case for the task force and wouldn't be available even for telephone calls until tomorrow. Rod stopped by Elsie Dorr's office and asked Elsie for any new information on the Megan Williams case. Did the police even have Megan's current address? Elsie pulled Megan's case file and Megan's last known address was the recently vacated apartment she had listed after leaving the hospital. "Sorry," said Elsie. "It's a cold case. We're still looking for the perps, but we're not actively looking for the victim."

Last, but not least, Rod tried the public library. Unfortunately, the city directory was only published once a year in the spring, and Megan's old apartment address was the one currently listed. Rod spoke with a reference librarian who did a search of several residential databases. Megan Williams was listed in one of them, but at the same old address. Megan was reported in the last census as residing with her parents and sister in a single-family dwelling on East Riverside Boulevard. Rod entered the house number in his notebook. Maybe Megan's mother still lived at that Riverside address. Did Megan's mother know the whereabouts of her youngest daughter? It was worth a try. Rod looked up Megan's picture in old Twin Rivers High School yearbooks buried in musty library stacks. Megan—blonde, beautiful, and full of potential—was a smiling seventeen in her senior photograph. He was surprised to note that Megan had been the editor-in-chief of her school newspaper. Rod, too, had been on his high school newspaper staff, though not the editor. He had reported weekly sporting events and club meetings. More than half-a-century later, Rod was doing much the same thing he had done as a teenager. The more things changed, the more some things remained the same.

People were creatures of habit. What were Megan's life-long habits? If she had edited her high school newspaper, that meant she once read newspapers from front to back. Did she still read newspapers? Would she read about herself in the *Twin Rivers Gazette* if Rod ran her picture on the front page and devoted next week's entire Reminiscences column to Megan's tragic story? Would Megan contact Rod at the *Gazette* to set the story straight after the story ran under a "Missing Megan" banner head?

Not only was Megan Williams the victim of a violent attack, she could now be legitimately classified as a missing person. Rod could slant the story to imply Megan had disappeared because the four rapists had come back to finish the job. Had they abducted Megan? Was Megan Williams dead? Or was she alive and hiding out in fear that the four would come back to finish her off? Inquiring minds wanted answers to those questions.

Rod made photocopies of the pictures in the old yearbooks. He headed to the *Gazette* office to write the story and try to convince Tim to run Megan's photo on the front page. Would Joel Giffords and Elsie Dorr feel betrayed when Rod pointed out in print that police weren't perfect in their case clearance record? Probably. But Rod needed to find Megan before the killers found her. Finding Megan was an obsession with him now.

Rod had felt powerless to protect Helen from the ravages of cancer, but he believed the power of the press would protect Megan Williams from being ravished again by the same rapists and killers who had nearly cut her to pieces. Those four men were like a cancer to the community, not only to the women of Twin Rivers but to women in all of the surrounding suburbs where the four raped and murdered with impunity even today. An informed citizenry could help bring them to justice.

Tim was at his desk designing ad copy when Rod entered. Rod took a seat at his own desk and began composing his columns for next week's edition. He hammered away at his keyboard the way he had pounded the keys on a manual typewriter. Tim shot Rod an angry look. Tim had never worked in a real newsroom where dozens of writers, editors, rewritemen, and copyboys vied to be heard over the incessant clatter of clacking typewriters and constantly chattering wire service terminals. From time to time, UPI or AP or Reuters would announce an important breaking story with loud alarm bells: five bells for urgent and ten bells for flash priority messages. Newsrooms were meant to be noisy. Rod ignored Tim's looks until Tim couldn't stand it anymore.

"Shut the fuck up," Tim shouted across the room. "Can't you see I'm trying to work?"

"So am I," said Rod. He stopped pounding the keys to read what was written on the screen. He went back and revised his lead paragraph.

Who: "Megan Williams, 18."

What: "was raped and physically mutilated."

When: "four years ago on August 6th."

Why: "by four young men out for kicks who were looking to rape Megan's twenty-one-year-old sister and found Megan instead."

Where: "in the apartment Megan shared with her sister at 514 Fifth Street in Twin Rivers."

How: "The four men entered the apartment before midnight, discovered Megan home alone, and cut her repeatedly with a hunting knife while also raping her. They left Megan for dead, but she survived."

Next paragraph: "Megan Williams was recently reported missing and is feared dead. Anyone who has any information about Megan Williams and her current whereabouts is urged to contact Rodney Engleworth at the Twin Rivers Gazette." Rod included the *Gazette*'s office telephone number.

Follow-up paragraph: "Megan Williams is described as blonde, five feet and seven inches tall, weighing approximately one-hundred-and-twenty pounds, and presently twenty-two years of age. The last known photograph of Megan Williams appears above. Megan had extensive plastic surgery to her face and may appear differently today than in her picture."

Next paragraph: "Police are actively searching for four Caucasian men between the ages of twenty and twenty-nine. All four men are wanted for multiple rapes and homicides in the Twin Rivers area."

Rod had a start. Now he had to turn his copy into the kind of human-interest story that people would be certain to read. He wanted people to discuss Megan Williams and what had happened to her. He wanted people to lock their doors and report any suspicious activity to the police.

And he wanted anyone who knew where Megan lived to contact him immediately.

New paragraph: "Megan Williams made news when she miraculously emerged from a coma after more than a year. She described her four assailants to the police: The leader was tall, clean-shaven, with black hair and hazel eyes, approximately 24 years old (now 28); another was medium height, skinny, had long red hair, bright blue eyes, and he was approximately 22 years old (now 26); a third man was described as good-looking, medium build, with blond hair, blue eyes, and a beard, approximately 21 years old (now 25); and the fourth man was approximately sixteen or seventeen (now possibly 21) with acne on his face, and his hair and eyes were brown."

Rod knew Joel Giffords would be angry if he wrote about the recent murders and mutilation of men in Twin Rivers. But he wanted more than just women to read the story, so Rod added brief paragraphs about each of the murders, implying that the recent mutilation murders were all linked to the four men who raped Megan. He felt there was some kind of link, but he had no clue what that link might be. He also implied that Megan Williams, now 22, might be afraid the rapists would come back to silence her, and she was hiding where those four men couldn't find her.

When he resumed typing, his touch to the keys was considerably softer than before. Filled with inspiration, Rod's fingers literally flew over the keys like angels dancing on the heads of pins. He finished writing the whole story, leaned back in his chair, and scrolled through thousands of words on the monitor's screen. He proofed the story once, made a few minor corrections, and sent the digital copy to Tim as an e-mail attachment. No need to call a copy boy to hand-deliver the copy to the editor's desk. It flew across the room at the speed of light with a single touch to the return key. It had been called the return key on the IBM Selectrics Rod had used at the Daily News. Now it was called the enter key on his computer's keyboard.

Rod had lived in the digital age for several decades now, but he still missed the old way of doing things. He knew the very existence of the *Gazette* depended primarily on replacing people with technology. Rod and Tim were the only staff, and Rod survived on the pittance Tim paid solely because Rod got monthly social security checks from the government. Tim drew a meager salary himself. He had bought the bankrupt *Gazette* from the previous owners six years ago, turned the resurrected title into a free weekly instead of a subscription-based daily, and digitized the entire operation. He had invested every penny of the money he had inherited when his father died, and he was only now beginning to show a small profit.

Tim, like Rod, held a journalism degree from Northwestern's Medill School of Journalism. Tim had gone on to earn a master's in graphic design from the University of Illinois at Chicago's Circle Campus. He had worked at a downtown Chicago advertising agency for a year or two before his father died. Tim quit his job as soon as probate was settled, bought the *Gazette*, and hired Rod to help revive the newspaper. Rod had been freelancing as a stringer for a dozen different papers, and he had seen an ad for "Writer Wanted in Twin Rivers" in the *Chicago Tribune*'s daily suburban edition's classifieds. Rod had rushed down to Tim's newly-rented office and applied. Tim had hired Rod on the spot.

The two men worked well together. Rod had mentored Tim in the newspaper business, and Tim had tutored Rod in using computers and surfing the net. Tim was the son Rod never had, and Rod was the father Tim had lost. Rod wrote all of the news copy and headlines, and Tim did all of the ads and page layouts. Together, they were a team.

But Tim never let Rod forget that it was paid advertisements that kept the paper in business, not hard news. By the time the *Gazette* appeared in print it was all old news anyway. Rod's job was to write the kind of human interest stories that made good filler. People *liked* to read about local people, local events, and local business establishments. Every time Rod ran a favorable story about a local business, that business took out a new ad.

Stories about serial rapes and murders and genital mutilations were hazardous to the paper's health. The chamber of commerce would be all up in arms about the *Gazette* sullying Twin Rivers' spotless reputation. Advertisers would feel betrayed. No one wanted to patronize businesses in locations where they might get raped, murdered, or castrated.

Rod felt it was essential to tell as much of the story as possible and as accurately as possible, so he named names and included ages and addresses. He wanted people to be on the lookout for both Megan Williams and the killers. Maybe someone would report Megan's current address. Maybe Megan herself would call. Maybe a tip would help catch the killers.

Maybe the power of the press was still alive and living in Twin Rivers.

Rod didn't wait around for Tim to read the story. Tim would only rant and rave and ask if Rod were trying to kill the goose that laid the golden eggs. But, in the end, Rod knew Tim would run the story just as Rod had written it. There was still something of the newsman in Tim Goodman that recognized an important story when he saw it. Tim wasn't in the newspaper business solely for the money. He could have made lots more money investing his inheritance in the stock market.

Rod desperately needed a cup of coffee. Tim didn't allow coffee or soft drinks around the computers in the office, and Rod felt he needed a drink badly. Instead of heading for a bar, however, Rod drove directly to Terri's Restaurant. It was already after five, and he wanted to have dinner and maybe a slice of delicious pecan pie along with his coffee. Bars, for Rodney Engleworth, were a thing of the past.

And, of course, he could see Susan at Terri's. He wouldn't find Susan in a bar.

As he entered the restaurant, Rod spotted the girl with the hoodie sitting in a booth in the front section. Was the girl trying to look goth? She was dressed entirely in black: black sweatshirt with a hood over her head, black jeans, black running shoes. Rod checked out her fingernails to see if she also wore black nail polish. She wore lacy black gloves that covered both hands, and Rod couldn't see her fingernails. But he bet they were painted black, too.

All he could see of her face was the tip of her nose. The rest of her face was hidden in shadow. Even her eyes were hidden, but Rod had the feeling the girl was looking straight at him while he was looking at her. He smiled and nodded in her direction. Then he took a seat at his regular table in Susan's section at the back of the restaurant.

"I had no luck at the hospital, the police station, nor the library," Rod said when Susan brought his coffee and a menu. "No one knows Megan's current address. If they do, they're not saying."

"Thanks for trying," said Susan. "Your usual tonight?"

"Open faced roast beef with mashed potatoes and gravy," Rod told her, not bothering to look at the menu. He was a creature of habit. Was he that predictable? He supposed he was.

When Susan brought the plate of food, Rod asked her about the girl with the hoodie.

"She's a regular," Susan said. "She comes in several times a day, always sits in the front, and always wears something covering her hair and part of her face. Sometimes it's a scarf. Lately, it's been that black hoodie or another like it. She's not a street person because she has money. And she bathes. She doesn't smell."

"She walks with a limp. Do you know why?"

"I've never talked to her. She doesn't sit in my section."

"I'm just curious," said Rod.

He finished his meal and ordered dessert. Rod felt the girl's eyes on him, watching every move he made. Once or twice he looked her way and tried to see her face. She didn't turn away.

What was wrong with the girl anyway? Nice people didn't stare at other people. Last night the girl had stared at the pimply faced boy at the counter. Tonight she was staring at Rod.

Rod knew the girl had a physical disability, a limp. Did she have a mental disability too? Something sure wasn't right about that girl. Was it drugs? Rod knew absolutely nothing about the goth subculture. Did goths do drugs? Rod had no clue.

Susan refilled his coffee cup. "Does she stare at everyone?" he asked Susan.

"All the time. She doesn't read. Most people who come in here and stay for a long time bring a newspaper or a book to read after eating.

She just stares. When she isn't staring at someone, she's staring off into space."

"She ever talk to the waitresses?"

"Only to order."

"She comes in every day?"

"Every day I've been here. I can't speak for Sundays and Mondays."

"Strange," said Rod.

"We get all kinds in here," said Susan. "I'm glad I don't work the night shift. After the bars close, drunks stagger in. They try to paw the waitresses, and sometimes they puke all over the floor and the waitress has to clean it up. As long as she doesn't bother anyone and pays her bill, she's welcome to stare all she wants. We only ask her to leave if we get real busy and there's a line waiting for tables. Otherwise, she can sip coffee all day, for all any of us care. Some days, she does."

"You ever see her face?"

"Only part of her face. She wears something covering her forehead and hair even in summer. Some days she wears sun glasses even inside the restaurant. Lately, she's been wearing sweatshirts with hoods. I've seen her wear blue, green, brown. Yesterday she dressed all in blue. Today, she's wearing black. She changes her wardrobe, and she's always clean. I don't think she's homeless."

"I thought maybe she was goth since she's all dressed in black."

Susan laughed. "If you want goth, you should see some of the teens who stop in on their way home from school. They have spiked hair all kinds of colors, and they wear tight leather pants or leather skirts. Most have multiple rings on their fingers, through their ears, noses, eyebrows, even lips. They dress that way to show off, not to hide."

"You think that girl is trying to hide?"

"Don't you?"

"I think a busy restaurant isn't the best place to hide," said Rod.

Susan moved around to other tables to refill coffee cups and check on customers. The girl in the hoodie momentarily shifted her attention from Rod to Susan.

Rod wondered if the girl might be gay. A lot of men, Rod included, came to Terri's to see Susan. Rod got the distinct impression Susan was the reason the girl came to Terri's, too. Maybe it was something in the way the girl's demeanor softened when she looked at Susan. Her body language seemed less uptight, less angry. Then the girl looked straight at Rod again, and her back stiffened, her fingers curled into fists. Rod felt pure hatred radiating in his direction.

That girl obviously had a problem with men. Rod had misjudged her yesterday when he thought she had a crush on the pimply-faced guy at the counter. She didn't have a crush, she had a grudge.

The girl glanced at the clock on the wall. It was eight-fifteen. She got up, dropped a buck tip on the table, and paid her bill at the cashier's stand. Rod watched her limp out of the restaurant and turn right. She was headed for the bus stop.

Rod's nose for news wasn't just twitching, it was itching like mad. Did this girl know Megan Williams? He sensed a connection to Susan and Megan.

Rod decided to follow the girl. He left a five under his coffee cup, paid his bill, and saw the familiar figure sitting at the bus stop as he ambled toward his car. Rod watched her from the front seat of his Ford Focus. The eight-twenty-five bus stopped at the corner but the girl did not get on.

What the hell is she waiting for? Rod wondered. She sure wasn't waiting for the bus.

Rod got the uncomfortable feeling the girl was waiting for him. She stared straight at him, her face hidden beneath that damned hood like some medieval monk. She didn't make a move, and neither did he.

Time ticked by. The clock on the dash read eight-forty-five. Then eight-fifty.

Finally, the girl got up and walked slowly toward Rod in the Focus, dragging her left leg behind her. When she reached the passenger side of the car, she knocked on the window. Rod turned the key to auxiliary and lowered the passenger window.

"It's not polite to stare," the girl said. Her voice sounded hoarse like she had a sore throat and was about to lose her voice entirely.

"You were staring at me," said Rod.

"I stare at everybody," said the girl. "Why did you follow me?"

"You intrigue me," admitted Rod. "I was wondering what your face looked like."

"Open the door and I'll show you."

Rod unlocked the passenger door.

The girl slid into the seat. "Do you live around here?" asked the girl, making no move to remove the hood from her face.

"I own a house in Twin Rivers."

"Is it far from here? Take me to your house and I'll show you my face."

"I'm not sure that's a good idea," said Rod.

"I won't show you my face unless you take me to your house."

"What's your name?" Rod asked.

"What's yours?" demanded the girl.

"Rodney Engleworth."

"The newspaper guy?"

"That's right."

"My name's Megan," said the girl.

Rod's mouth dropped open. "Not Megan Williams, Susan's sister!"

"No," said the girl. "I'm not the same Megan Williams that was Susan's sister."

"Do you know her? Are you related to that other Megan Williams?"

"Yes, I knew her. Take me to your house and I'll tell you all I know about the other Megan Williams."

Rod couldn't believe his luck. His old nose for news hadn't let him down. He had sensed a connection between this girl and Megan. He started the Focus, shifted into drive, and headed for his house.

"I've been looking all over town for Megan Williams," said Rod. "It's fortunate I found you. Do you know where Megan is now? How do you know Susan and her sister?"

"I grew up with them," said the girl. "Are you taking me to your house?"

"I'll take you wherever you want to go to talk."

"Take me to your house and we'll talk there."

Rod pulled into his driveway and parked in front of the garage. He opened the garage door and led the girl through the dark garage into his cozy kitchen. "Take a seat at the table," he said, flipping on the overhead fluorescent in the kitchen. "I'll make a pot of coffee. Then we'll talk."

The girl sat at the kitchen table and fiddled in her purse while Rod scooped fresh coffee grounds into the machine. He filled the reservoir with water and switched the machine on and left it to perk. He took two clean cups down from the cupboard and set them next to the coffee-maker.

"Now will you show me your face?" said Rod. "Take off the hood that hides your face."

The girl reached up and pulled the entire sweatshirt over her head. She wore nothing beneath the sweatshirt to cover the bare flesh of her upper body. Rod stared at twin mounds of badly-scarred flesh that looked more like a patch-work quilt than female breasts.

"It's not polite to stare at a girl's breasts," said the girl named Megan.

Rod moved his eyes upward and focused on her equally-scarred face where multiple scars decorated her forehead, her cheeks, her chin. There was a long scar on her throat.

He didn't notice the gun until the girl shoved the barrel between his eyes and cocked the hammer.

"Let's go into the bedroom," the girl said. "And I'll show you and tell you everything."

"You're Susan's sister, aren't you?" Rod said. It was as much a statement of fact as a question. He should have realized it sooner. How could he have been so blind?

"I was," admitted Megan Williams. "But now I'm someone else."

"You need help," said Rod. "Let me help you."

"You want to help me, old man? Put your hands together and hold them out in front of you. That's right. Just like that." Rod watched her reach into her purse with her free hand and bring out a roll of silver-colored duct tape. She wrapped the tape around his wrists a half-dozen times. Then she cut the tape with a pair of pinking shears.

"I don't want to shoot you, but I will unless you go into the bedroom and lie down on the bed." She snipped off another piece of duct tape and slapped it over Rod's mouth. She shoved Rod through the living room and into the bedroom Rod had shared with Helen. Rod knew what was coming next, and in a way he welcomed it. Soon he would see Helen again, and he would be with her forever.

He was only sorry that wouldn't be able to tell Susan he'd found her sister.

Megan Williams pushed him down on the bed and wrapped duct tape around his ankles.

She undressed completely and stood naked in front of him while she slipped a pair of rubber gloves over both hands. Then she opened her purse and took out a box-cutter and a butcher knife.

CHAPTER TWELVE

I told you what I would do to you if you didn't leave my sister alone, old man. Don't say I didn't warn you.

I'm no longer the same Megan Williams I once was. Those men who raped me changed me. You can see the scars. You said you wanted to see. Take a good look. Look at all of me. Look at my face. Look at my breasts. Look at my vagina. Look at my scarred thighs. See what I've become.

The old Megan Williams is dead. She died four years ago.

Now I want to see all of you. Since I've duct-taped your hands and feet, I'll have to cut your clothes off. You don't mind, do you? You won't need clothes anymore. You won't need anything after tonight.

Pinking shears work better than knives to cut fabric. I'll slice up the front of the trouser legs. Let me get that belt out of the way. There. Now I can cut the pants all the way up to the waist. We'll do the same with your shirt. Then your t-shirt and boxers.

Now you're as naked as I am.

How does it feel to be naked and helpless? I can tell by your eyes that you know what's coming next. Did you see what I did to those other two men? You did, didn't you?

Should I try to arouse you? Would it do any good if I played with your penis? I don't mind touching you when I'm wearing latex gloves. I see you've already been circumcised. Did it hurt when they cut off your foreskin? Or was it done when you were a baby and you don't remember?

Where shall we begin? How about your nipples. Men don't need nipples anyway. Let's just cut them off.

Now I'll use the box-cutter to slice open your inner thighs. Oh, don't struggle so much! It won't do any good.

I'm working my way up to your private parts. Your penis tries to hide like a turtle drawing its head into its shell. We'll use the pliers to pull it back out. Does that hurt? Oh, good. I want it to hurt.

I don't have a lot of time to waste tonight. I've got to get home and wait for the four men who raped me to come back to do Susan. So I'll get right to the root of the problem, cut to the chase, so to speak. We'll use the pinking shears to snip off your penis. There. All gone.

Now roll over and I'll do the backside.

So much blood! Who knew you'd be a bleeder? Your little heart must be pumping like crazy. You'll be dead in no time at all.

I read that your wife died. Too bad. Who will find you? Do you have children? No? Maybe you'll just lie here until you rot. Someone will find you eventually.

You men are all alike. I saw the way you looked at my sister. You look old enough to know better. But you didn't listen when I warned you to stay away from Susan. You kept coming back to see her. I saw you make her cry. For that alone, you deserve to die.

You'll get what you deserve. I won't let anyone hurt my sister.

You don't mind if I use your bathtub to wash up, do you? Of course, you don't mind.

You don't mind anything anymore.

Do you know what I miss? I miss feeling the tingles I used to feel when I soaped my breasts and washed between my legs. I don't feel much of anything anymore. It's like I'm as dead as you. I might as well be dead.

Will tonight be the night I get my revenge? Will those four men who raped me come to Susan's apartment tonight to do to her what they did to me? I hope so. I know exactly what I'll do to them when I see them again. I won't be as quick with them as I was with you. I'll make them suffer the way they made me suffer.

Since I'm already as good as dead, what difference does it make if I'm caught in the act? All that keeps me going, all that keeps me alive, is the thought of revenge. Once I've had my revenge, I can die happy.

What is death like? Can you still see and hear and feel? Are you watching me now from the Great Beyond? Or did everything end for you when you died? Did the pain go away? Do you see nothing but emptiness? Or do you have dreams?

I was in a coma for nearly a year. During that entire time I dreamed. Are you dreaming now? Are you having nightmares? Are you reliving the last moments of your life again and again? Is that what hell is like?

I know you're in hell. You had impure thoughts. Any man who has impure thoughts goes straight to hell.

Women, too, go to hell. I've lived in hell for the past four years.

Maybe I'll go to heaven after I die. Maybe I've already suffered enough. Do you think that's possible? Or, maybe, because I've broken the most important of the Ten Commandments and taken lives, I'll join you in hell. Would you like that? Would you like to see me again? No? Why not?

Now I must leave you. I have to hurry home before Susan gets home. I want to be waiting for those men when they arrive. I've washed your blood from my knives and the box-cutter and the pinking shears, but I want to sharpen them up again. I want to be able to cut through their flesh like butter so I can finish all four before the police arrive. By the time I'm done, the blades will be dull again.

If those men don't come tonight, I'll wait for them until they do. I've been patient, and I can be patient a little longer.

I'm nothing if not patient.

CHAPTER THIRTEEN

Tim Goodman went ballistic when he read Rod's story.

Tim had spent the entire afternoon and evening writing advertising copy, illustrating ads with photos and clip art, adding store logos, and formatting ads so they fit into the next edition exactly where buyers paid to have them placed. Tim always imported ads into InDesign first, then Rod's filler copy could flow seamlessly into whatever available space remained on each page. Sometimes Tim had to cut the last couple of paragraphs of Rod's column, but Rod always included the important stuff in the opening paragraphs and merely recapped near the end. Rod normally waited until Monday to file his copy for the Wednesday edition. Tim couldn't remember a single time when Rod had delivered both his lead story and the two weekly columns he composed this far in advance of his deadline. Today was only Thursday. Rod must not be feeling well.

Tim put off reading Rod's stuff until after a dinner break. Tim kept a small refrigerator and a microwave in the *Gazette*'s back rooms that doubled as his bachelor apartment, and he popped a frozen entre into the microwave. Tim thought about Rodney Engleworth while waiting for the microwave to signal the food was ready to eat. He hoped Rod wasn't coming down with the flu. Older people were especially susceptible, and the flu virus had been spreading around town since night temperatures dropped below freezing earlier this week.

Hiring Rod to write for the *Gazette* was one of the best decisions Tim had ever made. The old man had never once missed a deadline, not even when his wife was dying of terminal cancer. A few times, when Rod had been drinking heavily, Tim had needlessly worried that the story would be for shit or the old man would miss the Monday deadline, but the stories were always professional and competed on time.

Since Rod had stopped drinking, his stories had been even better than some of the award-winning stories Rod wrote in the distant past for big-city dailies. Rod's sixteen-week "Reminiscences of Helen" column had increased circulation and brought in dozens of new advertisers. If this kept up, Tim would be able to afford to give Rod a much-deserved raise and maybe give himself a raise, too.

Rod had taught Tim a lot about journalism, much more than any of the courses—hell, more than all of the courses combined—he had completed at Northwestern. Tim had been enamored of newspapers all of his life, but by the time he had grown up and was ready to become a journalist himself, almost all the great newspapers were badly hurting or going out of business and it was impossible to get a paying job as a cub reporter anywhere in the country. Unpaid internships were the new rage. So Tim had gone on to graduate school and studied graphic design and went into advertising instead. Advertising paid good money, and Tim's father was proud his son could support himself and have enough money left over to pay off his school loans.

When Tim's widowed father died and left a sizable insurance policy, pension settlement, and the suburban Twin Rivers house where Tim had been raised to Timothy Mark Goodman, his one and only child, Tim bought the bankrupt local daily paper he had grown up reading, got out of the advertising rat race, and hired a washed-up old newspaperman to help him. Tim had gambled his inheritance and his future on a long-shot.

But that long-shot was finally paying off, thanks to Rodney Engleworth. Circulation had doubled, ad revenues had increased accordingly, and Tim had visions of earning enough money to someday get married and have kids. Marriage had never seemed important to Tim before Rod wrote his "Reminiscences of Helen." Tim's parents had seemed happy enough together, but Rod and Helen were romantic ideals made real. They had lived and loved through adversity, stayed together through sickness and health, and the marital memories Rod had shared seemed priceless. Tim hoped someday to have the same kind of memories.

But Tim Goodman had been too busy keeping the struggling paper afloat to think about dating, much less marriage. He had dated a number of girls in high school and college, even lived with a girl for two years during grad school. He still chatted occasionally on Facebook with a few of those old girlfriends, but he felt he couldn't take time away from selling ads and formatting the weekly paper to actually go out on a date. Maybe now, when he had sufficient advertisers locked into annual or monthly contracts, he could look around for someone he wanted to date.

Tim wolfed down the TV dinner and opened a Diet Pepsi. He had been far too sedentary lately and the few extra pounds that filled out his waistline made his pants feel tight. He still wasn't fat. But he didn't want to become fat, either. Tim was thirty-three, going on thirty-four. He didn't want to die of a heart attack at fifty like his mom or a stroke at sixty like his father.

Tim had never been athletic. He had always been average height for his age and skinny, much too lanky and physically awkward—probably because he was a southpaw in a right-handed world—to successfully play football or baseball. He felt too short to play basketball. Besides, he had been terribly nearsighted and wore eyeglasses he was always afraid of losing or breaking. He couldn't see much of anything without his glasses.

As an only child, he had spent much of his childhood reading instead of playing with other kids. He became social only in high school and college. Being social still wasn't part of his comfort zone.

After Tim's father died, Tim developed a single-minded obsession with becoming a newspaperman. Running a newspaper had been his dream as a kid. The closest he could come to realizing his dream, however, was to buy the *Gazette* and turn it into an advertising medium. But Rodney Engleworth had helped make Tim's dream come true and Tim loved the old man despite their occasional disagreements.

But now, when Tim read Rod's story for next week's paper, Tim called Rod every name in the book. That no-good son-of-a-bitching fucking bastard had stabbed Tim in the back. That god-damned drunk must have fallen off the wagon. Where did that cock-sucking faggot get the idea that serial-rapists and serial-killers were at work in Twin Rivers? Was he out of his ever-lovin' mind? Tim had heard nothing from anyone reliable about murders and castrations in Twin Rivers ever, nor anything about a Megan Williams being raped and mutilated four years ago. Surely, if something like this happened in town everyone would know about it. It would be the talk of the town.

And didn't Rod write a story just last week about the phenomenal case clearance rate of Twin Rivers police? Tim had heard nothing about a Benjamin Willard or a Bill Murphy being murdered, much less castrated. He did see an obituary for Willard just yesterday. But the obit said nothing about the way the man had died.

Tim couldn't possibly run this story. The newspaper could be sued if Rod's copy weren't completely factual and verifiable. Tim had deliberately stayed away from running hard news stories because of possible litigation. Big papers like the *Chicago Tribune* kept a whole team of libel lawyers on retainer. The *Gazette* couldn't afford to hire a single attorney.

Tim picked up the telephone and dialed Rod's home number. The phone rang and rang and was finally answered by a machine. God damn that old bastard. Why didn't he have a cell phone like the rest of the civilized world?

Tim was so angry, he stormed out and drove straight to Rod's house and jabbed the doorbell and pounded on the door. It was after eleven. Why didn't the old guy answer the fucking door?

If Rod was out of the house, where would he go this late? The only place Rod had ever talked about was Terri's Restaurant. If Rod wasn't home or in a bar, he was drinking coffee at Terri's. Tim drove down to Third Street and parked in front of the restaurant.

Tim had been inside Terri's dozens of times to eat or run ads by the owner, and he knew the restaurant was laid out in sections, booths in the front, tables and coffee counter near the back. In fact, Terri's had just renewed their advertising contract with the *Gazette* for another year, and Tim had personally talked with Terri Gilchrist only last week. Tim walked through the entire restaurant and didn't see Rod anywhere, not even at the coffee counter.

Did the guy really fall off the wagon? Was he soaking up suds in one of the many downtown bars or passed out in an alley? Tim tried every bar he could think of, but Rod wasn't in any of them.

It was after one in the morning when Tim returned to Rod's house and knocked on the door again. Rod still wasn't answering his phone when Tim dialed Rod's home number with his cell, and Rod didn't respond to Tim's incessant knocks on the door. Now Tim was beginning to get worried. Rod wasn't young anymore. Had he suffered a heart attack like Tim's mother or a stroke like Tim's father? There were lights on in the house. Rod had to be home.

Was the old guy passed out drunk on the floor? Had he fallen and couldn't get up? Visions of Rod lying helpless while suffering a massive heart attack or a stroke drove Tim to smash a kitchen window and climb into the house through the three-foot by four-foot opening. "Rod! Where the fuck are you?" Tim shouted. "Answer me, damn it!"

Tim moved from the kitchen to the living room and called out again. Still no answer. He walked into the bedroom and nearly vomited from the coppery smell of coagulating blood, the acrid ammonium smell of urine, and the stink of feces.

And then he saw Rod's naked body on the bloody bed, saw the gaping hole where Rod's genitals should have been, and all of that partially-digested microwaved TV dinner spewed forth from Tim Goodman's stomach and out his open mouth with enough force to project a good four feet.

Tim fought off the dizziness that threatened to topple him. Unlike Rod, Tim went nowhere without a cell phone. He speed-dialed 911, identified himself, described the nature of the emergency, gave the residence address, and clicked off. Then he began snapping pictures with his cell phone camera.

Wasn't this exactly what Rod had written about and Tim had refused to believe without corroboration? Obviously, someone in Twin Rivers had covered up both previous murders plus the rape of Megan Williams. That same person or persons would certainly try to cover up this. Tim wanted documentary proof that the mutilation and murder of Rodney Engleworth had actually happened exactly this way. He e-mailed copies of the photos from his cell phone to his desktop computer at the *Gazette* office. He also saved copies of the photos to the cloud.

Tim found a whole pot of freshly-brewed coffee in the kitchen. Either Rod had made the coffee for himself and never had a chance to pour a cup, or he made coffee for a visitor or visitors. Since there was no evidence of a break-in other than the window Tim himself had broken, Tim surmised Rod knew his assailant, had voluntarily opened the door for him or her, and had fixed a whole pot of fresh coffee for both himself and his company. That meant the killer was someone Rod knew and trusted, not some hopped-up drug-head looking for kicks or drug money.

And the fact that none of the fresh coffee had been touched meant the killer had attacked Rod while the coffee was still perking. Tim knew Rod was a die-hard coffee-drinker from way back, and he had become even more so since he'd foresworn alcohol. Rod would have poured himself a cup as soon as the coffee-maker finished perking. Tim also noticed two clean coffee mugs waiting on the counter adjacent to the coffee-maker.

Tim heard sirens in the distance. He took a quick glance around the rest of the house while waiting for the police to arrive. Rod's study was in the spare bedroom, and it was piled so full of old newspapers that he found it almost impossible to walk around the room. The bathroom light was on, and the bottom of the bathtub still looked wet, as if someone had showered recently. One of the towels on the towel rack also appeared slightly damp.

Had Rod taken a shower tonight because he was expecting company?

Tim went to the front door and opened it for the police. Two squad cars, their red and blue MARS lights blazing, pulled into the driveway behind Tim's Jeep. A fire department ambulance followed and parked on the street.

"He's in the bedroom on the right," Tim told the uniformed cops and paramedics who paraded through the open door.

A moment later the paramedics returned to their ambulance. There was nothing they could do now but wait for the coroner to arrive. Several minutes later, a dozen more squad cars came and the entire block was cordoned off with crime scene tape and traffic rerouted elsewhere. An unmarked police car followed the coroner's van twenty minutes after that, and both vehicles were admitted to the crime scene.

Tim recognized Joel Giffords from the photos that had accompanied Rod's feature story in last week's *Gazette*. Giffords looked like a cop. He was six-two, two hundred pounds, and he wore a navy-blue London Fog trenchcoat over a blue suit and striped tie. Giffords was in his early forties, about ten years older than Tim, and Giffords wore his hair cut very short compared to Tim's.

Tim watched Sergeant Giffords and the medical examiner take pictures of Rod and the crime scene before turning the body over and taking additional photographs. The doctor measured both body temperature and ambient air temperature to determine time of death. Rod had been dead for about four hours. Close-up photographs were taken of each cut on Rod's mutilated body, plus the marks left on Rod's wrists and ankles and lips from restraints that had been removed after death.

"I'm afraid I contaminated your crime scene with vomit," Tim said. "The left-over dinner you see on the floor came from me. I'm also the one who broke the kitchen window."

"Are you Goodman?" asked Giffords.

"Yeah," said Tim. "I'm the one who found him and called 911."

"You the same guy who runs the *Gazette*?"

"That's right. I needed to talk with Rod about a story he turned in. I got worried when he didn't answer his phone or his door. I guess I was right to worry."

"When was the last time you saw Engleworth alive?"

"Maybe five or six tonight. I was working on creating ads, and I didn't pay much attention. He filed next week's copy and left the office."

"He have any enemies you know about?"

"None that are still alive. He did write some stories decades ago that involved mobsters. But those bozos all died of lead poisoning, or died in prison, or expired of old age."

"Was he working on any kind of story now?"

"Rod was always working on stories," said Tim. "He didn't share what he was working on until it was ready to see print."

Giffords nodded. "Engleworth was a good reporter," said the cop. "He held his cards close to the vest until he played them. Looks like this was one hand he didn't win."

"Why would anyone do this to an old man?" Tim asked.

"Revenge might be one possible motive," said Giffords. "Or sticking his nose for news where the killer thought it didn't belong. Either Engleworth rubbed someone the wrong way, or he was in the wrong place at the wrong time and saw something he shouldn't have."

"He was killed at home in his own house. He didn't have his nose in anybody's business but his own."

"This wasn't random. It wasn't a robbery gone wrong. This was deliberate. It was all planned out in advance. Someone came here specifically to kill him. Engleworth must have seen someone do something elsewhere, and that someone followed him home."

"Have there been similar incidents involving torture and murder in Twin Rivers?"

"I'm not at liberty to say," said Giffords. "I can't comment on ongoing investigations."

"So there have been," said Tim.

"I really can't say," repeated Giffords like a broken record.

"Rod meant more to me than just an employee or colleague," said Tim. "He was my friend. I'm going to help catch his killers whether you want me to or not."

"Stay out of this, Goodman, I don't want another newspaperman's corpse on my hands."

"Rod was helping you, wasn't he? You think he was looking for this mutilation killer and got too close. You just said you think the killer followed him home."

"I already told you. I can't comment on an on-going investigation."

"And I told you I was going to find Rod's killer. We can work together or we can work separately, but I'm not going to let this drop."

"Then go talk to Elsie Dorr tomorrow," said Giffords. "She handles all press inquiries."

"I will," said Tim. "And I'm going to ask her about other recent murders in Twin Rivers and about the rape of Megan Williams."

"What do you know about the Williams case?"

"I know that someone did to her what was done to Rod. I know Rod wasn't the only man to be mutilated and murdered and Megan wasn't the only woman to be raped and mutilated."

"How do you know this?"

"I have my sources."

"I think your primary source died tonight," said Giffords. "I think you're clutching at straws. I wish I could help you, but I really can't."

"Aren't you going to look for the killer?"

"Of course. I'm going to do everything within my power to bring the murderer of Rodney Engleworth to justice."

"Then help me. Let's get the word out to everyone in Twin Rivers that there's a maniac killer on the loose."

"I really wish I could," said Giffords. "I live here, too, you know. I have a wife and two kids to protect. But I want to protect them, not panic them. Do you really think releasing everything we know to the press will get us closer to catching the killer or killers? We'd be inundated with more phone calls and false leads than we could possibly handle. What will catch Engleworth's killer or killers is good old-fashioned police work, plus some help from modern forensics."

"How close are you to catching the killer now?"

"I'll know more once we have a chance to examine all the evidence."

"Do you think the person or persons who raped Megan Williams killed Rod?"

"I can't really say."

"Why not?"

"Because I told Rodney Engleworth what I knew, and now he's dead. Go home, Goodman. Go home and wash the puke off your chin and the front of your shirt."

Tim looked down and saw stings of vomit dangling from his chin to the front of his sweatshirt. He wiped it away with his sleeve.

"You're out of your league here, Goodman," said Giffords. "If an old pro like Rodney Engleworth struck out playing in the big leagues, what chance does a rookie like you have of hitting a home run?"

Tim stormed out of the house and found his car was boxed into the driveway by two police cars and the coroner's van. He wasn't going anywhere soon, even if he wanted to. Tim opened his car door and climbed inside. He sat in the front seat and silently watched all the activity inside and around the house. Crime scene technicians were carefully searching the grounds with flashlights. Fingerprint technicians were dusting the doors and windows. The whole thing looked like something out of an episode of *CSI*.

He couldn't believe Rod was gone. Rodney Engleworth was like a father to him, and though Tim's own father had died, Tim had believed Rod would be around forever.

Whoever had killed Rodney Engleworth hated the old man as much as Tim had loved him. What was it Rod had seen or done that drove someone to hate Rod enough to emasculate him? Giffords was right about one thing: whoever it was, had planned this in advance. He or she had brought tools with him to bind Rod's hands and feet, cut through the fabric of his clothes, and cut off his genitals. The killer or killers had made deep cuts into the flesh of Rod's inner thighs, sliced off his penis and testicles, and opened up his torso. Who was capable of doing such an inhumane thing to another human being?

Someone who was really sick, that's who. Someone who didn't see Rod as a kindly old man but as a threat.

Someone Rod knew and trusted.

Rod had opened his door to the killer. He had made coffee so they could talk. He had taken out only two coffee cups, one for himself and one for his visitor. Did that mean there was only one other person in the house with Rod? Yes, it did. Of course, that one person could have admitted others after Rod was subdued. But there was only one person that Rod personally had invited into his home.

And that one person was young enough and strong enough and demented enough to bind Rod with what Tim concluded had to be duct tape, force Rod into the bedroom, and do all of that damage to the old man's body.

Tim waned to kick himself for being so wrapped up with selling advertising that he hadn't paid more attention to Rod's private life. Who were Rod's friends? Tim had attended Helen's funeral, and he had seen only a bunch of old folks mourning Rod's loss of his true love. After Helen died and Rod quit drinking, did he socialize and make new friends?

And what about the stories Rod was currently working on? Tim had been so upset by the implications of Rod's revelations in the stories Rod had submitted today that Tim had barely considered any implications beyond a potential loss of advertisers and a possible libel suit. Someone named Megan Williams had been raped, mutilated, and left for dead four years ago. Now she was missing. Two men had been mutilated and murdered in Twin Rivers in the past month, and Rod implied a connection with the disappearance of Megan Williams. What did those stories have to do with the death and mutilation of Rodney Engleworth?

One way to find out was to run Rod's story as written, not changing a word. Tim also wanted to run a memorial to Rod in next week's *Gazette*. That meant adding another four pages to the paper, bringing it up from 64 pages to 68. What Tim had intended to be a raise for Rod would pay for the additional pages. With Rod gone, Tim would have to write the copy himself. Did he have a current photograph of Rod in *The Gazette's* files? He'd have to look when he got back to the office.

What he knew he did have were pictures of Rod and Helen together from before Helen got really sick. Rod had supplied those photos and Tim had run them with Rod's "Reminiscences of Helen" columns. Tim would include those pics along with any other pictures of Rod he could find.

The memorial to Rodney Engleworth would run in the center of the paper, a four-page pull-out section that readers might want to keep. The lead story on the front page of the paper would remain the banner head with the high school picture of Megan Williams and Rod's lead paragraph that included the five w's and one h of good journalism. Readers would need to turn to inside pages to read the entire story. When they got to the exact center of the paper, they'd find Rod's photos and obit along with Tim's "Reminiscences of Rod."

Who else knew Rod and might want to contribute memories? Nurses at the hospital, of course. The waitresses at Terri's Restaurant. Certainly the Mayor, whom Rod's favorable stories helped elect and kept in office. Tim would interview them all.

The coroner and his assistants came out the front door carrying a black body bag. The mortal remains of Rodney Engleworth were on their way to the county morgue. Tomorrow, Rod would be cut open once again at autopsy. Then he would be put on ice until the cops released the corpse.

Tim wondered who would claim Rod's body for burial. Did Rod have any remaining family? Helen had passed away and Rod had no children. Did Rod have a brother or sister? Or was he an only child like Tim?

Why hadn't Tim been more interested in Rod's personal life while Rod was alive? Rod had talked plenty about his career as a journalist, but he had talked little about any family except Helen. Tim had never asked, and Rod had never offered, to talk about family and friends.

Who would claim the body for burial if Rod had no one? Tim knew that Rod owned two cemetery plots at the Twin Rivers Cemetery. Helen was buried in one, and the other was for Rod. If no one else claimed Rod, Tim would make certain Rod got a proper burial.

After the coroner's van left and the two patrol cars blocking his way went back to patrolling downtown streets, Tim was able to back his Jeep Wagoneer all the way out the driveway onto the street. He headed home to the *Gazette* office to add four pages to next Wednesday's edition. It was after five AM when he walked in and took a seat at his computer. He reread Rod's copy from beginning to end, looking for clues to Rod's killer.

Rod had been one of the best investigative journalists in the country back in the heyday of investigative journalism. Jack Anderson, Woodward and Bernstein, Seymour Hersh, and Rodney Engleworth were often mentioned in the same breath and with the same reverence by newspapermen everywhere back when Tim studied journalism at Northwestern. It was a shame that almost no one remembered Rodney Engleworth today.

But this final piece of reporting would be his testament and epitaph. Rod had left this as his legacy, and Tim promised himself to follow up Rod's story until the killers were caught.

Tim opened up a new Word document and began composing.

"Rodney Engleworth was a great journalist," he wrote to begin his first "Reminiscences of Rod" column. "But, more than that, Rodney Engleworth was a great friend. He was my friend and a friend to all the residents of Twin Rivers. Rodney Engleworth will be missed, but he will not be forgotten."

CHAPTER FOURTEEN

I'm disappointed. I thought sure you would come tonight and I would have my revenge. I hurried home to wait for you. I was at my window, watching and waiting, before eleven. But you never showed.

I'm losing my patience.

I could have taken more time with the old man. I could have made him suffer more. I had all the time in the world. Instead, I hurried. I rushed home to wait for you. I want my revenge. I want it now. Why the fuck didn't you come tonight so I could have my revenge?

Susan came home shortly after one AM. I saw her park her Toyota in the alley, watched her climb the stairs to her apartment, watched her turn all the lights out at 2:30. She's safe and sleeping soundly.

I wish I could sleep. Do you know how long it's been since I've had a good night's sleep? Four years. That's right. I haven't slept without waking from nightmares since you raped me.

You say I was asleep for a whole year? You're wrong. Doctors claim I wasn't asleep. I was in a catatonic stupor, a coma-like state, for more than a year. But that wasn't normal sleep. It was more like being dead. And I dreamt all that time, every minute, reliving over and over again what you did to me. My mind turned off my ability to feel anything at all, or I would have gone completely crazy. My mind shut out the outside world entirely, and I lived solely inside myself. My brain remained active. My body did not.

Parts of my body continued to function normally. I breathed. My heart beat. I urinated. I defecated. I didn't eat. I was fed plasma and glucose and saline and vitamins and minerals by tubes in my arms, and my body managed to metabolize nutrients just like normal. What I didn't have was voluntary motor function. That part of my body and brain shut down when excessive trauma turned off my ability to feel. It didn't start up again until I knew exactly what I was going to do to you when I found you again. As I lay in that hospital bed, neither asleep nor awake, my subconscious decided it needed to revive my nerves and muscles so I could hold a gun and a knife. I emerged from my dissociative-fugue state in order to take my revenge.

I'm tired of being patient. I want my revenge.

Do you know what I'm doing now? I'm sharpening all my knives. I'm sharpening the pinking shears, too, and changing the blade on the box-cutter. My tools get dull when they slice through flesh. I want them sharp when I see you again. Oh, I agree that dull and rusty can take longer and be more painful. But I might not have a lot of time to cut all four of you the way I want to cut you before someone calls the police. I'm willing to sacrifice some of my enjoyment for the satisfaction of castrating all four of you.

You can suffer while bleeding out from the holes where your genitals used to be. You can suffer the way I suffered. I want you to feel helpless, to know that your life is ebbing away and there is absolutely nothing you can do to save yourself. I want you to know you'll never have children. I want you to know I'm the one who took your life away from you. I want you to hate me the way I hate you.

That's all I've lived for these past four years. You took everything else away from me.

I know you will come for Susan again soon. Perhaps you didn't come here tonight because you have a busy schedule at work tomorrow. Tomorrow—today, actually, since it's already morning—will be the end of the work week. Will you come for Susan on a Friday night because you don't have to work on Saturday? Will you wait until Saturday night? My patience is wearing thin.

You don't know I'm waiting for you, do you? How could you possibly know? You don't even know I'm alive. You think I bled out after you raped me and cut me up. You went about your ordinary lives as if nothing happened. You went to work in the city, mingled with people who had no clue you were rapists and murderers, and you came back to the suburbs only when you wanted sexual thrills you couldn't get elsewhere. You think it's exciting to take a woman against her will, don't you? Are you all such losers that you can't find a woman who will have sex with you unless you hold a knife to her throat? You are, aren't you?

How many other women have you raped since me? Dozens? Hundreds? Do you rape a different woman each week?

No, I think you only rape a few women each year, one a month at most. You look to find a woman who turns you on. You're very selective.

When you see a woman you like, you watch her for weeks. The four of you take turns following her. You fantasize about what you're going to do to her when the time is right. You follow her home to her house or apartment. You want to be certain she lives alone. You study her personal habits. You know where she works and when she's at work. You know what time she goes to bed each night because one of you follows her and watches her every night for at least a week, maybe even a month or more. You make sure she has no husband, boyfriend or roommate. You fucked up with me, didn't you? You had no idea I'd want to stay with my sister until I could find a place of my own. I had just turned eighteen. I couldn't stand to live with my parents' constantly bickering anymore so I left. I had only moved out of my parents' house and into Susan's apartment two days before you raped me. You missed seeing me move in because I did it in the daytime while you were working. I didn't go anywhere at night. I was a good girl. I stayed in the apartment and read.

You came to that apartment on Fifth Street to rape Susan, not me. You intended to enter Susan's apartment and surprise her as soon as she got home from work shortly after midnight. But you were the ones who were surprised. You didn't expect anyone to be in that apartment. When you saw me, you held a knife to my throat and told me not to scream. It turned you on to control me, and you couldn't stop once you began. So you raped me instead of Susan.

But you never forgot Susan, did you? You finally came back to see if she was the same as you remembered, and you followed her home and discovered she had moved.

You take elaborate pains to make sure your victims are alone. You can't afford to be seen by anyone who might live to identify you. Do you, the leader of the four, have a high-profile job? Are you afraid someone will recognize you?

And who are your buddies? Are you related in some way? Brothers, perhaps? Cousins?

Pimples could be your younger brother. Now that he's cut his hair, I do see a slight resemblance. Are the other two co-workers? Neighbors? What brought the four of you together to rape women in the suburbs anyway? Did you start on a dare? Did you do it just for kicks? Or are you all sick sociopaths who found you have similar tastes?

I don't really want to know. All I want is revenge.

I will wait as long as it takes. What choice do I have? I don't know your names. I don't know where you live. I have no way to trace your license plate number. All I know is you will come sometime in the future to rape my sister.

And when you do, I will be waiting.

CHAPTER FIFTEEN

Tim Goodman waited at the police station for Elsie Dorr to arrive for work on Friday morning. Officer Dorr was scheduled to begin work at 9 AM, and she arrived at 8:49. Tim liked that she was early. That indicated she loved her job. People who hated their jobs were habitually late.

Tim had been late nearly every day he had worked for that Windy City advertising agency northeast of the loop. So had most of the people Tim had worked with. It was a miracle that agency ever sold any ads. But the agency raked in big bucks and owned the entire Michigan Avenue skyscraper where its sumptuous offices overlooked the lakefront from the building's top four floors. People worked there mainly for the money, not because they loved—or even enjoyed—their jobs.

He recognized Elsie Dorr immediately when she entered the front doors of the police station. Rod had taken digital photographs of key police personnel and ran them with captions as part of last week's story about Twin Rivers' remarkable case clearance record. Dorr was identified in Rod's caption as the police department's community relations and public information officer.

"Ms. Dorr," Tim said as he followed her to her office. "I'm Tim Goodman from the *Gazette*. You may or may not have heard yet that Rodney Engleworth was murdered last night. I need to talk to you."

Elsie Dorr stopped dead in her tracks. When she turned to face Tim, she tried to blink away tears from her hazel eyes.

"I'm sorry," she said softly. "And, no, I hadn't heard until you told me just now."

Elsie Dorr had fiery red hair tied back in a girlish ponytail. Tim guessed she was close to his own age, somewhere around the Big Three-oh. Despite the blue uniform and the gun on her hip, she didn't look like a cop.

For one thing, she was too petite—short and skinny—to be a cop. For another, Tim thought Elsie Dorr was the most beautiful girl he had ever seen in his entire life.

Maybe it was the combination of green eyes and red hair that attracted and held his attention. Maybe it was the way her eyes glistened with tears that melted his heart. Maybe it was the freckles on her nose and the kissable lips that made him want to take her into his arms and nuzzle those lips and that upturned nose. Or maybe it was simply because Tim had just lost his best friend and he hadn't had any sleep all night long, and he was feeling very emotional right about now.

"Detective Giffords said I should see you this morning and ask you for details of the recent homicides in Twin Rivers. Joel seemed to think Rod's murder was directly related to the mutilation deaths of Willard and Murphy and the rape of Megan Williams four years ago."

"He told you that?" asked Dorr. "He said there was a connection?"

"Not in so many words."

"Those are on-going investigations," said Dorr. "Giffords shouldn't have said anything at all about them, certainly not to the press."

"He told me to talk to you. He said you'd fill me in."

"Why don't you have a seat next to my desk while I check with Giffords."

Tim waited while Dorr called Giffords and left a message on his cell phone. If Giffords had been processing the crime scene most of the night and then writing his report, he was probably at home and asleep.

"Tell me, Mr. Goodman," she said as she dropped her own cell phone into a leather holster on her belt next to her gun, "about Rodney Engleworth. How did he die?"

"I found him in his house around one this morning. He was naked and parts of his body had been cut off."

"Genitals?"

"Yes."

"And you talked to Sergeant Giffords? He investigated the crime scene?"

"Yes."

"Do you know who might be responsible for Engleworth's murder or why?"

"No."

"What were you doing at his house at one in the morning?"

"I needed to talk to Rod about a story he wrote. When he didn't answer his telephone and he didn't answer his door at eleven, I looked for him at his usual haunts. But he wasn't in any of them. So I went back to his house and tried again. I was worried he might have had a heart attack or stroke, so I broke a kitchen window and went inside. I found him dead on his bed in the master bedroom."

"How long had he been dead when you found him?"

"About three or four hours."

"Did you notice anything suspicious when you were at his house around eleven?"

"Only that there were lights on inside the house but Rod didn't answer the door. Come to think of it, I did see his car in the driveway. I should have known he was home. I guess I thought Rod had taken a cab to a bar because he intended to get drunk and didn't want to drive home intoxicated."

"He had a drinking problem?"

"He did. Rod quit drinking after his wife died. I thought maybe he had a relapse."

"He didn't seem like an alcoholic. He was sober the few times I met him."

"He's been sober for more than two years."

"What made you think he had a relapse? Was something bothering him?"

"I don't know. He turned in his story very early this week. That wasn't like him."

"Giffords wasn't who told you about Megan Williams and the two homicides, was he?" she asked, her eyes probing Tim's. "Rodney Engleworth told you."

"Rod didn't say a word to me, but he did mention Willard and Murphy in a story Rod wrote about Megan being missing."

"What story?"

"The one Rod turned in yesterday before he was killed."

"He promised Giffords he wouldn't write anything until we officially released information to the press. He said the *Gazette* didn't publish hard news stories."

"We don't," said Tim. "But this is different. I think Rod believed it was important enough to write the story, and I believe it's important enough to see print."

"I can't tell you what you can and cannot publish," said Elsie Dorr, "and I won't even try. But if you print that story now, you might harm our on-going investigations and put the public at greater risk."

"How? How will informing the public damage your investigation and put the public at greater risk?"

"By encouraging copy-cat killers. It seems obvious someone is imitating what happened to Megan Williams, except the latest victims are males instead of females. The department is worried that there are other nuts out there who might do the same. It's hard enough to solve the previous cases. If you print details of the Williams rape and the Willard and Murphy slayings, some weirdo might get the idea that raping and castrating can be fun. We don't have the manpower to track down more than one serial-killer at a time."

"Can't you get help from the state police and the FBI?"

"They're already assisting with analyzing evidence."

"But you're afraid to invite their investigators in because you think they'll take over the cases?"

"We have to maintain jurisdictional boundaries."

"I thought the task force was created to overcome the limits of jurisdictional boundaries."

"It was."

"And how is that working out for you?"

"Not well, I'm afraid."

"Why not?"

"Although we have a say in what cases the task force investigates, our voice is only one of many in the decision-making process. When we need their help here, the task force investigators may be busy elsewhere working cases in other jurisdictions. They're backlogged right now. With crime rampant in other suburbs, Twin Rivers is the least of their worries."

"I saw Giffords at the local crime scene last night."

"That's only because he came out on his own time. He has a vested interest in what happens in Twin Rivers. Joel is spread really thin right now trying to work task force cases in other suburbs and keeping up with what's happening here. It's like he's working two jobs."

"Don't you have your own homicide team?"

"No. We have a major crimes division that investigates homicides, rapes, assaults, car thefts, armed robbery, and narcotics trafficking. We've fortunately had too few homicides in the past to dedicate officers just to investigate homicides. Giffords was the best suspicious death investigator we had. He was trained in the army and at the FBI's National Academy. But we lost him to the task force and the department hasn't found a replacement."

"Is that why Giffords asked for Rod's help?"

"Mr. Engleworth was once a police reporter. He was good at finding things police officers missed. He did help Joel, but strictly off the record. He promised not to print anything until the killers were caught."

"Obviously, they haven't been caught. One or more killed Rod last night."

"Obviously," said Elsie Dorr.

"I think Giffords feels guilty for involving Rod in the case. He warned me to stay out of it."

"But you won't," said Elsie with a smile. "You newspapermen are all alike."

"Freedom of the press," said Tim. "You can't stop me."

"My father was a reporter in New York City," said Dorr. "He died investigating an arson case. The entire building collapsed on top of him.

When rescue crews dug out his body, they discovered evidence of arson. Unfortunately, the police never did find out who actually torched the building."

"Is that why you became a Twin Rivers cop?"

"One of the reasons. My mom moved us to Chicago after my dad died. I couldn't make the height and weight requirements for the Chicago force. But the Twin Rivers police department hired me. I was a patrol officer for two years before I became the public information officer."

"Rod spoke highly of you," said Tim.

"I liked him. He was a lot like my father."

"He was a lot like mine, too."

"Was your father a newspaperman?"

"No," said Tim. "My dad was foreman in a factory. Before that, he was a machine operator."

"Why did you become the owner and publisher of the *Gazette*?"

"Because I loved to read newspapers when I was a kid."

"So this is a childhood fantasy come true?"

"Something like that."

Dorr smiled. She had a beautiful smile that brightened the building like the sun emerging from behind a cloud. Tim smiled back.

"I can't release any information to you without the approval of the investigating officer or my captain," said Dorr. "I hope you understand."

"You're worried about a copy-cat killer? You think someone is imitating the men who raped Megan Williams?"

"It's a possibility," said Dorr.

"What really happened to Megan Williams?"

"She was sexually assaulted in her sister's apartment. When the four men finished raping her, they cut her up badly and left her for dead."

"But she survived?"

"Her sister found her in time and she was rushed to the hospital. She was in a coma for a year before she revived. I can't comment on the extent of her injuries."

"But there are similarities between her injuries and the men who were castrated?"

"Some of the cuts appear similar."

"So either the men who raped and cut Megan Williams are the same ones cutting up men, or someone who knows exactly what happened to Megan is killing the men."

"That seems a logical assumption."

"What about Megan Williams? Could she be the one cutting up men?"

"It's not likely. She lost a lot of the function of parts of her lower body. I understand she's partially paralyzed."

"What about Megan's sister?"

"She has iron-clad alibies for the approximate times of death of each of the men. She works three to midnight at Terri's Restaurant. I don't know about last night, but dozens of people saw her working in the restaurant when Willard and Murphy were killed."

"What you're saying—correct me if I'm wrong—is there's already one copy-cat killer, plus the original four rapists, running around Twin Rivers killing people?"

"And we don't want another."

"I'm running Rod's story on Wednesday. That gives Giffords five days to catch the current crop of killers before another copy-cat can get ideas."

"Can I see the story before you print it?"

"I don't need your approval to publish the story."

"Nor will I give it. I just want a heads-up before it hits the stands."

"Let me think about it."

"Call me when you decide," said Dorr, handing Tim her business card. "If I'm not in the office, my cell number is also on the card."

"Here," said Tim, handing Dorr his own business card. "That's my cell number, too. Call me if you learn anything more about Rod's death that you can share."

"I'll do that," said Dorr, standing up and offering Tim her hand. "It was nice meeting you, Mr. Goodman. Please stay in touch."

"Yeah," said Tim. "Nice meeting you, too."

Then Tim left the police station and drove to the hospital to interview nurses for Rod's memorial tribute.

CHAPTER SIXTEEN

All the long-term care nurses were shocked to learn of Rod's murder. "He was such a nice man," one of them said after Tim told them about Rod. "So faithful to his wife. He visited her every day. He really loved her."

"I saw him just yesterday," said another. "I can't believe he's gone."

"Rod was here yesterday?" Tim asked. "Why?"

"He inquired about that Williams girl who was here in a coma for a year and then miraculously woke up. He wanted to know what she looked like after reconstructive surgery. We didn't see the Williams girl after she healed physically. She had plastic surgery and went through physical therapy and psychological counseling as an outpatient."

"She healed physically? Completely healed physically?"

"Except for the partial paralysis of her lower limbs. She couldn't move her left leg at all at first, but before she left long-term care we had her standing up and moving around. She dragged that left leg something fierce. Physical therapy probably helped some, but that leg was never going to be right again. The nerves were severed at the base of her spinal cord. The neurologist said she might eventually learn to compensate by adapting other neural pathways. But the messages from her brain would take longer to reach her left leg than her right."

"That poor girl," said one of the other nurses, "went through hell. She had nightmares every night, and she often screamed herself hoarse.

Some days she was so depressed she couldn't do a thing. And other days she seemed so determined she wasn't going to let her disabilities get her down that she seemed almost normal."

"She'll never be normal," said another nurse. "After what she went through, how could she be normal?"

"Her parents stopped coming to see her after she had been in a coma for six months. Her sister came—not every day but maybe a couple times a week—but her parents just stopped visiting."

"I heard her parents got divorced," said the third nurse. "The father found a new girlfriend and moved out of town. But the mother still lived here in Twin Rivers. She just never came around."

Tim asked each of the four nurses their full names and requested their permission to quote their personal memories of Rod in the memorial section of Wednesday's *Gazette*. They provided glowing quotes of Rod's devotion to his wife while she was terminally ill. "I think the cancer was as hard on him as it was on her," one of the nurses said. "But he never missed visiting a single day. Not all husbands are like that."

Tim returned to the *Gazette* office. He telephoned Lola Wainwright, the mayor's press secretary, and asked if His Honor would like to make a statement about Rodney Engleworth's valuable contributions to the community. Lola said she was sure the mayor would be happy to make a statement. She'd fax it over later Friday afternoon.

Tim reread Rod's copy again. Once this story broke, the mayor wouldn't be quite so happy. People moved to Twin Rivers from the city and other suburbs because Twin Rivers was one of the safest places to live, raise kids, and shop in all Chicagoland. Twin Rivers' phenomenal growth was as much a result of its low crime rate as its prime location on the Metra line. There were lots of other commuter communities to choose from. If residents didn't feel safe here, they would rapidly relocate to another suburb. Twin Rivers could become a ghost town overnight.

In light of what Elsie Dorr had revealed this morning, Tim suspected politics had rendered the once-promising crime-fighting task force ineffective. Not only had the task force failed to find Megan Williams' rapists after four years, they had hindered Twin Rivers' ability to solve murders by sending Joel Giffords, Twin Rivers' best homicide investigator, elsewhere to apprehend drug dealers and car thieves. No wonder Giffords had asked Rod for help in solving the recent homicides.

But Giffords was feeling extremely guilty for involving Rod. Would Rod still be alive if he'd kept his nose out of what the killer felt was none of his business? Probably. Rod could have continued covering local politics and sporting events or writing his reminiscences and nobody would have cared.

Tim set aside the story while he worked on ads. He made several telephone calls to potential advertisers, sent e-mails with attached ad copy to clients for approval, and fell back into the familiar territory of advertising copywriter. Finally, lack of sleep took its toll, and Tim wandered into the back room and collapsed on his bed. Five minutes later, he was fast asleep.

When Tim awoke, it was already nine PM. If he wanted to interview the waitresses at Terri's Restaurant and talk with Megan Williams' sister, he needed to hurry.

He ran an electric shaver over his whiskers, took a quick shower in the shower stall he had installed in the back room, and dressed in jeans and a Northwestern sweatshirt. Tim hated to wear a suit and tie, and the

166 · PAUL DALE ANDERSON

best benefit of owning his own business and working primarily from a computer was he could dress as he pleased.

He threw on a light jacket and headed out the door. For the first time since he had purchased this office and living space, he took time to lock the door behind him. Twin Rivers—the place where he was born and lived most of his life—no longer felt safe.

Now Tim knew why Giffords and Dorr were hesitant about inform-ing the public about rapes and murders in Twin Rivers. Despite the vigilance of local police and constant patrols of city streets, police couldn't be everywhere. Criminals could easily enter the office while Tim was away, steal all the expensive computer equipment on desks, and abscond with the loot before Tim got back. It hadn't happened yet in the more than six years Tim had owned the *Gazette*. But Tim was aware it could happen now.

Rod's death had made Tim see a lot of things differently. No longer was the sleepy little suburb a place of safety. It had suddenly become, practically overnight, a violent and dangerous place to live. Someone had entered Rod's home while he was present, mutilated and murdered Rodney Engleworth in his bed, and escaped before anyone knew what had happened. The same killer had likely done something similar with Willard and Murphy. And someone had raped Megan Williams and left her for dead four years ago and still was on the loose. If it could happen to them, it could happen to anyone.

Tim found parking on the street a block north of Terri's. During the day, parking was practically impossible to find on downtown streets. People were willing to pay substantial parking fees to use the municipal lot near the Metra station. But, at night, free parking was usually avail-able on the street within reasonable walking distance of businesses.

Terri's was crowded at ten o'clock on a Friday night. Young people stopped in for a slice of pie after a movie date, and seniors came in later than usual for a discounted evening meal. Commuters stopped in at all times of the day and night, and shoppers came by after the malls closed at nine. Tim had to wait to be seated.

Terri Gilchrist had expanded her restaurant from the tiny long and narrow hole-in-the-wall Tim remembered from his childhood into a bustling business that occupied three downtown storefronts. Terri had purchased the properties on both sides of her original restaurant, knocked out the walls between buildings, and created a huge dining room that legally seated three hundred people in booths, at tables, and along the long coffee counter in the back near the kitchen. There were two sets of restrooms, one on the north wall and one on the south wall. In the front was a small waiting area and the cash register. Terri herself worked the register in the mornings when commuters consumed big breakfasts or ordered only coffee and a sweet roll to go while waiting for trains. One of the older waitresses acted as the hostess and cashier tonight, directing patrons to recently vacated tables or booths as soon as the previous occupants paid their checks. Waitresses hustled to clear tables and take orders as quickly as they were able.

"Is it always this crowded on a Friday night?" Tim asked the older waitress as she showed Tim to an empty stool at the counter.

"High school football game just ended and the theaters let out practically at the same time," explained the harried waitress whose name badge identified her only as "Sally."

Tim took the open seat at the coffee counter. A girl with long blond hair who looked to be about twenty-five brought Tim a menu and a glass of water. Her name badge read "Susan."

"Are you Susan Williams?" Tim asked.

"Yes," she said, suddenly wary of someone she'd never met before knowing her name. "How on earth do you know my last name?"

"Just a guess. Rodney Engleworth told me all about you. I'm Tim Goodman, publisher of the *Gazette*."

Susan's face relaxed. "I read your paper every week, Mr. Goodman," she said. "Rod delivers them on Wednesdays."

"What does Rod usually order when he eats here?"

"The open faced roast beef sandwich with mashed potatoes and gravy."

"I'll have that and a Diet Pepsi."

Susan brought him a large glass of Diet Pepsi. Then she went into the kitchen and placed his order.

Tim watched Susan work the counter and twelve large round tables in the back section of the restaurant simultaneously. She was very efficient, and it was obvious she had done this kind of work for some time and enjoyed talking with the customers.

When Susan brought his food, Tim said, "I'd like to talk with you about Rod when you have time."

"I'm pretty busy right now," she said. "If you're still here after midnight, I'll have time for a cup of coffee with you before I go home."

Tim glanced at his watch. It was already ten-forty. He could eat slowly and order a piece of pie when he finished the sandwich. He'd make sure he was still here when Susan's shift ended.

The restaurant began to thin out after eleven-thirty. By midnight, there were only a handful of people remaining in Susan's section. Even after midnight, Susan continued to refill coffee cups as a new waitress took orders and gradually assumed control of the counter and surrounding tables. Tim finished the last of his pie and looked at his bill. Twelve dollars for the meal, two dollars for the Pepsi, and six dollars for the pie. Twenty dollars plus tax total. Tim left four dollars for a tip.

After he paid his bill at the cash register, he walked back to find Susan sitting at an empty table.

"Rod was killed last night," Tim said as he took a seat next to Susan. "How well did you know him?"

Susan's face suddenly turned ashen as all the color drained away. Her eyes filled with tears and rivers ran down her cheeks. Tim didn't know what else to do but put his arms around Susan while she sobbed like a baby on the front of his sweatshirt. The waitress at the counter came over to see if Susan was okay.

"He du...du...died," Susan told the waitress without looking up. "Heh...heh...he was in here last night," she mumbled into Tim's sweatshirt. "He had his u...u...usual. I talked to him. He left a big t...t...tip,"

"Who died?"

"Rodney Engleworth."

"The old guy who writes about his wife in the newspaper?"

"Yes."

Now it was the new waitress' turn to look distraught. "I loved the way he wrote about his wife," she said. "You could tell he really loved her. Love like that doesn't happen often, does it? It's too bad they both died."

"He did love her," Tim said. "She meant the whole world to him."

"Did he have cancer, too?" asked the waitress.

"No," answered Tim. "He was murdered."

"Murdered? Oh, my God! Where?"

"In his home. Here in Twin Rivers."

"Oh, my God!" said the waitress again.

"I'm the publisher of the *Gazette*, and I plan to run a four-page tribute to Rod in next Wednesday's paper. May I quote what you said?"

"About how he really loved his wife?"

"Yes."

"Sure. I thought it was real romantic. Kind of like a love story in a book."

Susan's tears were slowly ebbing. She wiped her eyes with a paper napkin from the table. "Why would someone kill such a sweet old man?" she asked. "Was it robbery? Was he killed during a robbery? Did somebody shoot him?"

"He wasn't shot. Police don't yet know why he was killed. It doesn't appear to be a robbery."

"I gotta go take care of customers," said the other waitress. "Will you be all right, hon?"

"Yes," said Susan.

"I didn't want to say anything while she was close enough to hear," Tim told Susan after the other waitress left, "but Rod was cut up similar to the way your sister was cut up four years ago."

"Oh, no," said Susan.

"I know this is hard for you Ms. Williams, but try to remember. Who, besides you, knew what happened to Megan and exactly how and where her body was cut?"

"Why?"

"Police suspect there may be a copy-cat cutting up people for thrills. They think Megan's injuries gave the copy-cat the idea."

"The paramedics who responded to my 911 call saw her cuts. The police. Doctors and nurses who cared for her at the hospital. My parents. Megan didn't have many visitors, other than me. She didn't want to see anyone after she came out of the coma. She did talk with several police officers. I don't think she showed them her cuts."

"Whom did you tell?"

"No one. I told Rodney Engleworth a week ago that Megan was raped and mutilated, but I didn't go into detail."

"No one else?"

"No."

"So the only ones who knew the extent of Megan's injuries were the first responders, the staff at the hospital, and your parents?"

"Yes."

"So, if there is a copy-cat, it must be one of those people? That doesn't seem very likely."

"No, it doesn't."

"I suppose your parents or one of the paramedics may have told someone. Or someone may have overheard them talking about Megan's injuries among themselves."

"I suppose."

"Do you wish to give me a quote about Rod I can use in next week's paper?"

"He was the nicest man I know. He was like a father to me. He knew how to listen. Most men don't listen. And he knew how to tip. He always left more than twenty percent. We don't earn much salary, half of minimum wage, so we live mostly off tips. He was a very generous and caring man."

"He was like a father to me, too."

Tim handed Susan his business card. "Call me if you think of any-thing else. Are you all right to drive home? Do you need a lift?"

"I'm fine," said Susan.

"You sure? I can follow you home, if you like. I want to make sure you get home safely."

"I don't live very far from here. Just over on Eleventh Street."

"Then let me follow you home. It will make me feel better to know you made it home safely."

"All right."

Tim waited as Susan collected the last of her tips and said goodbye to the other waitresses. Then he walked her out to her car.

"It's the red Toyota," she said.

"I'll be right behind you in my Jeep Wagoneer. When I see you enter your apartment, I'll leave."

Tim followed the Toyota to an alley between Tenth and Eleventh Streets. Susan turned into the alley and parked. Rod followed and kept Susan in his headlights as she walked to the back stairs and climbed up the stairs to the third floor. She gave Tim a wave as she opened the back door to her apartment. When Susan was safely inside her apartment, Tim drove out of the alley and headed back to the office.

CHAPTER SEVENTEEN

Who are *you*? I've never seen your car before. Why are you here? Why are you following Susan? Why doesn't she seem worried that you followed her home? I saw her wave to you. She knows you. Why don't I know you?

I stayed home tonight to wait for the four rapists to return, but they didn't show last night or tonight. Now I see you instead. Who are you?

The four rapists drive a dark blue Dodge van. Your car does look a little like theirs, except yours is black, a cross between a station wagon and a van. Is it a Jeep? I think it is. It isn't real new, but it isn't really old, either. Who are you? What do you want with my sister?

I couldn't see you well from this angle, but you seem to be only a little older than my sister. You're not ancient like the old man. You're much younger. You have a full head of dark hair. Are you Susan's boyfriend? Does she even have a boyfriend? What does she see in you?

Susan was popular in high school, and she dated lots of guys. I did, too. We didn't know any better then. We thought guys were nice. We didn't know what men were really like. We didn't know that men only wanted to use us, to hurt us.

Susan doesn't date much since she began working the three to midnight shift at Terri's Restaurant. She works every weekend, and her prime dating hours are spent waitressing at the restaurant. She stays home Sundays and Mondays to rest up for the workweek, or she uses those days for shopping. She hasn't had a steady boyfriend since high school.

After I was raped, Susan became afraid of men. She puts up with men at work because she must, but she wants nothing to do with men personally. I was glad when she told me that. I don't want to see Susan hurt. That's all men want from women: to hurt women and make them so afraid of being beaten that women will do whatever the men want. Men think they can get away with anything because they are stronger than women. Men are wrong.

Women aren't the weaker sex but the stronger sex. Maybe we're not physically stronger, but we're definitely stronger mentally and emotionally. Women are built to endure the pain of childbearing. Can a man endure that kind of pain? I don't think so.

I'm in pain constantly, but I don't let it stop me. I could take those powerful pain medications doctors prescribed for me and become pain-free. But I would be a complete zombie. I'd become a mindless automaton. Men would like that, wouldn't they? Men want women to be mindless.

Most men have superior upper body strength. Men have muscles where women have mammary glands. Men think muscles are everything. They're wrong.

Determination is everything. I am determined to have my revenge. That makes me stronger than any man.

Plus, I'm patient. Most men are impatient. Men demand instant gratification. If they can't get what they want from one woman when they want it, they'll look around for another. Is that why the four rapists haven't returned? Have they found another woman to rape? How many women do they watch at the same time? How many women do they follow home from work? Why doesn't someone stop them? Why aren't the police doing their jobs?

If I had transportation, I would drive around until I found their dark blue van. But I have no way to find those men until they come for Susan. I do have their license number. I wonder, if I gave the license plate number and a description of the van to the police, would the police arrest those men?

I have no faith in the police anymore. Most police officers are men, and I trust no man. If the police haven't caught the rapists in four years, are they still looking for the men who raped me? Probably not.

It's up to me to see justice done. An eye for an eye, a tooth for a tooth. It's up to me to ensure those men never rape another woman again. It's up to me to make certain all four suffer for their crimes.

I made that old man suffer last night. I wanted to make him suffer more, but I was in a hurry to get home. He shouldn't have made Susan cry. He deserved to die for that, if for nothing else. But he didn't suffer enough. He didn't really struggle and plead with his eyes the way the others did. Oh, he felt the pain the same as the others. But when I cut off his penis, it didn't seem to matter to him. Nor did dying seem to matter. He seemed almost happy to die. Is that what happens when you get old? It doesn't matter if you live or die?

I'll never get old. I expect to die as soon as I finish those four men who raped me and left me for dead. If the police don't shoot me, I'll shoot myself. I have the Beretta. I know how to shoot.

But I can't die yet. Not until I have my revenge.

CHAPTER EIGHTEEN

Elsie Dorr telephoned Tim's cell phone at 1:42 on Saturday afternoon.

"Can I see your story?" she asked. "The one Rodney Engleworth wrote?"

"Of course," Tim said. "I've thought it over, and I was planning to show it to you before it went to press. Give me your e-mail, and I'll send you a .pdf copy of Rod's story as an attachment."

"Can I come to your office and read it in your office?"

"Sure. But you don't need to."

"I want to."

"When?" Tim asked.

"Now? I'll be there in ten minutes." She clicked off before Tim could reply.

Since today was Saturday, Tim hadn't planned to shower or shave. He was dressed in the same beat-up old Northwestern sweatshirt and jeans he wore last night at Terri's Restaurant. Tim usually spent all day Saturdays and Sundays in the *Gazette* office positioning ads in InDesign. Each newspaper page consisted of four two-inch wide columns. Although Tim had a master's in graphic design and knew how to use pica measurements in typography, he preferred to use common English inches to sell and position ads. Advertisers understood inches. Picas and points were foreign languages to ordinary folks. A pica was simply 1/6th of an inch, and each pica contained twelve points. In the old days of hot type, picas and points meant something to typesetters and compositors who inserted slugs to justify type. In the digital age, picas and points were a thing of the past.

Tim sold advertising by the column inch. He had only two full-page advertisers each issue, and maybe a dozen half-page ads. He saved room to include birth and death announcements, wedding anniversaries, and the weekly schedule of local events. He copied the police blotter directly from the city's website. The remaining ads, classifieds, and Rod's columns began on page two and filled the white space left by the contract ads. The front page of each issue was for that issue's feature story (last week it was the police department's amazing clearance rate) that Rod wrote. Rod included local-interest captioned photos, and he wrote the feature story's front page banner headline that ran beneath the *Gazette*'s masthead. Rod's feature story continued on inside pages wherever space permitted. Rod also wrote two regular columns that ran near the back of the paper. One included his favorable reviews of local dining and drinking establishments, comments on local politics, and miscellaneous filler. The other was his "Reminiscences of Helen" column. This week Tim would run Rod's final columns in the four-page tribute section, along with Tim's first new "Reminiscences of Rodney Engleworth" column. This week's feature story was twice as long as normal, and Tim wanted every word to appear in print.

No one ever came to the *Gazette* offices on Saturdays or Sundays. Tim didn't need to dress up for people placing ads or obituaries like he did Monday through Friday. The newspaper's offices were officially closed on weekends.

He hadn't expected to see anyone today, especially not Elsie Dorr. Tim wasn't sure he wanted Elsie Dorr to see him unshaved and unwashed. But he didn't have time to shave and shower and change clothes in ten minutes. The best he could manage was to comb his hair.

Tim stepped into the back room and quickly ran a comb through his shaggy brown hair. He noticed he desperately needed a haircut. He decided the stubble that had grown on his chin since yesterday afternoon might make him look more rugged and manly. He thought for a moment about growing a full beard, and rejected the notion. He didn't think Elsie Dorr liked men with beards. He ran the electric razor over the stubble a couple of times and got rid of the whiskers. Now he looked more nerdy than manly. Maybe he should try contact lenses and ditch the eyeglasses.

He heard the door chimes sound as the office front door opened, They jingled again as the door slammed shut. Goddamn, that woman got here fast! Tim dashed out of the back room and barely recognized the woman who had entered as Elsie Dorr.

Elsie Dorr looked entirely different in civilian clothes. She, too, wore a heavy sweatshirt. Hers was pink and had the familiar breast cancer awareness logo stenciled on the front. She wore tight Levi's and a pair of black cowboy boots.

Her red hair was still up in a ponytail, but now it was half-hidden beneath the broad brim of a black cowboy hat. She removed the hat from her head and a leather purse and a blue-jean jacket from her shoulders, and tossed them onto a nearby chair.

She wasn't wearing a pistol that Tim could see. If she were armed, the gun was inside the purse she threw on the chair. Tim liked the way her slim hips curved in the tight jeans without the bulky gunbelt hiding her femininity.

"I rushed right over," she said, sounding out of breath. "I hope that's okay."

"Sure. I was just working on next week's issue. Have a seat at the desk over there. That was Rod's desk. I'll pull up Rod's copy from the hard drive so you can read it."

Elsie sat in Rod's chair, and Tim leaned past her and booted up the old Dell. He regretted not showering this morning. He hadn't even bothered to brush his teeth. He wondered how bad his breath reeked. He didn't want to think what his underarms must smell like.

Elsie Dorr, on the other hand, smelled wonderful. Tim breathed in the fresh scent of Irish Spring and some kind of flowery herbal shampoo. She didn't need to use perfume, and if she was wearing any, it was something extremely subtle.

Elsie Dorr was one of the few women Tim knew who made him feel tall. She was about five-four or five-five. He was almost five-nine. He was half-a-head taller than her.

Tim opened Word and found Rod's most recent file. He double-clicked, and the feature story opened and appeared on the screen, complete with the scanned photo of Megan Williams from her high school yearbook.

He handed Elsie the mouse and let her scroll through the story at her own pace. Tim returned to his own desk on the other side of the room where he could watch her from a safe distance. He didn't think she could smell him all the way over here. But the odor of Irish Spring lingered in his nostrils and his eyes followed the swish of her ponytail as Elsie Dorr moved her head to scan the words that scrolled across the screen. The movement of her red ponytail fascinated him like a moving string or a red laser dot might fascinate a kitten.

When she finished, she scrolled back and re-read parts of the story again. Then she swiveled in her chair to face Tim and said, "He was a good writer."

"One of the best."

"I can't officially comment on the accuracy, but I think it's factual enough to print. Are you still planning to run the story on Wednesday?"

"Yes."

"Good," she said. "It's time."

Tim was surprised. "You approve?" he asked.

"Officially no. Unofficially, yes."

"Why the change of heart?"

"Off the record?"

"Sure. This is just between you and me."

"There was another rape last night. Not here in Twin Rivers, but in one of the nearby suburbs. The MO was similar to the Megan Williams rape four years ago."

"Do you think the same men did it?"

"Joel Giffords does. This makes the sixteenth rape and homicide in four years with the exact same MO. There may have been others, too. Megan Williams was the only one raped within the city limits of Twin Rivers with that MO. The other rapes took place in southern or western suburbs of Chicago."

"What about male homicides? Were there other male homicides where the victims were cut and castrated like Rod?"

"Only Willard and Murphy. And all three castration murders took place in Twin Rivers."

"So it sounds to me like there are two separate, but equally-vicious, groups of killers out there. One group is mobile and selects female victims from various suburbs. The other kills men and concentrates on males residing in Twin Rivers."

"There are some similarities between the two groups," Dorr said. "All of the victims were killed in their own homes. All of the victims sustained psycho-sexual mutilations. All were bound with duct tape which was removed before the killers left the scene. No fingerprints were found at any of the crime scenes, and we suspect the killers wore latex gloves."

"The dissimilarities?"

"The sex of the victims. The female victims were raped. We have evidence that four men—the same four men—committed all sixteen rapes. Not all municipalities are as diligent in collecting and processing DNA in assaults and murders as Twin Rivers. We collected male DNA from each of the sixteen rape scenes within the task force's jurisdiction. We collected female DNA samples from Willard's and Murphy's houses. The female samples appear identical in both cases, indicating the same person killed Willard and Murphy, and in each of the male homicides, the killer showered immediately afterwards. We believe the copy-cat killer may be a female who acted alone. We don't have results yet on the DNA found in the bathtub drain at Engleworth's house, but I bet it's female and identical to the DNA found at the Willard and Murphy crime scenes. None of the rapists showered at the scene. We found their DNA on the victims, or on the bed, or elsewhere at the crime scene, never in the bathtub drains."

"Why are you telling me all this? Aren't you placing your job at risk?"

"I spoke with Joel Giffords on the phone just before I called you. Joel phoned my home to inform me about the rape and murder that occurred last night in a nearby suburb. I told Joel you were planning to run the full story on Wednesday. We agreed it was time the public was warned. Neither the Twin Rivers police nor the regional task force is close to apprehending the killers. We hope Engleworth's story will generate leads."

"Aren't you worried about more copy-cats? Aren't you worried about being inundated with telephone calls from false-confessors?"

"Of course, we are. But we think the risk is minimal compared to doing nothing. People need to be warned. If the police can't protect our citizens, people need to protect themselves."

"Who put the lid on information? The police chief?"

"The chief and the mayor."

"I thought so. It's politics as usual, and public safety be damned."

"I'm not here today in an official capacity. I'm here as a concerned citizen."

"I won't tell anyone you were here or what we discussed."

"I'm really sorry about what happened to Rodney Engleworth," she said. "He was actually a big help to Joel."

"How did he help?"

"He discovered a picture of the female murderer riding in Willard's car the night of the murder. It helped establish a more accurate time of death, and it showed the murderer was a young woman with light-colored hair."

"How did Rod get the picture?"

"Our public safety cameras at major intersections captured Willard's car on video. There was a woman riding in the front seat with Willard."

"Rod mentioned in last week's article that you credited the cameras with keeping the crime rate low. But I didn't know he looked at any of the videos."

"We capture a lot on video. But we don't realize the significance of what we've recorded until an incident occurs and we review the recordings."

"You have cameras at every intersection?"

"Not yet. Just the major intersections in the downtown area. We don't have cameras in most residential areas. We had a camera not far from Willard's apartment because it was close to downtown, but nothing near Murphy's house."

"Anything near Rod's home?"

"No."

"Too bad."

"Thanks for giving me a preview of next week's front page. I appreciate the heads up. I know we'll get calls. You will, too. I noticed Rod asked readers to contact the *Gazette* if they had any information about Megan Williams or the murders."

"I'll let you know if I get any useful information," promised Tim.

"What do you think happened to the Williams girl? I checked with her former landlord, and he said she just moved out without advance notice and left no forwarding address. She was renting month to month. He said that kind of thing happens a lot. People move from suburb to suburb when they change jobs or just want a change of scenery. He found a new renter right away because the apartment is relatively inexpensive and close to the Metra station."

"Rod said Megan's sister hasn't seen her in more than six months. She could have moved anywhere, I guess. Do you think she's still in Twin Rivers?"

"I have no clue."

"Neither did Rod."

"I should be going," said Elsie Dorr. "I've been here too long already." She got up from Rod's desk and put her jacket on. Then she slung the purse over her shoulder and positioned the cowboy hat on her head.

"You look like you're from Texas," Tim remarked.

"Upstate New York, actually," she said. "I graduated from Syracuse University's Newhouse School of Public Communications."

"I thought you said your mom moved the family here after your father died."

"She did. But I went back to dad's alma mater to get my degree. Then I became a cop instead of a journalist."

"Why the cowboy hat?"

"It's comfortable. And it doesn't make me look or feel like a cop on my days off. No one wants to date a female cop. Guys get all worried I'll arrest them if they make a move on me."

"Would you?"

"Depends on the move. And the guy."

She touched a hand to the brim of her hat in a mock salute and turned to open the door.

"Thanks, Ms. Dorr," said Tim as the chimes tinkled when she pulled on the door.

"You can call me Elsie when I'm off duty," she said as she exited.

Tim wanted to tell her to call him Tim instead of Mr. Goodman, but she slammed the door behind her and the tinkling chimes reminded Tim of sleigh bells jing, jing, jingling on Rudolph's harness at Christmastime. Tim stared at the closed door where after-images of Elsie Dorr's shapely behind lingered the way her scent had lingered earlier in his nostrils.

Tim sat at his desk and switched his gaze from the closed front door to the blank computer screen. Elsie Dorr had risked her job by coming here today and revealing details of the murders police didn't want made public. She had implied that she had come here with Joel Giffords' blessings. The rape and murder of another woman last night, following so close on the heels of Rodney Engleworth's mutilation death, had been the last straw for Giffords. Joel Giffords was ready to go public and accept any help he could get.

Rod had claimed to have a nose for news. He said he could always sniff out a story wherever it hid. Tim's nose wasn't nearly as sensitive as Rod's, but Tim could smell something rotten in Denmark all the way from here in northern Illinois.

Twin Rivers police had woefully underreported serious crimes through misclassification, delay, and deliberate neglect. Megan Williams' rape wasn't reported either as an attempted murder or as a rape four years ago. It was classified and reported only as an aggravated assault on an eighteen-year-old female. That could mean anything from pushing and shoving, to coping a feel, to date rape. Aggravated sexual assault was closer to what happened, but police had left the sexual part off the report. The Willard and Murphy murders hadn't been reported at all yet, according to the official police blotter. Tim had downloaded the blotter earlier this afternoon to include in Wednesday's paper. He published the weekly blotter under the title "Police Reports" in every issue. Local funeral homes had supplied obituaries of both Willard and Murphy. Neither obituary listed cause of death. The obits listed only dates of birth and death, names of surviving relatives and friends, and significant accomplishments in the decedent's life. Both obits ended exactly the same: "Died suddenly in his home." Anyone reading that would naturally assume death came from a heart attack or stroke. Nothing could be further from the truth.

Evidently, Giffords and Dorr had been aware of the deliberate cover-ups for some time, and their consciences were bothering them. The mayor and chief of police were in collusion on this, and they had ordered police officers to lie or be vague on official reports. Twin Rivers wasn't the safe place people thought it was.

Rod's story would break the cover-up wide open. State and federal investigators would have to investigate the cover-up once the story appeared in print. Maybe they'd even step in and take over all current cases.

Now Tim knew why the Twin Rivers chief of police didn't want the FBI and Illinois State Police involved. Outside investigators would discover that the regional task force, rather than helping solve major crimes, not only diluted the manpower of each police force but reduced the open case load of major felonies. Once local law enforcement turned over a major case to the task force, city police no longer actively pursued the perpetrators. Nor did individual departments need to report the cases as unsolved. They were reported as "case cleared by exceptional means." The task force was a sham created by politicians to make it appear the suburbs were tough on crime when all suburban politicians wanted was a way to look good on paper.

Honest cops like Giffords were stuck in the middle. Instead of devoting all of their time to solving local crimes, they now had dozens of cases to work over a much larger geographical area. The advantages of the task force—knowing about similar crimes in surrounding suburbs and having multi-jurisdictional authority—were offset by the volume and variety of crimes to investigate. Instead of solving murders, Giffords might spend most of his time busting drug dealers or car thieves.

Tim was reminded of the famous quote attributed to Juvenal, the first century Roman satirist. "Quis custodiet ipsos custodies" was often translated as "Who will guard against the guardsmen themselves?" or "Who watches the watchmen?" Traditionally, the free press informed the populace of political or police corruption and kept politicians and cops honest. But, with fewer and fewer independent newspapers, investigative reporters rarely reported the kinds of things politicians were doing in Twin Rivers and other suburbs. Few people knew, and even fewer cared. Besides, that sort of story damaged the image of one's home town and alienated advertisers. Better to keep quiet and hush it up.

Tim was ashamed to admit he had felt that same way just two days ago. He had invested his inheritance and his future in a newspaper that depended on the goodwill of advertisers. He had a vested interest in maintaining Twin Rivers' sterling reputation and couldn't afford to rock the boat.

But Rod's death changed everything. Now money was no longer important to Tim, nor was even the continued existence of the *Gazette* important. What mattered now was finding Rod's killer or killers and ensuring they would never kill anyone else ever again.

Rod's killer was probably female, and that explained why Rod had invited her inside his house. Rod had always seemed the perfect gentleman. He never would have suspected a woman of being a threat. Even if the woman were a stranger at his door, he would have invited her inside on a cold night. Gentlemen didn't leave women standing outside in the cold. They held the door open for them to enter.

But this woman was likely someone Rod knew because he put on a fresh pot of coffee and had taken two clean coffee cups down from the cupboard, one for himself and one for his visitor. Rod was expecting the woman to sit at the kitchen table and talk with him over coffee. He didn't expect the woman to tie him up with duct tape and emasculate him.

How did the woman get Rod to agree to be bound? Rod had speculated in his story that the killer had drugged Willard and Murphy. Had she managed to drug Rod? If so, how?

Rod was old and not as spry as he had once been, but he was spry enough to fight off a woman or to run away if necessary, so she didn't subdue him by physical force as a man might have. But Rod had neither fought nor fled. Had she brandished a knife or gun? Tim thought of the gun Elsie Dorr wore when she was in uniform. If Dorr pointed that gun at a man, the man would have to do as she ordered. Either submit, or risk being shot and killed. No man in his right mind would argue with a woman holding a gun.

How did the woman know where Rod lived? Rod had a land line so he was listed in the telephone directory. If the murder were premeditated, the woman could have looked up his address if she knew his last name. Did she drive to Rod's house? Tim supposed the police had already checked with neighbors about a strange car in Rod's driveway.

But Tim had parked twice in Rod's driveway that same night. Did anyone notice? No. None of the neighbors seemed interested in what took place at the Engleworth house until they heard sirens and saw flashing lights. Then they knew something was wrong and ventured outside to take a look.

Was the woman still in the house when Tim knocked on the door at eleven? Possibly. She may have been in the shower, or she may have heard Tim's car in the driveway and hid. If she hid, where was her car parked? Not in the driveway nor in front of the house. She may have left before Tim arrived at the house. Time of death was estimated between nine PM and midnight. If she had left, she hadn't been gone long. Tim may have missed her by minutes.

Tim tried to remember if he had seen anybody on the street near Rod's house that night. He had been too angry at Rod to pay attention to cars or pedestrians. He might have driven right past the killer and never noticed.

Rod felt the killings were linked, but it was obvious there were two separate sets of killers at work. One set consisted of four men who raped their female victims before pounding the crap out of them, cutting them all over their bodies, and finally allowing them to bleed out. The other set consisted of one woman who castrated her male victims, cut off both of their nipples, and cut out large chunks of flesh before letting the men simply bleed out and die. The rapists used hunting knives. The woman used a variety of household tools, including pinking shears, pliers, box-cutter, and both butcher and paring knives. The woman subdued her victims with drugs or held a gun on them. The men subdued their victims with physical force and a hunting knife. The men beat their victims with their fists. The woman didn't. Their methods were gender-specific.

The men entered residences by picking or forcing door locks. The woman was invited to enter by her victims. Some victims may even have held the door open for her to enter. Rod would have done that. Rod was a gentleman.

So how did Rod conclude both sets of killings were related? None of the victims appear to have known each other. True, both sets of killers physically mutilated their victims with sharp instruments. Both sets of killers tortured their victims until they bled out and died from exsanguination. Both sets of killers attacked their victims in their own homes when the victims were home alone. That indicated that none of the killings were completely random. The victims may not have known their assailants previously, but their assailants knew them. The killers stalked their victims. They had a chance to observe their victims before they acted. All of the murders were premeditated.

All five murderers—four men and one woman—have killed more than once and all five will surely kill again. They will keep on killing until someone stops them.

The rapists have been raping and killing for at least four years and perhaps even longer. The woman began killing only recently. Giffords believed the woman was merely a copy-cat killer, inspired by the four men who raped and cut women. If men could carry out their wildest fantasies and get away with it, she reasoned, why couldn't a woman? Women could be just as mean and cruel as men, maybe meaner and crueler.

How did she know about the four rapists and what they did to victims? Specific details were never released to the press or the public. Yet the woman mimicked many of the same wounds on her male victims that the rapists inflicted on their female victims. How was that possible?

Obviously, the woman serial-killer knew Megan Williams, either personally or second or third-hand. Had she heard about what was done to Megan from Susan? From Megan's parents? From the nurses or doctors at the hospital? From first responders who viewed Megan's naked body at the crime scene?

Tim had taken a couple of psychology classes in college—general psych and social psychology—but he had no idea what could possibly motivate a person to kill. That one human being could mutilate and kill another human being for kicks was beyond Tim's comprehension.

Did they kill because they had unhappy childhoods? Freud believed all pathology stemmed from childhood trauma.

Not everyone, Tim realized, had as happy a childhood as he had. Tim was an only child of doting parents, and both of his parents had lived until Tim was a senior in high school when his mother suddenly had a massive heart attack and died in the kitchen while preparing supper. She began to put on weight in her early forties, her belly and hips expanding gradually, and the excessive weight finally took a toll on her heart as she reached fifty. Up until his mother's death, Tim's home life had been idyllic.

His parents afforded him the luxury of exploring the world around him at his own pace and in his own way. Because he had no siblings, he had been shy around other kids in grade school and middle school. But, by the time Tim reached high school and began working on the high school student newspaper, he had outgrown most of his shyness and learned how to play well with others. He had seldom been bullied, and he had never bullied anyone else. He had seen instances of school bullying, however, and he suspected such things went on all the time. He was glad it had never happened to him, and he had never intervened when he saw it happening to anyone else lest he become a target himself. Tim had always been one to mind his own business. But he supposed if someone were bullied often enough, it could have a significant psychological impact. He had heard that bullying was learned behavior and all bullies had been bullied themselves sometime in their past.

Tim had spent much of his youth with his nose buried in books or newspapers. He learned to love the smell of newsprint, and one of his girlfriends had told him he had ink in his veins instead of blood like other boys. It wasn't until years later that he realized her remark was meant as a put-down and not as a compliment.

Tim had excelled in high school, and he earned a partial academic scholarship to Northwestern. Uninterested in sports, he had devoted his spare time to *The Daily Northwestern*, a publication of the Medill School of Journalism. Tim also edited a student literary journal. He fell in love with the process of putting a publication together and ushering it into print. It was a lot like birthing a child. First came the conception, then the gestation period, and eventually the birth. The printed word was a living, breathing thing to Tim's mind. But once a publication saw print, it was already time for Tim to move on to father his next brainchild. Since taking over publication of the *Gazette*, Tim had generated a new child every single week. He was both the father and the mother of the *Gazette*, and he also acted as the midwife when he delivered printed copies to drop-off points around town.

Even now, he felt next week's issue growing within him. He had lots to do to nourish the fetus before Wednesday's delivery date. He had four additional advertising-free pages to fill with reminiscences of the life and legacy of Rodney Engleworth. Tim had called the printer yesterday and added the pages to his print order. He began filling the InDesign template with a picture of Rod and Helen that Tim took of the two of them when they celebrated their fortieth wedding anniversary. Helen's cancer had been in temporary remission, and both were smiling and looked happy to be alive. It was difficult for Tim to believe they were both gone, Helen's body ravished by the cancer and the effects of its treatment, and Rod's body ravished by some knife-wielding maniac.

Tim worked non-stop until after ten PM. He stopped only when his stomach loudly reminded him he had eaten nothing all day. He walked into the back room and searched the small refrigerator for something microwavable. He decided he wouldn't be able to stomach another frozen TV dinner after throwing up the last one. Tim remembered only too well what that half-digested regurgitation had looked and smelled like on the floor of Rod's bedroom. There wasn't much else in the fridge. Was it too late to go out and grab a quick bite someplace nearby?

Terri's Restaurant remained open twenty-four-seven, and suddenly Tim wanted an open-faced hot roast beef with mashed potatoes and gravy, allegedly Rod's favorite meal. Tim jumped into the shower. Fifteen minutes later, he brushed his teeth and rinsed his mouth with Listerine before putting on clean underwear and a different sweatshirt. He splashed on some after-shave, and he was in the Jeep and on his way to the restaurant before eleven.

Tim had inherited the Wagoneer from his father. He loved this all-weather workhorse that worked so well to haul newspapers all over town every Wednesday year-around, come hell or high water. He could throw dozens of bundles of papers in the open hatchback and the Wagoneer never complained about the excess weight. And it plowed through winter snows with four-wheel drive as if city streets had been cleared when they weren't. Tim's father had bought the Wagoneer new a month before he died. The vehicle was eight years old and had less than a hundred-thousand miles on the odometer. Other than oil changes and replacing the tires, Tim hadn't had to spend anything on maintenance. He hoped he could coax another fifty-thousand miles out of the engine before he had to trade for a new model.

Terri's was slightly less busy tonight than last night. Tim was able to take a seat at the coffee counter without waiting, and Susan brought him a menu and a glass of water as soon as he sat down. He ordered the open-face hot beef sandwich and a Diet Pepsi. Susan turned the order in to the cook in the kitchen and brought Tim his soft drink.

"Have you heard from your sister recently?" Tim asked.

"No," said Susan.

"I'm running your sister's picture on the front page of Wednesday's edition. We're asking people to call the newspaper office if they have any information about Megan."

"Do you think that's a good idea?" asked Susan. "I don't think Megan wants to be found."

"Rod thought it was important that we speak with her. We need to know who, if anyone, she may have told about her injuries. Does she have any friends she might be staying with?"

"I don't think so. She didn't want to see anyone, or anyone to see her after the rape."

"Whoever killed Rod knew about Megan's injuries. That same person killed two other men in the past three weeks. All of the victims had their genitals removed, their nipples cut off, and knife wounds on their faces, backs, and inner thighs."

Susan blanched. It was as if all of the blood had drained from her face. "Megan had her nipples cut off. She had knife wounds on her face, chest, back and inner thighs."

"It was as if the same four men who cut your sister four years ago came back to cut Rod and the other two male victims," Tim said. "Only it wasn't those four men. It was a woman who killed Rod. Police know it wasn't you, because you were working when those murders took place. It was another woman who knew exactly what had happened to Megan."

"I don't know who that could be," said Susan.

"Rod thought Megan might know," said Tim. "That's why it's important to find her."

"I've been trying to find her. I've looked everywhere I can think of. I've called all of her old friends. No one knows where she is, not even mom."

Tim finished his supper while Susan went around to occupied tables refilling coffee cups. Tim decided to skip the piece of pie tonight. The sandwich and potatoes were enough to fill him up. His waistline didn't need the extra calories.

Tim left three dollars for a tip and took his check up front to the cash register. The hairs on the back of his neck prickled. Was someone staring at him? Who? Why? For how long?

As the cashier rang up his payment and counted out change for a twenty, Tim glanced around the restaurant. There were still more than a dozen people occupying booths near the front of the restaurant, and three times as many seated at tables in the back. Six people remained seated at the coffee counter. It was almost midnight on a Saturday night. Terri's probably wouldn't be really busy again until the bars closed at two. Then the place would be swamped with people trying to sober up before driving home.

Only one of the people in the entire restaurant appeared to be looking Tim's way. He couldn't see her face because her features were shrouded in shadows beneath the hood of a heavy dark-colored zip-up sweatshirt. But she was obviously female and relatively young. Did he know her? She was looking straight at him as if she knew him.

Tim thought about walking over to the booth and taking a closer look at her face, but he decided it was getting late and he had better things to do.

He walked out of the restaurant and felt the woman's eyes follow him as he turned left and headed for his car. When he drove past the restaurant, he saw the same woman paying her bill at the cash register. Her face was still hidden by the hood. But she looked like she was about to leave, and Tim wanted another look when she got outside.

Tim drove around the block. He saw the woman walking toward the bus stop on the corner. She walked with a limp and her left leg seemed to drag slightly behind. Did he know anyone who walked with that kind of limp? No one came to mind.

She didn't wait at the bus stop but crossed the street. She continued walking east on Foster. Should Tim follow her? Should he offer her a ride?

Tim was stopped by a red light at the corner of Third and Foster. If he were going to follow the woman, he would need to turn left when the light changed. He could make a right turn on red and be back at the office in less than five minutes. Which should he do? He had work to do at the office. He wanted to work some more on his "Reminiscences of Rod" before going to sleep.

He waited for the light to change and turned left to follow the girl, but she had disappeared completely, as if she were merely a ghost or an apparition and not a real woman at all.

CHAPTER NINETEEN

You can't see me, but I can see you.

I hide in the shadows and watch you drive slowly by where you think I should be. I'm practically invisible in my dark sweatshirt, dark jeans, and dark shoes. While you were stopped at the corner stoplight, I ducked into this alley and blended into the shadows. You can't see me, but I can see you.

I saw you enter the restaurant just after eleven. I saw you take a seat at the counter in Susan's section. I saw you talk with her. I couldn't hear what you said to her, but she was obviously upset by your words. Her face turned ghastly white with shock at whatever you said. Did you tell her you wanted to ram your penis into her until she screamed? Is that what shocked her?

I thought about letting you pick me up tonight. I could tell you wanted to. I saw you drive around the block and come back to pick me up.

Not tonight, dear. Maybe tomorrow night. Tonight I must get home and be there before Susan arrives. I thought those men would come for Susan last night, but they didn't. Maybe they'll come tonight. Tonight is the last night of the weekend. They won't come for Susan tomorrow night because they have to work on Monday morning and Susan doesn't work Sundays. They mostly scout on weeknights, but they might want to rape Susan only on a weekend because they know she won't be home until late and they don't have to hurry to get to work the next day. Did they not rape her last night because they saw you following her home?

Will they try to rape Susan tonight? I hope they come tonight. I want my revenge.

How far did you get on Foster before you realized you had missed me entirely and decided to turn around? I see you driving back this way, looking into the shadows. But I know you can't see me. Are you frustrated? I hope so.

I expect you'll drive around the block one more time before giving up. Then I can leave my hiding place and walk home. I have time to wait. Susan won't leave until the last of her customers leave their tips on the counter or tables. She makes good money working for tips. Some nights she gets four hundred dollars or more. Some nights she doesn't make shit.

Fridays and Saturdays are good nights for tips. She serves between thirty and forty people an hour on average. If each person leaves her three or four dollars, she pockets more than a hundred dollars an hour during peak periods. Some people put tips on their credit cards. Then Susan has to wait until after her shift is over and the cashier banks out to collect her tips. She doesn't get the full amount, either. The restaurant deducts credit card fees and withholds taxes. I always leave cash tips. Of course, I have bad credit and can't get a credit card, so I have to leave cash.

I see you drive by again. Still can't see me, can you? I know your car. I know your license number. I'll know you when I see you again.

And now you drive by me for the last time, going back the other way. It's time for me to emerge from the shadows and walk the seven remaining blocks to my apartment.

I walk past the apartment on Fifth Street and remember what those men did to me. I feel pain in places where the nerves were cut and I can no longer feel anything real. Pain is the only sensation my vagina re-members. My breasts—the artificial reconstructions that pass for breasts—know only pain, never pleasure. If I were able to have chil-dren, I would not be able to nurse.

I pick up my pace. I know there is still plenty of time before Susan leaves work, but I hurry home anyway. I want to be there long before Susan arrives. I want to be there before the four rapists get to Susan's apartment. I want to be certain what happened to me does not happen to my sister.

I reach my apartment building on Tenth Street and walk slowly up the stairs. I can't walk up stairs like a normal person. I have to step up with my right leg and deliberately will my left leg up to stand alongside the right in literally a two-step process. I don't have the luxury of sub-consciously knowing exactly where my left leg will be at any given moment. When specific nerve receptors connecting muscle spindles to my brain were severed by a rapist's knife, I lost proprioception in my left leg. I can no longer feel those muscles respond. Muscle memory remains intact, and the muscles move. I just can't sense how much they move nor in which direction. I have to look down to see where my left leg is and then will it to move to where I want it to be. Normally, that entire process would happen automatically, without need to think it through with each step. But I need to consciously make the process hap-pen with my left leg. My right leg works just fine.

When I first regained full consciousness after a year, I couldn't walk at all. But physical therapy taught me how to walk again despite my inability to feel much in that leg. I will never be able to walk normally, but at least I can walk.

I hobble into my own apartment and take up vigilance at the window. I see neither Susan's car nor the rapists' van in the alley. I use my binoculars to make sure I haven't missed seeing the van. It's not in the alley.

Of course, the rapists could park on the street and walk into the alley. Now that they know which apartment is Susan's, they can come in from the street and hurry up the stairs to the third floor landing. I'm on the third floor of the apartment building directly across the alley from Susan's apartment. I can see into her apartment with my binoculars when the lights are on and the window shades open. But with the lights off, I can't see anything inside that apartment.

I worry that the rapists might have arrived while I was away. They might have left the van on the street, already entered Susan's apartment, and they're inside waiting for her to come home. Everything is quiet and still. Outside floodlights aimed at the alley cast sinister shadows onto brick walls behind stairs. I tell myself to be patient. When Susan arrives home and opens the door to her apartment, she'll switch on two overhead fluorescent tubes in her kitchen. I'll be able to see inside the apartment.

It's already nearly two, and Susan isn't home yet. She should be here any second now. I'll see the headlights of her Toyota when she enters the alley. I'll be able to watch her park the car, climb the stairs, unlock the back door, and enter.

And then I see headlights turn into the alley from Addison Avenue. It's Susan's red Toyota. Her usual parking place is taken tonight and she parks in the next available space. I watch her lock the Toyota, amble up the alley toward the back of her own apartment building, and climb the stairs to the third floor as any normal person would walk up stairs. I'm envious of my sister.

She opens the door without incident and turns on the kitchen lights. There is no one waiting in the kitchen.

The lights come on in the bedroom, and I see Susan walk to the window and lower the shades. I can see her shadow move about in the bedroom. The light comes on in the adjoining bathroom. Everything seems normal.

I continue to watch. I love my sister. When I was a child, I watched Susan constantly and tried to be just like her. Susan has always been a good three years older than me, and she was my role model. When I was ten, Susan was already a teen. I learned to love the music she loved, and I would watch her dance around her bedroom and I would try to mimic her and imitate her moves as best I could. Perhaps it was the age difference that made her seem so much more graceful then me.

When I was thirteen and Susan was sixteen, she told me all about boys and what they wanted from girls. Susan was a bit of a tease in high school, and she had lost her virginity to a football player who acted like he didn't know what "Stop" and "No" meant. Susan worried for nearly a month that she might be pregnant. It scared her so much that she stopped being a tease.

It scared me, too. I knew that my father had married my mother only because mom was pregnant with Susan. Mom loved dad, but mom was never sure that dad loved her or merely married her out of obligation. Mom was always worried that dad was seeing other women. When mom discovered her worries were factual, she made life difficult for the entire family.

I swore I wouldn't have sex until after I was married. That way I'd be certain the man I married loved me. I'll never be able to marry anyone now. The men who stole my virginity and took away my ability to have children also took away any hope for love. Now I hate all men.

Men are cruel. It's time men learned that women can be cruel, too.

My heart is stone. It's as if those men ripped my heart out when they cut open my breasts. Surgeons replaced my broken heart with one that has no feeling. I still live and breathe, but I feel nothing.

I live for revenge. I live to act as an instrument of justice and divine retribution. Police have done nothing to punish the men who did this to me.

I was so sure they—the rapists—would come last night or tonight. Why didn't they? What kept them from trying to rape my sister?

I take the Beretta out of my purse and fondle it. The metal is cold to my touch. I yearn to point the gun at someone.

I think of the man who followed me tonight. If I knew where he lived, I would go there and point the gun at him. I would bind his hands and feet and mouth with duct tape. I would do to him what I did to the old man, what those four rapists did to me. And I wouldn't hurry. I'd make certain he felt every bit of pain I've felt for four long years.

Perhaps I will see that man again. Perhaps he will follow me and try to pick me up. Next time, I'll let him.

Meanwhile, I must be patient. I know those four rapists will come for Susan sooner or later. When they do come, I will be ready for them.

I'm nothing if not patient.

CHAPTER TWENTY

Tim spent all day Sunday writing his tribute to Rod. He wanted every word to be absolutely perfect. He went over his copy again and again until he was satisfied all the words were right. Rod would have sat down at his desk and knocked out the same kind of tribute, the same number of words, in record time. Rod had a way with words that Tim envied. It took Tim all day to write one original tribute column. Rod usually did two compete columns—including "Reminiscences of Helen"—in less than three hours.

Tim's natural talents were more visual and kinesthetic than verbal. He had a unique gift for spatial orientation that allowed him to visualize relationships he found difficult or impossible to put into words. He simply moved things around until he found where they fit. Sometimes he found exactly where each word belonged. If that didn't work, he went back to the drawing board and tried again.

Rod had often said investigative journalism was exactly like putting together pieces of a giant jigsaw puzzle. "You gather pieces from various sources and try to see how they fit together. When you get enough pieces, you try to grasp the big picture. If you can't see the entire picture, you have to keep adding pieces until you can. Once you have the whole picture, the remaining pieces easily fit into place with no pieces missing and no extra pieces left over. If you have pieces missing, you don't yet have the entire story. If there are pieces left over, you may be seeing the wrong picture entirely."

As hard as he tried, Tim couldn't visualize the big picture. He saw only scattered pieces, small parts of the whole. He saw the mutilated bodies of Rod, Willard, and Murphy. He saw the faces of the four rapists as Megan Williams had described them to the police. He saw the face of Megan Williams from her high school yearbook photograph. He moved those pieces around, but they didn't begin to hint at the picture that connected them all.

Rod had been certain there was a connection between all those pieces, and Tim trusted Rod's instincts. Rod must have discovered a possible connection that brought Rod too close to the killer. That was the only reason Tim could think of why Rod was brutally murdered. Rod knew too much.

Or, as Giffords had put it, the killer felt Rod had stuck his nose where it didn't belong.

Wherever that place was, it was someplace real close to home. Hadn't Susan Williams said she had talked to Rod the night he was killed? Didn't she say she had served him his usual hot roast beef sandwich with mashed potatoes? Tim wondered what time Rod had left the restaurant. If Susan had said the time, Tim didn't remember.

Rod must have encountered the killer sometime between when Rod left Terri's Restaurant and the time he invited the killer into his own house to talk and have a cup of freshly-brewed coffee. If the medical examiner determined approximate time of death to be between nine PM and midnight, where could Rod have gone in the brief intervening time period? He didn't have time to go far. What prompted the killer to follow Rod home? What did Rod see on Thursday night that got him killed?

Tim thought about asking Susan if she knew the exact time Rod left the restaurant. Rod had e-mailed next Wednesday's columns and feature story to Tim at exactly five-forty-seven. Rod left his desk almost immediately after sending his copy to Tim. If Rod drove straight to Terri's Restaurant from the office, he probably entered the restaurant shortly after six PM. Tim visualized Rod sitting at the coffee counter, ordering his usual from a smiling Susan Williams, and sipping a cup of hot coffee while waiting for his meal. Susan was very efficient and put Rod's order in at the kitchen around six-fifteen. Depending on how crowded the restaurant was at dinnertime on Thursday, Rod had his plate of hot beef and mashed potatoes well before six-thirty. He had cleaned his plate by seven, and likely ordered a piece of pecan pie. Rod often raved about Terri's pecan pie, and Rod would want to celebrate the early completion of next week's copy with pie. Before Helen's death, Rod would have celebrated at one of the local bars. After Helen died and Rod gave up drinking, he developed a sweet tooth and a fondness for pecan pie. Tim imagined Rod talking with Susan while savoring his pie as long as it lasted.

Susan would have interrupted her conversation with Rod to take care of other customers. When Rod finished his pie, he would have continued drinking coffee. Terri's was as well-known as the home of the bottomless coffee cup as it was known as the best place for pie in all Chicagoland. Customers got free refills, and they were welcome to stay and drink coffee until they floated away. Tim imagined Susan refilling Rod's cup while Rod pumped Susan for information about restaurant regulars. Investigative reporters developed bartenders and waitresses as valuable information sources. "When you want to really know what's going on around town," Rod had often said, "talk to a bartender or a waitress. They see and hear everything."

Had Susan given Rod a lead that he followed up on when he left the restaurant? What did Susan Williams know? And did she even know what she knew? What did she tell Rod that got him killed?

Police had speculated that Susan, not Megan, had been the intended target. The four rapists had seen Susan at Terri's Restaurant and followed her home to learn where she lived. On the night Megan was raped, Susan was much later than usual leaving work for home. The rapists who had planned to enter Susan's apartment to wait for her discovered Megan alone in the apartment. They raped Megan instead of Susan.

All of the local murders were linked to Megan Williams' violent rape nearly four years ago. The wounds on Rod, Willard, and Murphy were too similar to Megan's wounds to be coincidence. No other unsolved rapes had occurred in Twin Rivers since Megan was raped, though dozens of similar rapes and murders had occurred in surrounding suburbs. Whoever murdered Rod, Willard, and Murphy knew exactly what had happened to Megan and he or she copied Megan's injuries when she murdered men.

Tim was certain the killer was someone who knew Susan and Megan Williams personally. Whoever the killer was, he or she was someone Megan or Susan had confided in about the rape. Did Susan know who the killer was? Did Susan tell Rod whom she had informed of Megan's injuries?

Tim rushed from the office and drove straight to Terri's Restaurant to ask Susan the same questions he had just asked himself. What time had Rod left Terri's Restaurant on Thursday night? What had he asked Susan? What had Susan told Rod? Who did Susan tell about the extent of Megan's injuries? Who might Megan have told? Who did Susan personally know who was capable of murder?

Tim found a parking place almost in front of Terri's Restaurant. Downtown Twin Rivers was practically deserted on Sunday night at nine. Tim wasn't surprised to learn that Susan didn't work Sundays or Mondays. He asked Sally, the older waitress who worked the cash register, for Susan's home phone number. Sally said she couldn't give that information out to customers even if she knew where Susan lived. Tim asked Sally for a telephone directory and looked Susan Williams up in the phone listings. Susan Williams wasn't listed. Neither was Megan.

Tim remembered where Susan Williams lived on Eleventh Street. He had followed her home once to make certain she arrived home safely. He wanted to drive to Susan's apartment right now and grill her until she remembered the answers to all of the burning questions Tim needed answered.

Tim got in his Wagoneer and started the engine. Then he had second thoughts.

If Rod had been murdered after speaking with Susan Williams, visiting Susan at home might not be a good idea. Police had speculated that the rapists had watched Susan's Fifth Street apartment for some time before entering to rape and murder her. Both Rod and the police believed Susan was the original target of the rapists, and the four rapists would be back someday to do to Susan what they had done to Megan. That it hadn't happened yet didn't mean it wouldn't happen soon. Tim didn't want to be caught in Susan's apartment if those killers came back.

Nor did he want to tip off his hand to the man or woman who had killed Rod. Rod had been murdered almost immediately after speaking with Susan last Thursday. That killer had followed Rod home and done terrible things to him because she felt Rod was getting too close to the truth. Tim didn't like to think of himself as a coward, but he knew he was. When he had seen other kids bullied in school, Tim had looked the other way. When he thought a story would jeopardize ad revenues, he refused to run the story. As much as he would like to be, he admitted he wasn't a crusading journalist, a real newspaperman, like Rod. He was an advertising man and a business owner. Joel Giffords had warned Tim to keep his nose out of other people's business, lest Tim's nose get chopped off like Rod's penis. This wasn't some game that kids played. These killers were playing for keeps. Tim could lose everything—including his life—if he continued to pursue the killers.

Tim should take what he knew or surmised and give that information to the police. He should talk to Giffords in the morning and let Giffords interview Susan. He should keep his nose and his private parts where they belonged. But Tim knew Giffords was limited in what he could do. He was being run ragged with task force investigations, and he had no time to follow up on what was merely speculation. What proof did Tim have that Susan Williams and her sister were the keys to the recent murders in Twin Rivers and surrounding suburbs? What did he really know for certain?

He knew that Rodney Engleworth, the man who had been Tim's friend and mentor and surrogate father, was brutally murdered in his own home by a person or persons unknown. Tim had witnessed Rod's mutilation with his own eyes, and he had digital pictures to prove it. He had Susan Williams' testimony that Rod had been in Terri's Restaurant and talked with Susan the same night Rod was killed. He had Rod's written story that implied a link between the current murders and the rape and mutilation of Megan Williams four years ago. And he knew that Megan Williams was indeed missing. She had moved out of her apartment without telling anyone where she was moving, and she had simply disappeared off the face of the earth like that limping hooded woman Tim had tried to follow last night had disappeared in the dark.

If Tim went to the police, he should talk to someone other than Joel Giffords. The only other cop Tim knew was Elsie Dorr. Should he talk to Dorr? Would she accompany Tim to Susan's apartment if he asked her politely?

Tim remembered the business card Elsie Dorr had handed him on Friday at the Twin Rivers police station. Dorr's cell phone number was on that card, and she had practically begged Tim to call her. So what if she only asked Tim to call her if he decided to give her a preview of Rod's story? So what if she had already seen that story yesterday afternoon? So what if it was already late on a Sunday evening and getting later with every minute? Tim felt he needed to talk with someone. If he couldn't talk with Susan Williams or her sister, he needed to talk with the police. Elsie Dorr was a Twin Rivers police officer, wasn't she? She had told Tim to call her, hadn't she?

Tim took out his cell phone and Dorr's printed business card he had shoved into his wallet where he could find her phone number when he needed it. He needed it now. He keyed the cell phone number from the card and pressed the talk button on his phone. He also pressed save to enter Dorr's number into the cellular phone's memory.

"You have reached the cellphone number of Elsie Dorr, Twin Rivers Police community relations and public information officer," said Dorr's recorded voice-mail message. "Please leave a number where you can be reached and the purpose of your call, and I'll get back to you as soon as I can."

"Shit!" said Tim as he clicked off without leaving a message.

Tim decided to take a big risk and visit Susan Williams in her apartment on Eleventh Street. If the rapists hadn't come back for Susan yet, what were the chances they would come for her tonight? Tim needed answers to his many questions. Susan could supply some—if not all—of those answers. Tomorrow Tim needed to completely finish designing Wednesday's issue and put the entire 68-page newspaper to bed before ten AM on Tuesday. He had less than thirty-six hours before deadline. He was almost out of time if he wanted to add anything to Rod's story. If he didn't get answers now, he wouldn't have a chance to get anything else into print for at least another week.

He drove to Eleventh Street. He didn't know how to reach Susan's apartment through the front door, or even which third-floor apartment was hers. Susan's name was probably on a mailbox in the lobby, but the building lobby was likely locked. It was too late at night to ring doorbells randomly in the hope someone might buzz him inside. He would have to park in the alley behind Susan's building and walk up the back stairs. He had seen which door on the third floor Susan had entered from the rear. He could climb the three flights of stairs and pound on her kitchen door until she opened it, assuming she would open it instead of calling the police to report a prowler. It was a risk he was willing to take. He could always explain to the police what he was doing vising Susan's apartment late at night uninvited. He was certain Susan would be understanding once he explained.

He drove around the block and entered the alley from Addison Avenue. He saw a parking spot near the stairs to Susan's apartment, and he felt the hairs on the back of his neck prickle as he pulled into the empty parking space.

He looked around but saw no one in the alley. Someone must be watching him from one of the windows. Most of the windows in Susan's building were still lit, and so were nearly all of the windows in the apartment across the alley. Whoever was watching him was in one of the few dark windows because Tim saw no face in any of the lit windows. And, because he felt eyes on the back of his neck, he was certain he was being watched from the building across the alley.

It was still relatively early yet, not quite eleven. Tim was sure Susan was still awake. There were lights on in her apartment. Why was he so afraid to go up there? If he wanted answers, he needed to go up there now.

Tim made up his mind. He put a trembling hand on the driver's door handle, pulled up, shoved the door open, and stepped out into the cold cruel night.

CHAPTER TWENTY-ONE

I see you driving down the alley in your black Jeep SUV. Didn't I warn you to stay away from my sister? Why doesn't anyone listen to me?

If I see you take one step up those stairs, you're a dead man. I can shoot you from here. I have the loaded Beretta in my hand, the safety off. I'll wait until you're on the stairs where I can't miss. I'll lift the window, stick the muzzle out the opening, and fire until I see you fall. I won't let you hurt my sister.

What are you waiting for? I know you want to get out of your SUV, climb up those stairs, and knock on Susan's door. Is she expecting you? Did she invite you to visit? Oh, God, I hope not.

It occurred to me that Susan might someday have a boyfriend. Are you her boyfriend? You look older than Susan, but not too much older. Susan always liked boys a year or two older than her. The football player who almost got her pregnant was a high school senior when Susan was a junior.

No, I don't think you're Susan's boyfriend. You're not her type. For one thing, you're too short. Susan is an inch or two taller than you. Plus, Susan is absolutely gorgeous, and you're an insignificant little nobody in glasses. Susan likes football players. She falls for tall men with broad shoulders and strong arms. You're nothing like that. You can't be Susan's boyfriend.

But I bet you want to be. I watched you closely last night in Terri's Restaurant. You sat at the counter with your back to me. You were looking at Susan. You didn't see me, but I saw you.

It wasn't until you paid your bill that you noticed me. I don't want people to notice me, but you turned around and looked straight at me in my booth. What did you see when you looked at me?

Did you see my scars? How could you? I had my head hidden by the hood, my body covered with the sweatshirt and jeans.

I saw you look at my breasts. Are breasts the first thing a man notices about a woman? My breasts aren't real, but you couldn't tell that when I wore my sweatshirt over them. Did you want to lift my sweatshirt and stare at my breasts? I bet you did.

Come here, and I'll show you my breasts. I'll show you my entire body, scars and all. It will be the last thing you'll ever see.

What are you waiting for?

I see you looking up at the windows. I see you turn around in your seat to look back at my building across the alley from Susan's. Are you a peeper? Are you trying to see women's naked breasts in the lit windows?

Is that why you're here? Are you going to wait in your car until you see Susan's bedroom lights come on and Susan appear in the lit window? It won't do you any good. Susan always lowers the window shade before she undresses for bed.

You can't see me because my window is dark. But I can see you in your car, partially lit by the floodlights that light up the alley. I could shoot you now as you sit in your car.

But I won't shoot until you make a move toward Susan's apartment on the third floor. I don't want to take a chance the bullet might miss. I will shoot you if you attempt to enter Susan's apartment. I won't let anyone hurt my sister.

Shooting you will delay my revenge. I don't care. I can wait. I can be patient. I'm nothing if not patient.

What are you waiting for?

Susan doesn't have to work until three tomorrow. She won't go to bed before one or two. If you're waiting to watch her take off her clothes before bed, you'll have a long wait. Or are you waiting for Susan to go to bed so you can break into her apartment and rape her? Are you like those other men? Do you want to fuck my sister?

Maybe I should shoot you now. Maybe I should riddle your car with bullets. Police will know where the bullets came from. They'll know the shots originated from my apartment. But I'll be gone before the police arrive. I can find another apartment. I can start all over again. I've done it before. I'll do it again if I have to.

At last I see you take off your seat belt and move your left hand to open the car door. The overhead light comes on in your Jeep as you shove the door wide open and swing your feet out. You slam the door shut and take the first step toward the stairs.

I open the widow sash and cold air floods into my apartment. Temperatures have continued to drop after the sun went down. Winter is coming, but you won't be around to see it.

What are you doing? You walked around the car to get to the stairs and you stopped behind the car where I can't get a clear shot at you. I can only see the top of your head over the roof of the car. You're not moving forward. You're standing still.

I see now that you're holding a cell phone to your right ear. Who are you calling? Are you calling the other four rapists and telling them Susan is alone in her apartment? Are you acting as their scout tonight? Will they come to rape Susan tonight? It's still early. They'll think they have plenty of time to rape Susan and still make it to work in time tomorrow morning. Is tonight the night I get my revenge? Will I have to kill five men tonight instead of four? I can do that. I have enough bullets. There are fifteen bullets in the Beretta. That's three bullets for each of you.

Are the men in the van waiting around the corner for your call? Should I go downstairs now to be ready for them when they arrive? Let me get my purse with the tools I plan to use. I'm all dressed in black tonight. I'll slip the sweatshirt hood up over my hair and go down the back steps and wait downstairs for your friends to arrive. There. I've closed the window. I can go through the kitchen and out the back door. My entire apartment is dark, and you won't see me exit the kitchen.

I'm outside now on the third floor balcony looking down at you. I have the Beretta in my hand and the purse with the knives and box-cutter slung over my shoulder. I'm ready for you and your friends.

I see you put the cell phone away. I watch you walk back to your car and get into the driver's seat. Are you going to wait in your car for your friends? I don't blame you. It's too cold to wait outside for long.

I hear you start the motor. Did you do that because you want to run the heater? Now I see you turn on the Jeep's headlights and I watch you angle out of the parking space. Are you leaving? Aren't you staying to watch your friends rape my sister? Are you leaving before the fun begins?

I will wait right here in the cold for them to come. They are the ones I want. When you learn I've cut off their dicks and they died from excessive blood loss, you'll think twice about trying to rape Susan on your own. But if you come back, I'll do you, too.

It's really cold out here tonight. My teeth are chattering. Although I can't feel much else, I do feel the cold.

I'm ready and waiting. As soon as I see all four men get out of their van, I'll go the rest of the way downstairs and shoot them all in the legs. I'll aim for their kneecaps.

Then I'll pull their pants down and do them right where they fell. I'll cut off their dicks and make them eat their own flesh. I'll make sure they swallow, too.

I've waited a long time for my revenge. I can wait here in the cold as long as it takes.

I'm nothing if not patient.

CHAPTER TWENTY-TWO

Tim's cell phone rang. He pulled the phone out of his jacket pocket, looked at the caller ID, and was surprised to see Elsie Dorr's cell number displayed on the screen.

"Did you call me?" Elsie asked when Tim pressed talk.

"Yes," said Tim. "I remembered today that Rod talked with Susan Williams the night he was killed. I think the woman who killed Rod followed Rod home when he left Terri's Restaurant."

"You think the killer was in Terri's? Why?"

"I think the killer was watching Susan Williams and happened to see Rod talk with Susan. I think the killer believed Susan had told Rod something that would positively identify the killer."

"What did Susan tell Engleworth?"

"I don't know. I want to talk to Susan again to see if she remembers exactly what she told him and when. I don't think she even knows what it is she knows that's so important. But I thought if I could learn what she and Rod discussed, that might give me a clue. I'm downstairs from Susan's apartment right now. Do you want to come over here to Eleventh Street and we can quiz her together? How soon can you get here?"

"I can't right now," said Dorr. "I just got out of the bathtub. That's why I didn't answer the phone when you called. I heard the phone start to ring just as I was getting into the tub. I knew I couldn't dry my feet and reach the phone in time to answer. So I just let it go to voice mail.

After I finished my bath, I checked for messages. When I heard no new messages, I checked caller ID for missed calls. That's how I knew you had called about an hour ago. I haven't dressed yet, my hair's still wet, and it's too cold to go outside with wet hair. But I definitely don't want you to talk to Susan Williams alone if what you suspect is true. Why don't you come over to my place? We'll talk about what we should do. If you still want to talk with Susan, I'll go with you. I live at 1404 North Riverside. It's a condo. I'm in unit B. I'll get dressed and wait for you at the door."

"I'll be there in twenty minutes," said Tim.

The hair on the back of Tim's neck prickled again as Tim returned to the Wagoneer, slid into the driver's seat, and started the motor. He looked up and thought he caught a brief glimpse of a shadow moving on the third floor balcony of the building behind him. He didn't want to take the time to investigate because Elsie Dorr was waiting for him. But traffic was light this late on a Sunday night. Tim managed to drive to Dorr's condo in ten minutes instead of twenty. He had plenty of time.

Riverside ran north and south alongside the east bank of one of the two relatively-small and almost-parallel rivers that gave Twin Rivers its name. The two rivers converged into one much-bigger river just south of the city, and the combined rivers then flowed into the Illinois River thirty miles or so farther south. On a map, the configuration looked like the letter "Y" with the city of Twin Rivers stuck in the valley just north of the middle of the letter.

The McKinley Avenue Bridge separated North from South Riverside and spanned both rivers. Construction along South Riverside Boulevard consisted mainly of expensive single-family dwellings in various subdivisions and gated communities. North Riverside Parkway was mostly apartments, duplexes, and condominiums. Elsie Dorr's condo at 1404 North Riverside was a medium-sized, medium-priced two-story red brick building with four apartment units built above four identical garages with attached storage spaces.

Elsie opened the door before Tim could ring the doorbell. She was dressed in a white cotton bathrobe, and her shiny red hair, not completely dry yet, was still down and not tied up in her usual ponytail.

"Come on in," she said. "I was just about to get dressed."

"I know it's late," said Tim. "You don't have to dress on my account. You look fine just the way you are."

She smiled. "I don't usually answer the door in my bathrobe, but I wasn't expecting you so soon. You must have broken every speed law in the book to get here that quick. I haven't had time to dress or even finish brushing my hair. Why don't you take a seat in the living room and make yourself comfortable? I can put on a pot of coffee, if you drink coffee this late at night. Otherwise, I have Coke and Ginger Ale in the refrigerator."

"A Ginger Ale would be nice."

Tim looked around the tastefully-decorated living room while Elsie walked to the spacious kitchen and rummaged inside the refrigerator. A large sofa with mahogany end tables on each side and a matching mahogany coffee table in front occupied half a wall. Two large comfortable-looking recliners and two padded arm chairs sat near another wall. The third wall had a 52-inch flat-screen television mounted on the wall itself, with an entertainment center containing high-end stereo equipment beneath the TV screen. The fourth wall opened up into a dining room with a large dining room table, eight marching chairs, a buffet table, and a china cabinet. The house and the furnishings looked like they cost a small fortune.

"Nice place you have here," Tim told Elsie when she returned from the kitchen carrying two cans of Canada Dry Ginger Ale.

"Thanks. It belongs to my mother. I have the whole house to myself from November until April every year while mom winters in Florida." Elsie handed one of the cans to Tim. "Pick a seat anywhere. I'm going to sit on the sofa and you can join me. Or you can sit in a recliner if you prefer."

Tim chose the recliner closest to the sofa. He discovered the recliner was as comfortable as it looked. Elsie placed her can of pop on the coffee table. Tim caught an eyeful of shapely thigh as she took a seat on the sofa and crossed her legs. She quickly pulled the robe tightly closed when she saw him looking.

"What time did Engleworth leave Terri's on Thursday?" she asked.

"That was one of the questions I wanted to ask Susan," Tim said. "I'm guessing between eight and nine."

"And the coroner estimated time of death between nine and midnight?"

"That's what I heard."

"What makes you think the killer followed Engleworth home from the restaurant?"

"Two things. One, Rod didn't have much time to go anywhere else. And two, I believe the killer was watching Susan Williams and happened to see Rod and Susan talking. I think the killer was afraid Rod had somehow learned her identity from Susan, so she—assuming Rod's killer was female—followed Rod and murdered him to keep him from talking."

"Why did she mutilate Engleworth's body? If she just wanted to keep him from reporting her identity, she could simply have killed him. She could have stabbed him or cut his throat. She didn't need to emasculate him."

"Rod thought the woman had a thing against men, a hatred of all men. She wanted to send a message to someone, and the mutilations were symbolic."

"What kind of message?"

"That women are as capable of cruelty as men. She was inspired by the rape and mutilation of Megan Williams. She wanted to show that a woman could be just as powerful, just as controlling, and just as mean as those rapists were."

"Interesting." Elsie took a sip of Ginger Ale.

"It all fits together," said Tim.

"If you're right," said Dorr, "we should be able to see the killer follow Engleworth from the restaurant. There are video cameras at the corner of Third Street and Foster Avenue. What time do you think Engleworth left the restaurant?"

"Sometime after eight PM."

"I start work at nine tomorrow morning," said Dorr. "How would you like to meet me at my office at nine-thirty? I can show you the communications center and we can take a look at last Thursday's recordings from the cameras near the Metra station."

"Why can't we go there tonight and look at the recordings?"

"First, because I need my beauty sleep if I'm to function tomorrow. Second, the Captain needs to approve showing the recordings to a civilian, and the Captain only works the day shift. Third, I'd like to have

Giffords join us. I can call Joel tonight and arrange for him to meet us in the communications control room at ten."

"I guess I'll have to wait," said Tim, unable to hide disappointment from his voice. When Elsie mentioned the video cameras at the corner of Third and Foster, Tim had high hopes of being able to add valuable missing pieces to the puzzle. If the face of a woman following Rod from the restaurant had been caught on camera, someone would surely be able to identify her. Tim wanted to get a picture of that face into Wednesday's edition. He was even willing to put that picture on the front page next to the high school photo of Megan Williams. He could even add a front-page sub-head that read, "Has anyone seen either of these women?"

"Whatever you do, Tim," said Elsie Dorr, "do not go anywhere close to Susan Williams. You might be right that the killer is watching her. I'll ask Giffords to place a stakeout on her apartment just in case." As Elsie stood up to remove her cell phone from a pocket in her robe, Tim was treated to another flash of bare flesh.

Tim was aware Elsie had just addressed him by his first name, and he found himself overjoyed to be on a first-name basis with such a beautiful woman. Had it been that long since he'd been intimate with a woman that simply catching the barest hint of what lay beneath Elsie's robe turned him on? Yes, he admitted. It had been that long.

Elsie had Giffords' cell number on speed dial. Giffords answered his phone almost immediately, and Tim listened to one-half of the conversation. Elsie informed Joel that Rodney Engleworth left Terri's Restaurant around eight on the night he was murdered, and Tim heard Elsie ask Giffords to meet with both her and Tim in the communications command center at ten on Monday morning to view videos. Giffords must have suggested eleven instead of ten, because Elsie said, "Okay, we'll meet at eleven." She asked Giffords to request a stakeout on Susan Williams' apartment on Eleventh Street as soon as possible. "For as long as necessary," said Elsie. "Okay," she agreed. "Only at night. I know we're short on manpower. But this could be important."

Despite the thick cotton of the white bathrobe belted to her waist, Tim could see enough of Elsie's fine figure to imagine what she would look like naked. He wondered what it would feel like to run his hands over every inch of her bare flesh. He had never felt this kind of attraction for a woman before in his entire life. Oh, sure, when he was in high school and his hormones had run rampant, he had been infatuated with half the girls in school. But he had never felt drawn to a woman like he felt drawn to Elsie Dorr. Not even Andrea Albright, a girl Tim had lived with in a Rogers Park apartment during his last year at Northwestern and his first year of graduate school at Circle, appealed to him as much as Elsie Dorr. Tim had almost married Andrea, and he probably would have if she hadn't received a job offer in Seattle she couldn't refuse. Tim was glad now he hadn't married Andrea Albright.

Andrea became a successful broadcast journalist in Portland, Oregon. They kept in touch via e-mail and Facebook. Andrea was still single and had made quite a name for herself as a weather girl on a local TV station before becoming one of the nightly news anchors at a rival station. She was still beautiful and still more interested in her career than in becoming a wife. Lately, however, she had mentioned to Tim how much she missed him and urged him to move out to the west coast so they could be together again.

But Tim was rooted to Twin Rivers and the Chicago area. He loved the way the seasons changed in the Midwest—fall yielding to winter,

winter becoming spring, and spring merging into summer. He loved the smells of the city, even when the ozone levels were so dangerously high from auto exhausts and airplanes taking off and landing at O'Hare that it was next to impossible to breathe. He was a Midwestern boy, born and bred. He couldn't imagine living anywhere else.

And Andrea would never give up her career to move back to Chicago. Oh, maybe she would if WBBM or WGN offered her a good-paying job in the Chicago market. But she wouldn't do it just to be close to Tim.

Tim had no illusions that women found him attractive. He had an ordinary face and an ordinary body. He wore eyeglasses and couldn't see far without them. He was thirty-three years old and hadn't made a name for himself as a journalist nor a fortune as a publisher. He owned no real estate, drove an eight-year-old car, and had less than ten thousand dollars in the bank. It was foolish to think Elsie Dorr might be interested in a romantic relationship with someone like him.

Tim's biggest problem, however, was his inability to want only sex with a woman. Rosie Palm and her five daughters worked fine for relieving his sexual desires. What he really wanted was a woman he could talk to, someone with whom he could share his dreams of success and even his fears of failure. Andrea had been the closest he had come to finding a woman like that.

But Tim couldn't deny he was sexually attracted to Elsie Dorr. He had met her less than a week ago, and he had thought about her a lot since. Had it been the tears he had seen in her eyes when he told her about Rod's murder that made him fall helplessly in love with her? Had it been her red hair up in a ponytail? Had it been the cute freckles on her nose?

All of the above, Tim decided. Most importantly, however had been her curiosity, the way she had asked questions, the way she had probed Tim for information like a good reporter. Deep down, he felt, Elsie Dorr and Tim Goodman were kindred spirits.

And when she had come to Tim's office on Saturday and disclosed information she shouldn't have, Tim had fallen in love with her all over again.

He couldn't keep his eyes off her. Her long red hair hung down over the collar of the white cotton bathrobe and loose strands danced around her neck and over the tops of both shoulders each time she moved her head. Tim wanted to run his fingers through that silky-smooth hair. He wanted to whisper words of endearment. He wanted her to love him as much as he loved her.

He knew he was Don Quixote tilting at windmills.

"We'll see you in the command center at eleven," Elsie said. She clicked off the phone and turned around to face Tim. "Giffords will be there. He'll arrange for a stake-out on Susan Williams' apartment every night from midnight to dawn, beginning tomorrow. Is there anything else you can think of we should do before we call it a night?"

There were plenty of things Tim could think of he'd like to do with Elsie Dorr, but he didn't dare suggest any of them. "No," he said. "I guess I'd better leave and let you get some sleep."

"Thanks for calling me, Tim," she said. "Now that we know where Engleworth was before he was murdered, we can check video to see where he went and who might have followed him. Giffords doesn't have any leads yet, and this could break the case wide open."

"I thought you should know," said Tim. "Thanks for inviting me to your house, and thanks for the Ginger Ale."

"I'm sorry I wasn't dressed when you got here."

Tim wanted to tell her that he wasn't sorry at all. Instead, he said, "You don't need to dress up for me. I didn't dress up for you when you came to the paper yesterday."

Elsie showed him to the door. "I'll see you in the morning," she said "Since we're meeting Joel at eleven, why don't you come by at ten. That'll give me a chance to show you around the command center before we view surveillance videos from Thursday."

"I'd like that," said Tim.

She didn't slam the door when he left, despite the cold. Tim saw her standing in the doorway watching him walk to his car. It wasn't until he pulled out of her drive that she closed the door on the cold.

Tim arrived at the Twin Rivers police station at 9:45 AM on Monday morning. He hoped Elsie didn't mind if he was early.

He had stayed awake for hours after he returned to the office, and he had saved two separate designs for Wednesday's edition. One was the original design with Rod's story as written. The other had blank spaces on the front page for a sub-head and any photos of the killer they might discover on the recordings. He thought the sub-head should read, "Has anybody seen these women?"

Elsie's hair was up in her usual ponytail. She was dressed in her sharply-pressed uniform and wore her gun on her hip. She smiled at Tim when he entered her office.

"You're early," she said. "You were early last night too. Are you always early?"

"Sometimes I'm a day late and a dollar short," said Tim. "I'm only early when I'm excited about something."

"Let me show you around the command and communications center. We've centralized command and control and integrated those functions with our dispatch center. There's always a senior officer in charge— usually an experienced Captain or Lieutenant—who can assume control and make command decisions in all emergencies. He or she can be in constant communication with the officers on the scene. Many police departments made similar changes after 9/11, and we did, too. Not only can the officer in charge, the OIC, communicate with our own officers, he can communicate with county, state, and federal authorities. Today, Captain Ed Gross is OIC. He's in his fifties, has been on the force for more than twenty-five years, and he's a graduate of the Justice Department's National Academy for Law Enforcement. He's interfaced with the FBI and state police for years, and he has a good rapport with both agencies. What we've added in the past couple of years is monitors to view live feeds from video cameras around the city. Plus, we have a real-time situation map that displays digitally the GPS location of each of our units. We know how close to a scene any officer is at any given time. We also have direct communications with the county-wide 911 call center. We hear and record all 911 calls. We dispatch the closest units immediately. We usually have a patrol car cruising high crime areas throughout the day and night, and we run unscheduled patrols of residential areas when we can. Not only do we have eyes in the sky, we have wheels and feet on the ground."

Elsie scanned her ID card to gain admittance to the control room. Tim was impressed by the high-tech atmosphere and the efficiency of the operation. More than a dozen civilian-attired personnel staffed the communications center, and two uniformed officers sat on a riser near the rear of the room where they could see everything that happened on big-screen monitors mounted on the walls. Everyone wore a headset with earphones and a microphone. Everyone had a computer and keyboard in front of him of her. Everyone and everything appeared wired and plugged in.

"Let's stand off to one side and watch for a while," said Elsie. "When Giffords gets here, we can ask the Captain to display the recordings from last Thursday.

During the one hour that Tim watched from the sidelines, officers responded to six minor traffic accidents, one reported car theft from a shopping center parking lot, one breaking and entering in progress at an unoccupied residence reported by the next-door neighbor, and one domestic disturbance where a wife claimed her husband had hit her on Saturday night and she waited patiently until her husband left for work on Monday to report it. She said she wanted the police to arrest him at work so everyone he worked with could see him in handcuffs.

"That's pretty typical for a Monday morning," said Dorr. "Things get much more exciting after dark and on weekends. On nights we have a full moon, things sometimes get crazy. But most days, all we respond to are misdemeanors and minor felonies."

Giffords arrived shortly after eleven. "Couldn't keep your nose out of it, could you, Goodman?" Giffords said, shaking his head. Then he broke into a smile and offered Tim his hand. "I guess I'll have to accept your help whether I want to or not."

"I told you I wouldn't stay out of it," said Tim, accepting Joel Giffords' hand. "Rod was my friend."

"Ed, can you bring up last Thursday night from the cameras around the Metra station?"

"What time, Joel?" asked the Captain.

"Let's start at eight PM and keep running the footage until we tell you to stop."

"Watch the wall monitor on the far left," said Elsie. "The screen will display four quadrants with a different camera angle in each."

"I see Rod's car," said Tim. "It's the light blue Ford Focus a few parking places back from the entrance to Terri's."

"If you look at the lower left part of the screen, you can see the view from the camera mounted on the roof of the Metra station," said Elsie. "You can actually see into the front of the restaurant as far as the cashier stand."

"I see it," said Tim. "I stood right there next to that register and talked to a hostess named Sally last night. You probably caught me on camera."

Tim watched the seconds and minutes roll by on the time and date display at the bottom center of each view. Eight-ten went by. Eight-eleven. Eight-twelve.

At eight-sixteen, a girl got up from a booth near the front and walked to the cashier to pay her bill. The girl walked with a slight limp and her face and hair were hidden from view by a dark hoodie.

"That girl must be a regular in Terri's," said Tim. "I saw her in there Saturday night, too. She sat in that same booth."

The girl left the restaurant and three of the four cameras picked her up on the street walking toward the corner bus stop.

Rod appeared at the cashier stand at eight-nineteen. A minute later, the cameras showed Rod on the street walking toward his Ford Focus. At eight-twenty-five, a bus stopped at the corner but the girl did not get on.

Now the girl was looking at Rod sitting in his Ford Focus. Her face remained hidden by the hoodie, but it was obvious by the way her head was turned that she was watching Rod. Neither the hooded woman nor Rod moved for nearly thirty minutes, as if the two were having a staring contest where neither was willing to blink or look away before the other person.

Finally, the girl got up and walked slowly toward Rod in the Focus, dragging her left leg behind her. When she reached the passenger side of the car, she knocked on the window. Rod rolled the passenger window down and spoke with the girl.

At nine-oh-three, Rod unlocked the passenger door and the girl got into the passenger seat of the Ford Focus. The two remained sitting in the car, presumably talking, until nine-seventeen. Then Rod must have started the Focus because the headlights came on. A minute later, the car moved out of the parking space and drove south on Third Street to the corner, turned right at the light, and disappeared from view as it drove west toward Rod's house.

"That has to be her," Tim said, excited that he was getting answers to some of his most burning questions. "Rod didn't admit a woman to his house when he heard a knock at the front door. He admitted a woman to his car when she knocked on the window. Then he drove her to his house and invited her in for a cup of coffee."

"Take it back to eight-fifteen, Ed," Giffords called across the room. "All four cameras, please."

They watched the events again. None of the camera angles showed the girl's face. The most they could see, even when the picture was enlarged, was the tip of the girl's nose.

"Now we know it was definitely a woman who murdered Rodney Engleworth," said Giffords. "And we know she's Caucasian and walks with a limp."

"You said you saw her on Saturday?" asked Dorr. "You saw her inside the restaurant?"

"Yes."

"Did you see her face?"

"She was wearing that same hood, or another one exactly like it. I couldn't see her face any better inside the lighted restaurant than we saw her face on camera. She was deliberately hiding her face."

"And you didn't think that was suspicious?"

"Of course, I did. I also felt she was staring at me inside the restaurant, probably because I had spoken with Susan Williams. I tried to follow her after she left, but she disappeared on Foster about a block east of the corner."

"What do you mean she disappeared?" asked Giffords. "How could she disappear?"

"She was all dressed in black, and she must have hidden in a dark alley or someplace where I couldn't see her. I drove up and down Foster twice, but I couldn't find her."

"What time was that on Saturday night?"

"About Midnight. Maybe a little before."

"Ed, bring up Saturday night at eleven-forty-five. Would you do that for us, please?"

The screen went blank for a moment, then the same four camera views were displayed. The date and time stamp showed Saturday at 11:45.

Tim watched the minutes scroll by again until he saw himself come into view in front of the cashier's stand. He saw himself scratch the back of his neck as if it itched, then turn around to look at someone sitting inside a booth. The girl wasn't visible at all on camera from this angle, but Tim remembered exactly where she was sitting.

She was the only person in the entire restaurant who appeared to be looking Tim's way. He couldn't see her face because her features were shrouded in shadows beneath the hood of a heavy dark-colored zip-up sweatshirt. But she was obviously female and relatively young. He wondered if he knew her.

Tim had thought about walking over to the booth and taking a closer look at her face. He should have done that when he'd had a chance, but he'd decided it was getting late and he had better things to do.

So he walked out of the restaurant. He had felt the woman's eyes follow him as he turned left on the sidewalk and headed for his car. He saw himself drive past the restaurant in the Wagoneer. On another camera, he saw the same woman pay her bill at the cash register. Her face was still hidden by the hood. But she looked like she was about to leave.

Tim saw himself drive around the block. He saw the woman walk toward the bus stop on the corner. She walked with a recognizable limp and her left leg seemed to drag slightly behind the right. She didn't wait at the bus stop but crossed the street. She continued walking east on Foster.

Tim saw the Jeep Wagoneer stop at the red light at the corner of Third and Foster. He saw himself wait at the corner for the light to change. He saw the Wagoneer turn left. On another camera, he saw the girl duck into an alley just east of the Metra station parking lot.

He saw himself return, going west on Foster. He saw himself drive the same route one more time. Not more than a minute after he had driven past the alley on his way back to the office, he saw the girl come out of the alley and resume walking east on Foster. He watched her until she disappeared beyond the camera's range.

"Very suspicious," said Giffords. "It's too bad we couldn't see her face even once. I really would like to know who she is."

"I know who she is," said Tim, remembering what one of the nurses at the hospital had told him about the partial paralysis of Megan Williams' left leg.

"Who?" asked Giffords and Dorr almost in unison.

"She's Susan Williams' sister. She's the girl who was raped and left for dead four years ago. I know it's her by the way she limps. Her left leg is partially paralyzed because the nerves were cut when four rapists rammed a hunting knife inside her vagina. That girl in the hood—the same woman who murdered Rodney Engleworth on Thursday—is the missing Megan Williams.

CHAPTER TWENTY-THREE

I've waited patiently for you to come back. But you haven't returned, and it's nearly daylight. You disappoint me. Why haven't you returned? Don't you know it's not polite to keep a lady waiting?

I'm cold. So very cold. I've waited out here all night. I was sure you'd come back tonight. I saw you talk to your friends on your cell phone. They didn't come tonight, either. Didn't you tell them Susan was home and all alone? Didn't you tell them it was safe?

You couldn't know I was here waiting for you and for your friends, the four rapists. I'm sure you didn't see me up here on this dark third floor landing. I'm above the glare of the floodlights. I'm dressed all in black. I have a hood to hide my hair and face. I'm invisible in the dark.

Sometimes I'm invisible in the light, too. People look away when they see my scars. People look away when they see me limp. It's as if I'm diseased and infectious, and they're afraid maybe they can contract what made me this way simply by looking at me.

What made me this way was men like you. I hate you. I hate all men. I hate those things men have that cause pain when men shove those things inside a woman. If I had my way, I'd take those things away from all men. I'd line men up for punishment, strip them naked, and I'd go down the entire line with a butcher knife and a pair of pinking shears. I'd cut off those appendages that make men do evil to women.

But I know I can't always have my own way. So I'm willing to settle for just four men, the four men who raped me. I can be patient. I know they will come for my sister Susan sooner or later. And when they do, I'll be ready and waiting.

I put the safety on the Beretta and drop the gun into my purse with the rest of my tools. It's time for me to go inside. The sun will soon rise in the east behind Susan's apartment building, casting out the dark, dissipating the shadows of the night. I don't think you or your friends will return this morning. I suspect Monday is a workday for them. Is Monday a workday for you?

I, too, have a job. This is my only job now. My job requires patience, and I'm highly skilled at waiting and watching. I worked a different job, a part-time job, while I was in high school. I was a clerk at that big bookstore out in the east-side mall. That job required different skills, skills I no longer possess. It required a pleasant and unscarred face, the ability to smile at customers including lecherous men who bought *Playboys* and *Hustlers*, and the ability to stand on both feet for long periods of time. But that bookstore went out of business the summer I graduated, and I was still looking for a full-time job when I was raped and mutilated. Thanks to men like you, I do have a full-time job. My new job requires the abilities to fire a Beretta, to carve with a butcher knife, to trim with pinking shears, and to watch men bleed until they die. You trained me to do my job, and I've had lots of hands-on practice. I can't wait to demonstrate what I've learned. But I will wait, if I must wait. I will wait for as long as it takes. I'm nothing if not patient.

Even inside my heated apartment I shiver from the cold. The chill of the night follows me everywhere. My heart is cold. My heart is made of ice.

When will you come back? When will I have my revenge?

Everything gets mixed up in my mind, and I can no longer tell the difference between you and the men that raped me. I see their faces on the faces of every man I meet.

I wish I could sleep. I doze off from time to time, but the nightmares awaken me. Sometimes I wake up screaming.

Today is Monday. I don't think you or your friends will return today or tonight. I will stay in my apartment today and watch Susan's apartment, just in case you do come back. Susan doesn't work today, so I don't need to visit Terri's restaurant. When I get hungry, I'll heat a can of soup. I'll stay near the window and watch. I'll practice dry-firing the Beretta. I'll imagine I see your faces. It will be easy to pull the trigger.

I feel no remorse for what I've done, no guilt for what I'm about to do. I feel nothing.

Time moves slowly for me. The sun rises. The sun sets. All days seem the same. I live for one thing, and one thing alone. I live for revenge.

That isn't entirely true, you know. I also live to protect my sister. I know you want to harm her. I know you want to do to her what you did to me. I will do anything to protect my sister.

It's dark again outside my window. Where did the day go? Did I sleep? Did I fall asleep while sitting at the window? The Beretta is still in my right hand, and I load the magazine of fifteen rounds into the Beretta and chamber a round. I make certain the safety is on and the hammer decocked. I wait at the window for four men to appear in the alley. I will wait here forever, if I must. I am nothing if not patient.

CHAPTER TWENTY-FOUR

When Tim saw Megan Williams get into Rod's Ford Focus with him and ride off in the direction of Rod's house on the night of Rod's murder, Tim had the missing pieces he had been looking for that tied everything else together. These new pieces of the puzzle fit together so perfectly that Tim could almost see the big picture.

Tim hadn't thought Megan physically capable of committing those murders. Not only was she physically handicapped, she owned no car. But Tim had witnessed Rod picking her up in downtown Twin Rivers and providing transportation directly to his house. She must have walked almost a mile to a bus stop after she finished. Tim had previously imagined walking any distance was impossible for a woman with a game leg. But Megan had shown on camera she was capable of walking well enough to get around. Had she also accepted rides with her other victims? Probably. Hadn't Rod discovered Megan in the front seat of Willard's car on another surveillance video? Yes, he had.

Megan's motive for killing all three men: she wanted revenge for what men had done to her. She had mutilated men the way she had been mutilated herself. She had acted out the nightmares that still plagued her by making others feel even more helpless than she had felt when she was raped. Wasn't that what bullies always did? They acted out on others what they most dreaded themselves.

Giffords asked Captain Gross to enhance each video frame where the hooded woman appeared and see if her face could be made visible. Gross said he'd have a technician make a duplicate of the videos, zoom in on the hooded face, and send printouts to Giffords for analysis.

"How long will that take?" asked Giffords.

"Five or six hours," said Gross.

Giffords invited Tim and Dorr to follow him to his office on the sixth floor. Tim was surprised to see that Detective Sergeant Joel Giffords had only a small wooden desk and several steel filing cabinets located all the way in the back of the major crimes squadroom. Unlike Dorr, Giffords didn't rate a separate office. He didn't even have partitions to separate his desk from the dozen or so other desks in the room. "I'm in and out most of the time anyway," Giffords explained when he saw the surprise on Tim's face. "All I need is a place to hang my hat when I'm in. Have a seat while I make a few phone calls."

Tim listened while Giffords put out an all-points bulletin to be on the lookout for Megan Williams, a twenty-two year-old Caucasian female believed to be armed and dangerous, wanted on three counts of premeditated murder. He called the regional task force headquarters and repeated the same information. He promised a full description of the suspect in a future bulletin.

"Now tell me all you know about Megan Williams," Giffords said when he hung up the phone. "Tell me again why you think Megan Williams was the girl on camera and why you think she murdered Rodney Engleworth."

"I don't believe Megan Williams ever fully recovered after she was raped, mutilated, and left to die," said Tim. "You saw the way she limped and dragged her left leg behind her. Some of the nurses at the hospital who cared for Megan while she was in her year-long coma and for months after she came out of coma told me about her partial paralysis. The nerves to her left leg had been severed. Messages from her brain took longer to reach the muscles in her left leg than her right be-cause they had to take a roundabout way to get there. The nurses also claimed Megan was so psychologically traumatized by her ordeal that she couldn't sleep, and when she did try to sleep, she often woke up screaming. She had horrible nightmares. She kept reliving the rape and feeling the pain of being cut and stabbed. I think that affected her mind and made her a killer."

"Why did she kill Engleworth?"

"Rod was in the wrong place at the wrong time. Megan saw him talking with Susan, and she may have thought Susan told him some-thing that identified her as the murderer."

"Or maybe," offered Dorr, "she thought Engleworth was stalking Susan and she killed him in order to protect her sister."

"Why did she cut off his genitals?" asked Giffords.

"So he wouldn't be able to rape anybody," suggested Dorr. "She saw every man who talked to Susan as a potential threat, a potential rapist."

"Why did she kill Willard and Murphy?"

"Maybe for the same reasons," said Dorr. "Willard was a known womanizer and Murphy died with his pants down when the strange woman he brought into his house while his wife was away cut off his cock. Even if those men weren't an immediate threat to Susan, Megan might have viewed them as a potential threat to other women. Maybe she thought she was doing the world a favor by killing them, by remov-ing the threat of their genitalia. After what she went through herself, she couldn't stand the thought of the same thing happening to anyone else."

"Where is Megan Williams now? How do we find her?"

"No one knows," said Tim. "I'm running a front-page story on Wednesday that asks readers to call the *Gazette* if they have any information at all about Megan's current whereabouts. Rod found an old picture of Megan in a high school yearbook to include with the story. I'd like to add a picture of her in that hoodie if you'll give me a picture of Megan from the videos. Will you give me a printout from the videos and allow me to publish it?"

"Let's see what kind of pictures we get after they're enhanced," said Giffords. "Maybe we'll get lucky and see her face."

"We know Megan hangs out at Terri's Restaurant," said Dorr. "She wants to keep an eye out for her sister's welfare. Maybe we can catch Megan in the restaurant. Shouldn't we stake out Terri's too?"

"I think," said Tim, "Megan's waiting for the four men who raped her to go after Susan. I think she's dividing her time between the restaurant and Susan's apartment on Eleventh Street."

"What makes you think that?" asked Giffords.

"When Megan was watching me in the restaurant on Saturday, I felt the hairs on the back of my neck bristle. Rod had a nose for news, and he could smell out a story wherever it was hiding. My nose doesn't work like Rod's. I have a feel for news, not a nose for news. I can feel when someone's watching me, and I felt someone was watching me in the alley behind Susan's apartment last night. I felt a tingle similar to what you get when you touch a live electrical wire."

"There were probably plenty of people who saw you through windows in their apartments," said Giffords. "They might have watched you to see what you were doing in the alley that late at night."

"If somebody was watching me through a window, I wouldn't have felt any tingle at all. Glass would have blocked the sensation because glass acts as an electrical insulator. No, whoever was watching me was outside or had a window wide open."

"You want me to believe you feel a tingle when people are staring at you?"

"Sure. Don't you feel a tingle when someone stares at you?"

"No," said Giffords. "I don't."

"I do," said Dorr. "I felt a tingle last night when Tim stared at my legs."

Tim blushed. "I wasn't staring," he said.

Dorr smiled. "I don't believe you," she said. "I do believe what you said about the tingle, but I don't believe what you said about not noticing my legs."

"Goodman made you tingle when he looked at you?" asked Giffords.

This time it was Dorr's turn to blush. "Yes," she admitted. "I felt a definite tingle."

"See?" said Tim. "I'm not the only one. Elsie, I mean Officer Dorr, studied journalism. She has the same feel for news I have."

"Okay," said Giffords. "Someone was watching you in the alley, and it wasn't anybody inside one of the apartments. I'll have a stake-out set up in the alley behind Susan Williams' apartment. Now that we suspect Megan of murder, we can justify the stake-out."

"And the restaurant," said Dorr. "Susan works three to midnight at Terri's Tuesday through Saturday."

Giffords picked up the phone again and requested the two stake-outs. "At least a week, Ed," he said. "I know we're short-handed. I'm talking about catching a killer, Ed. Okay, I'll settle for overnight stake-outs on the apartment and spot checks on the restaurant from three to midnight."

"I can watch the restaurant," Tim offered as Giffords hung up the phone. "After I put the paper to bed at ten tomorrow morning, I'll take a laptop with me to Terri's and work from there. Terri's has wi-fi, and I can access InDesign from the cloud. I can work from anywhere."

"I'll help, too," offered Dorr. "After I get off work at six, I can stop at Terri's for supper."

"All right," said Giffords. "We've done all we can do for now. Goodman, can you e-mail or fax me that high school picture of William?"

"I'll send it as soon as I get back to the *Gazette*."

"Then go do it. I want to include copies of the picture when I send out the next BOLO APB."

"When can I see the enhanced photos from the video recordings?"

"Dorr will drop off copies later this afternoon or early this evening. Is that okay with you Elsie?"

"I'll be glad to," said Dorr.

Tim returned to the *Gazette* office and e-mailed Megan's high school picture to Elsie to give to Giffords. He spent the rest of the afternoon putting the finishing touches on Wednesday's edition. He added a sidebar that said Megan Williams was wanted for questioning in the murders of Rodney Engleworth, Benjamin Willard, and William Murphy. All he needed now to complete the paper and put it to bed was a picture of Megan wearing a hoodie.

Elsie Door jingled the door chimes as she entered the office at 6:15. "I would have been here sooner," she explained, "but Giffords wanted me to go over all of the enhanced pictures—there were more than a hundred—and pick out the best to give you." She handed Tim an inter-office envelope containing a handful of photocopies from the enhanced printouts.

Tim dumped the contents onto his desktop. "Any of these show Me-gan's face?" he asked Elsie as he quickly glanced through the pictures.

"Not in detail," Elsie said. She walked behind Tim's desk and leaned over to leaf through to find the best three of the dozen pictures. "We can almost see her face in this one."

The camera caught Megan siting on the bench at the bus stop, and part of her profile was visible. Her nose looked nothing like the way it had looked in her high school picture. For a moment, Tim wasn't certain it was the same woman. Then he remembered that Megan had extensive facial reconstruction performed on her face by several plastic surgeons. Her nose had been shattered by repeated blows from the rapists. Doctors did the best they could do with what was left, but they didn't make her new nose look much like the old one.

"She was beat up pretty bad," said Dorr, as if reading Tim's mind. "There wasn't much left of her nose. Doctors must have rebuilt the bridge from scratch."

"I can almost see her chin in this second picture. And part of one cheek. Too bad we can't piece together an entire face from the parts shown in different pictures."

"Giffords is having a sketch artist do that. We should have a com-posite by tomorrow."

"We still don't know what her hair looks like. Or the shape of the back of her head. Or her ears."

"We're having patrol cars stop young women wearing hoodies on city streets and asking for identification, plus a look under the hood. Maybe they'll nab Megan tonight."

"I don't think so. I think she'll keep a low profile tonight. She's probably hanging out near Susan's apartment. She has no reason to go to Terri's tonight because Susan isn't working."

"We'll have an unmarked squad with two officers staking out the alley behind Susan's apartment, beginning tonight. They have instructions to question all women wearing hoodies. If she's anywhere in Twin Rivers, well get her."

"What about the rapists? Are you still looking for them?"

"Four men in their early to mid-twenties. Unfortunately, we have no pictures of any of them. All we have to go on is Megan's four-year-old description. They probably don't look anything like that now. People can change a lot in four years, especially when they're in their late teens or early twenties."

"I can't help but feel sorry for Megan," said Tim. "She's as much a victim as the men she killed. She's got to be all messed up inside her head. What will happen to her when you catch her?"

"That's up to a judge and jury. If she's found to be mentally incompetent, she might be confined to a mental institution and maybe she'll get the help she needs. If she's found guilty of first degree manslaughter, she'll go to prison for a long time, possibly for life. I doubt if she'll get any psychiatric help in prison. Illinois abolished the death penalty. At least she won't be executed."

"I'm glad of that. There's been enough killing."

"She has to be held accountable for her actions, Tim. Even if she is crazy, she can't just go around killing people."

"Have you eaten tonight?" Tim asked. "I haven't had anything all day, and I'm hungry. Would you like to go to Terri's with me for supper? We could continue talking while we eat."

"I'd like that," said Elsie. "Do I have time to run home and change first? I don't like to wear the uniform when I'm off duty."

"Sure. I can scan a couple of these pictures and crop them to fit into the space I saved on the front page. Why don't we meet at Terri's at eight? That should give you enough time to go home, change, and drive back downtown."

"It's a date," she said. "I'll see you at eight."

Tim watched her walk to the door and heard the door chimes jingle as she pulled the door open and chime again when she pulled the door shut behind her. Did she really think of their supper tonight as a date? It hadn't occurred to Tim that he was asking Elsie out on a date, but he supposed he had. And she had accepted his invitation to go on a date! Tim felt exactly like he did back in high school when a girl had agreed to go to the prom with him.

Did Elsie feel the same kind of chemistry around him he felt around her? She said she felt a tingle when Tim stared at her legs. Was it a good tingle or a bad tingle? Tim had only felt good tingles when he was in her presence. Did she feel the same electricity between them that he felt?

When Elsie told Tim in front of Giffords she had felt a tingle last night, Tim had been both surprised and embarrassed. Did Elsie think Tim was only interested in her for sex? He did want to have sex with her, but that wasn't all he wanted. He wanted to have a real honest-to-goodness relationship with Elsie Dorr. Not a one-night stand. Not just a wham-bam-thank-you-ma'am roll in the hay. He wanted to hold her and be held. He wanted to touch her mind as well as her body. He wanted all of her, body, mind, and spirit. And he wanted to give himself to her, all of himself.

How was it possible to feel this way about someone he had known for less than a week? He knew he was setting himself up for a big fall, but had already fallen. He had fallen helplessly in love with Elsie Dorr. What if she didn't feel the same way about him? How could she? She was the most beautiful girl in the world, and he was a nobody, a nerd in eyeglasses. How could she possibly love him?

Tim decided to leave scanning the photos for later. He had a little more than an hour to get ready for his date with Elsie. He locked the front door, walked to the back room, and ran his electric shaver over his five o'clock shadow. He shucked out of his clothes and jumped into the shower.

After drying himself off with a bath towel, Tim combed his hair and splashed a handful of after shave on his cheeks and chin. He rolled deodorant under his arms. Then he selected a dress shirt and a nice sweater to wear. Instead of his usual jeans, he put on a pair of dress slacks. Now he looked like he was ready to go out on a date.

Did he forget to brush his teeth? He brushed them again, just to be sure. He swished Listerine around real good, and spit the mouthful into the sink.

Now he knew he was ready. He still had ten minutes. He didn't want to arrive too early. He fidgeted around for five minutes before grabbing his good winter overcoat and struggling to get his arms into both sleeves at the same time. Why was he so goddamned nervous? It wasn't like it was a real date, for chrissakes. It was only dinner and conversation.

Tim left the lights on in the office, but he remembered to lock the door behind him. He drove the six blocks from the *Gazette* office to Terri's Restaurant in record time.

Elsie had taken a booth near the right side of the front of the restaurant, and she was already waiting with her back to the door when Tim arrived at eight on the nose. She, too, wore a sweater. Hers was light pink instead of navy-blue like his. And tonight she wore a dark green wool skirt and either nylon stockings or pantyhose. Her legs were crossed and her skirt was hiked up above the knees. Stockings, he decided when he thought he caught a glimpse of bare flesh as she suddenly turned around in her seat to smile at him.

Tim noticed just a touch of red lipstick on those kissable lips.

Tim awkwardly removed his overcoat and slid into the booth opposite her. He folded his coat and placed the coat on the bench next to him. "Been here long?" he asked.

"Just got here," she said.

The older waitress named Sally brought menus and asked if they wanted coffee. Dorr asked for decaf, and Tim ordered a Diet Pepsi.

"I've only been in here twice before," said Dorr. "What looks good?"

"Everything," answered Tim without looking at the menu. "I'm having the open faced hot beef sandwich with mashed potatoes."

"I think I'll have a grilled cheese and a cup of soup," she said after briefly studying the menu.

"You didn't have to dress up just for me," Tim said. "But I think that sweater looks good on you."

"And the skirt? Did you notice the skirt? And the heels? I almost forgot how to walk in heels."

"Yes. I looked at your legs."

She smiled. "I wanted to dress up for you," she said. "I don't often get a chance to look like a lady."

"You look very nice," Tim said.

"I left my hair in a ponytail. I think it makes me look younger than I am. Tonight I don't mind if I look young. I have to wear my hair up when I'm in uniform. The department has this silly rule that an officer's hair can't touch the uniform collar. So a lot of people who see me in uniform think of me as a kid because I'm so small and wear a ponytail. But I'm thirty-two."

"I'm a year older than you," said Tim. "I'll be thirty-four in January."

"I thought we were close to the same age. I was right. I'll be thirty-three in April."

Sally brought their drinks and took their order. "And I'll take the check after we order dessert," said Tim.

"Oh, don't be silly. I can pay my own way."

"And I can deduct the cost of the meal from my income tax as long as we talk business," said Tim. "Tonight's on me."

Elsie smiled again. "Okay," she said. "I guess I can act like a woman for a change and let the man pick up the tab."

Tim looked around the restaurant for Megan Williams. He didn't expect to see her, but he had to look.

"She's not here," said Dorr. "I already checked."

"This is the same booth she sat in on Saturday," said Tim.

"I know. That's why I picked it. Where were you standing when you felt her staring at you?"

"Over there next to the cash register."

"And you couldn't see her face?"

"No. She had that hood on over her head, and her face was cloaked in shadow."

"She was sitting where you are?" Elsie asked.

"Yes," said Tim.

"Go over by the register and let me sit in your seat. See if you can feel me staring at you."

"Why?"

"It's an experiment. When you feel a tingle, turn and look at my face."

Tim got up and walked to the register while Elsie took his seat. He turned his back to her and waited. Sure enough. He felt a tingle on the back of his neck. He turned around and faced her.

She looked into his eyes and he looked into hers, neither choosing to look away first. Finally, Tim walked back and took Elsie's former seat.

"What did that prove?" he asked.

"Just that I felt a tingle when you looked at me. And you felt a tingle, too, didn't you?"

"Yes."

"So I was right about last night. You were looking at my legs."

"Yes," Tim admitted. "I was."

"That's never happened before," she said. "Not to me anyway. I've seen men look at my legs, but I never felt anything. But I felt you. I felt you looking at my legs again when you came into the restaurant tonight. You did, didn't you? That's what made me turn around."

"I'm sorry," said Tim.

"No, don't be sorry. I'm not. It was a nice feeling. It made me feel all tingly and warm inside. I've never felt like that before with anybody."

"You haven't?"

"Look, Tim, I'm not a virgin. I've been around the block a few times. But nobody ever made me feel like that just by looking at me."

"Are we talking about the same kind of tingles?" Tim asked. "When Megan stared at the back of my head, I definitely felt a tingle. But it wasn't a nice feeling. It was kind of spooky and raised the hairs on the back of my neck."

"And what did you feel when you felt me staring at you a moment ago?"

"It wasn't the same at all. Of course, I knew it was you looking at me this time."

"And when you turned and looked into my eyes? What did you feel then?"

"Happy," he said. "I felt happy we were looking at each other."

"So did I," said Elsie. "I didn't want us to ever stop looking at each other."

Sally brought Elsie's soup and interrupted the conversation. "Your orders will be right up," she said. Then Sally left to tend to other customers.

Tim still couldn't take his eyes off Elsie's face. He kept staring into those beautiful green eyes as she tried to spoon soup from her bowl into her lovely mouth. Nor could she stop looking at him. She only dropped her eyes from time to time in order to dip the spoon into the soup bowl. But then her eyes returned to his as she mechanically raised the spoon and brought it to her open mouth. The spell was finally broken when she partially missed her mouth and some of the soup dripped down her chin. Tim instantly reached over with his napkin and wiped away most of the soup before any of it dripped onto her sweater. Elsie licked the rest off with her tongue.

"Thanks," Elsie said. "You have quick reflexes."

"I was afraid you'd ruin your sweater."

"I'm sure the dry cleaners could get the stain out."

"Will you join me here tomorrow night, too? I plan to eat here every night until Megan is caught."

"Only if you let me buy dinner tomorrow night. I'll go straight home after work and change. I can be back here by seven."

"You've got a deal," said Tim.

Sally arrived with two plates. She set the hot beef and mashed potatoes in front of Tim and the grilled cheese in front of Megan. She returned a minute later with a coffee pot to warm up Megan's decaf.

Instead of talking about Megan Williams as Tim had intended, Elsie asked Tim about himself. She said she wanted to know all about him. Was he born in Twin Rivers? Were his parents still living here? Did Tim live at home or in an apartment?"

"Are you trying to learn if I'm still single?" Tim asked. "I am. I was born in Twin Rivers. My parents are both dead. And I live in a back room of the *Gazette* office."

When Tim asked Elsie about herself, she revealed that she was also single. She lived with her mother in that condo on North Riverside. Her father died fifteen years ago when Elsie was still in high school, and her mother moved a year later to Twin Rivers and bought the condo with insurance money from her husband's life insurance. Elsie had two older sisters and a younger brother. Her sisters were married and her brother was a stock broker in New York City. Elsie housesat the entire condo while her mother vacationed in Florida. Her mother still received a monthly survivor's benefit check from her father's newspaper pension and she had just turned sixty-two and also collected social security. She could afford to winter in Florida.

"You never married?" asked Tim.

"I've been asked," admitted Elsie. "But I like what I'm doing too much to give it up. In my current job, I get to be both a cop and a news-paperwoman. I write press releases and interface with the media. I'm also privy to ongoing police investigations. I always worried when I was a street cop that I was too small to handle some of the things I encountered. So this job is perfect for me."

"The guys who wanted to marry you asked you to give up your job?"

"They didn't want to be married to a cop."

"I'd never ask you to give up your job. You're good at it."

"Sometimes I think about quitting," said Elsie. "Especially when I'm ordered to lie to the press."

"You've been ordered to lie to the press?"

"I've been ordered to withhold information. Especially about the re-cent murders in Twin Rivers."

"What's going to happen when Wednesday's edition hits the stands?"

"I'll be given the third degree. I'll be suspected of leaking the infor-mation."

"Why?"

"The Captain has seen me showing both you and Rodney Eng-leworth around the command center. A patrol car just drove by and the officers saw me in here talking with you while I'm off duty. I don't think the chief will fire me, but he'll probably limit my access to information in the future."

"Maybe you shouldn't eat with me tomorrow night."

"No, Tim. I want to. I want to be here with you and I want to help apprehend Megan Williams. I want to make Twin Rivers safe like it used to be."

"Has Twin Rivers ever been safe?"

"Bad choice of words. I meant safer than it is now."

After they finished their meals, Tim talked Elsie into trying a slice of pecan pie. He didn't want the evening to end.

Finally, at eleven o'clock, Megan said she needed to go home and get her beauty sleep.

"I think you're very beautiful," he said. He didn't want the evening to end. "You don't need sleep to look beautiful."

She reached out and touched his face affectionately. "And I think you're very brave for printing a story that might alienate advertisers. I know how the newspaper business works. We're both taking risks, aren't we?"

"Yes," he said, reaching out to touch the side of her face the same way she was touching his. "We're two of a kind."

"I've never felt this way before, Tim. You're very special to me."

"And you to me," he said, looking into her eyes. "I'm glad to know you, Elsie Dorr.

"I'm glad to know you, Tim Goodman. Will you walk me to my car?"

Elsie grabbed her purse and coat. Tim helped her into the coat, then struggled into his overcoat. He walked to the cashier to pay the check and felt Elsie's eyes on the back of his neck. Her gaze didn't prickle and irritate like Megan's had. Elsie's gaze felt warm and caressing.

Elsie drove a silver Subaru Outback, and it was parked two spaces to the left of Terri's entrance. Tim held the door open for her as she slid into the driver's seat. Her skirt hiked up and treated him to a show of bare thigh between the tops of her nylons and her panties. She looked up at him and smiled.

"You can kiss me, you know," she whispered. "I want you to."

He leaned in and pressed his lips to hers. He felt her open her mouth and her tongue danced with his tongue.

Tim's erection strained against his pants and he felt Elsie brush her fingers lightly against him as if she wanted him as much as he wanted her. Then she broke the kiss. "You can follow me home," she whispered. "I live all alone. You could stay the night."

Tim stood up and took a deep breath. "I can't tonight," he said. "I have a front page to finish and a paper to get ready to go to press."

"I understand," she said. "I'll see you tomorrow night at seven."

Tim reluctantly closed her car door and took a step back. Elsie started the Subaru and turned on the headlights. Tim watched her drive to the corner, turn left, and disappear from sight. He still had an erection.

Tim unlocked his Jeep Wagoneer and climbed inside the front seat. He drove slowly back to the office, thinking of tomorrow night.

CHAPTER TWENTY-FIVE

Who are those two men sitting in the bucket front seats of that black Dodge Charger behind Susan's building? They've been sitting down there in the alley for hours, looking up at Susan's apartment or looking at the entrance to the alley from Addison. Occasionally, one of the two men gazes all around and I have to duck out of sight. Even with the lights out in my apartment, I don't want to chance being seen.

They look nothing like the four rapists or the rapists' friend from last night. These are men I have never seen before, tough men, dangerous men. They don't belong here. Why are they in the alley I share with Susan? Why do they just sit there? Why don't they leave?

What do they want?

I saw that car enter the alley at midnight, drive all the way through the alley from Addison to Foster, and come back again a few minutes later. The Dodge Charger is a late model, shiny and solid black. All four hubcaps have been removed, as if someone has recently stolen them from an almost-new car when it was parked where it shouldn't be parked.

The men inside wear suits and winter overcoats. One has a big thermos of coffee and I see him fill a plastic cup and drink. The other is a smoker, and I see the glow of his cigarette as he inhales a lungful of smoke. He has the window cracked about an inch. Smoke wafts out the tiny opening like smoke from the brick chimney atop Susan's building across the alley. Smoking is a sick and disgusting habit. One of the men who raped me was a smoker. I remember the smell of stale cigarette smoke in his hair. I can't stand to be around the smell of cigarette smoke. It makes me want to vomit.

Why don't they leave?

I fear the rapists with their van won't come while there are other men in the alley who might witness them entering Susan's apartment. How can I get my revenge with those two men watching?

Tomorrow night I will go to Terri's restaurant and wait for the four men there. This time, as soon as I see all four together, I will shoot them. Then I will emasculate them. Will they come tomorrow? It has been nearly a week since they last came to see Susan. I was so sure they would return on Friday or Saturday. I'm disappointed they didn't.

I'm still patient, but even my patience wears thin.

And what about the man I saw last night, the rapists' friend? Will I see him in Terri's? If I do, I'll shoot him, too.

I have watched all night, and the men in the Charger are still there in the same place. The first time I saw them start the car's engine, I thought they were going to leave. They run the engine for about ten minutes every hour. I suspect it's only to get some heat. Nights have become frosty cold. The two men wear heavy winter overcoats, hats, and gloves. When they feel like they're freezing, they start the motor and run the heater.

As the first light of dawn brightens the sky, they start the motor again. This time they keep the motor running. Finally, the Charger leaves the parking space and I watch it drive out of the alley and turn right on Foster.

They stayed in the alley more than seven hours. That's almost an entire work shift.

As the light of dawn illuminates the alley, it becomes evident to me that the two men in the Charger were police officers. For some reason they were assigned to watch Susan's building. Were they sent to guard Susan? Why? Why after all of this time?

I don't trust the police. They did nothing to catch the men who raped me. And the cops who interviewed me in the hospital made me feel like I was the one responsible for what happened, not the four men who raped me and cut me up. "What were you wearing?" the cops asked. "What did you do to attract their attention?" When I told those cops I was in bed wearing only my shortie nightgown and panties, they gave me a look like I should have known better than to dress like that. Can't a woman dress the way she wants, the way that makes her most comfortable, in her own home? Must women wear a lead-lined bra and a chastity belt to go to bed and sleep in peace?

Now I wear men's clothing. I wear jeans and sweatshirts and sneakers I buy at a nearby resale shop. I wear a sweatshirt and sweat pants to bed. I wouldn't be caught dead in a skirt.

I still do carry a purse. Some men carry briefcases, and workmen often carry toolboxes. My purse is my toolbox. Inside are pliers, knives, pinking shears, a box-cutter, and my loaded Beretta. They are the tools of my trade.

My job—since I am not qualified to do anything else—is to mutilate and kill men. I do this work free of charge as a public service. My satisfaction comes from doing my job well enough to ensure men are never able to rape women ever again.

My job will continue until I'm dead or until the four men who raped me are dead, whichever comes first. I do not intend to die until I have my revenge.

Now that I know policemen are watching, I must be more careful. Is it possible that they are not here to guard Susan but to look for me?

I'm positive policemen take the mutilations and deaths of men more seriously than the rape and mutilation of a woman. Police won't stop looking until they catch the person who castrated and killed three men. Police stopped looking for the men who raped me long ago, as if what happened to me was unimportant. The only one who is looking for those four men is me.

Now that the sun is up, I will try to sleep. Susan will be safe during daylight. It's only dangerous at night.

I lie on my mattress on the bare floor. I remain fully dressed. I keep my toolbox near my right hand, within easy reach. The Beretta is loaded. If anyone tries to enter my apartment, I will defend myself.

When I close my eyes I see your faces, each of your faces. I smell your breath, your sweat. I taste your semen. I feel you—each of you—between my legs. I feel the big hunting knife cut into my flesh, the blood spurt out. Just as you woke me from a sound sleep that night four years ago, you wake me every time I lie down and try to sleep. I desperately need sleep. I would kill for a good night's sleep.

But I cannot sleep. Not yet. I will wait to sleep when I'm dead. I can be patient. I'm nothing if not patient.

I need to revise my plans. If you won't come to Susan's with those policemen watching the alley, I'll have to kill you in Terri's or outside the restaurant. It's been nearly a week since you have checked on my sister. I'm certain you will check on her again before you make your move to do her the same way you did me.

Will you come tonight? I can watch the restaurant tonight from inside the Metra station. It's too cold to sit outside on the bench at the bus stop. I'll wait until it gets dark, and then I will walk to the Metra station and take up my vigil. When I see you, I'll sneak up on your van. You won't notice me in the dark with my black hoodie. I'll shoot each of you. Then I will teach you the meaning of pain.

I have lived in pain for four years because of you. I am an expert on pain.

You, too, are an expert on pain. But only on inflicting pain. Have you felt pain yourself? Excruciating pain? Do you know what it feels like to have your flesh ripped apart? Do you know what it feels like to have your tendermost parts cut and stabbed? Let me show you what pain is really like.

Come to me tonight. I will be waiting for you.

CHAPTER TWENTY-SIX

Tim imported the recent scan of the hooded Megan Williams into the front page layout of the InDesign template. He captioned the first photo from her high school yearbook, "Megan Williams five years ago," and the scanned photo of Megan wearing a hoodie, "Megan Williams today."

Tim read over the entire issue, proofing for typos and misaligned graphics. When he was satisfied with the way everything read and looked, he saved the 68 pages as a .pdf file and e-mailed a copy to the printer before noon.

Tim had rounded out Rod's original story with an update. Megan Williams was no longer a victim. She was now a hunted fugitive, a cold-blooded killer who was considered armed and dangerous. Tim promised to tell why in next week's issue of the *Gazette*. He promised to tell Megan's story in full as soon as she was apprehended and he could arrange an interview.

Tim transmitted the story to the printer at ten AM. Then he began work on next week's edition

Tim collapsed in bed at 12:32 on Tuesday afternoon, intending to sleep for only three or four hours before taking a laptop with him to Terri's restaurant. He had stayed up all night brooding over what had turned an innocent teen into a cold-blooded murderer. He decided he didn't have enough information to accurately describe what had happened to Megan, so he wrote "To Be Continued" at the end of the sidebar titled "Megan Williams Wanted on Suspicion of Murder."

Tim awoke at 6:08 PM. He had just enough time to shower and shave. He selected another dark blue sweater to wear, and he found his last clean pair of jeans and stepped into them. He grabbed his overcoat and his Lenovo laptop and headed out the door, remembering to lock the door only after he was in the car and on his way to meet Elsie at Terri's Restaurant. He didn't bother to go back.

Tonight he beat Elsie by five minutes. He arrived in such a hurry he forgot the laptop in the Jeep. He decided to leave it there. Elsie arrived at 6:57, and Tim was already seated in the same booth as last night. He wanted to try the exact same experiment Elsie had tried last night, and sure enough he felt her eyes on the back of his head when she came through the front door.

She looked even lovelier tonight than she had looked last night, if such a thing were possible. She had let her hair down, and she had brushed the long red hair out to curl seductively about her narrow neck. Tonight she wore a low-cut white sweater (and it was very obvious to Tim she didn't wear a bra beneath the cotton sweater by the way her boobs bounced with each step). She had on a black pleated skirt that stopped at her knees. Again, she wore nylons. Tonight, however, she wore flats, whereas last night she had covered her feet with medium-heeled pumps.

"I felt you come in," Tim said as she removed her coat. "You gave me warm tingles."

"That's because I was looking for you," she said. "And I couldn't keep my eyes off you once I saw you."

"You are so incredibly beautiful," Tim said, reaching for her hand.

Tonight, instead of sitting opposite him, she slid into the booth next to him. "Much better," she said as she snuggled up close on his left side.

A different waitress than last night—this one was a few years younger and her name badge read, "Dottie"—brought them menus. "Coffee?" she asked.

Elsie ordered decaf, but tonight Tim felt brave and ordered regular coffee. Maybe coffee would help him feel more alert. If he hadn't planned to meet Elsie at seven, he would certainly have gone back to sleep. Tim's sleep patterns had been irregular at best since he had discovered Rod's cut-up body on Friday. Tim was feeling somewhat sleep-deprived and more than a little stressed out.

"Did you get the *Gazette* put to bed on time?" Elsie asked.

"I made my deadline," he said.

Dottie placed two cups of steaming coffee on the table in front of them. Elsie took her decaf black, but Tim diluted his leaded high-octane caffeine with two spoons of sugar and a dash of cream. "Whatcha gonna have, hon?" Dottie asked.

"What's your soup tonight?" Elsie asked.

"Vegetable beef barley," Dottie said. "It's really good."

"I'll take your word for it. I'll have a grilled cheese and a cup of soup."

"And I'll have the open faced hot beef with mashed potatoes and gravy," said Tim.

As Dottie ran off to the kitchen to put their orders in, Tim's left hand accidentally bumped into Else's right hand when both reached for their coffee cups at the same time. He barely felt Elsie's hand touch his before her fingers became intimately intertwined with his own fingers. Tim peered into her beautiful green eyes. He saw his own happiness reflected back at him. Both faces broke into big smiles at the same time.

"I've never felt this happy before," Tim said.

"Nor have I," she said, sounding amazed. "When you look at me, I get goose bumps all over."

"Maybe you're just cold," he said. "You just came inside from twenty-degree temperatures outside."

"Do you think I'm cold?" she asked. "Maybe I am. I'm actually trembling. You could put your arm around me and help keep me warm. But only if you want to."

He released her hand and slipped his left arm around her shoulders, pulling her even tighter against him. "That better?" he asked.

"It's a start," she said. "I feel warmer already."

Dottie brought Elsie's soup, and Tim quickly removed his arm. He took a sip of coffee while Elsie tasted the soup.

"That's Susan Williams over there behind the coffee counter in the back of the restaurant," Tim said.

"She's gorgeous," said Elsie. "Tall, thin, blonde, and absolutely gorgeous."

"You're much better looking," Tim said.

"No way," she said. "But thank you for saying so anyhow."

"No. I really mean it."

"Have you seen Megan anywhere in the restaurant? I haven't looked for her until now."

"She's not here. I checked when I came in."

"Do you think she'll show tonight?"

"If she's watching Susan to protect her, she'll be somewhere close."

"Where else could she be?"

"I don't know," said Tim.

Dottie returned with their plates. "Enjoy," she said.

"Maybe we should switch seats," Tim suggested. "Since I'm left handed and you're right handed, it will be easier to eat if I sit to the left of you. That way we can still sit close while we eat, but we won't constantly bump arms."

Elsie got out of the booth and so did Tim. Then Elsie sat back down first and Tim slid in next to her.

Tim put his right arm around Elsie's shoulders and he ate with his left. Tim had survived on one meal a day for nearly a week, and he wolfed down the meat and potatoes like a starving man.

"I've been thinking about the men who raped Megan," Tim said between bites. "If they were after Susan, why haven't they come back to try again?"

"They've been busy elsewhere," said Elsie. "We're pretty certain they raped a woman in another suburb last Friday."

"How many women have they raped?"

"At least sixteen."

"Over a four-year period?"

"Yes. They may have raped others, but we can definitely link their DNA to sixteen crime scenes."

"And all of those rape victims were murdered?"

"All except Megan. And she would have died if Susan hadn't found her in time."

"How close is the task force to catching them?"

"Not very. The only description we have is what Megan furnished a year after she was raped. We're not certain it's accurate."

"I think you're right in thinking Megan wants to protect Susan from rapists and potential rapists. I think that's why she killed Rod and the other two."

"I've never been raped," Elsie said, "but I've had men try to force themselves on me. I think every woman has. Not every man is as polite and kind as you, Tim. Some men are animals. I can understand why Megan would want to kill her rapists. If they did that to me, I'd want to kill them, too."

"Megan killed three innocent men as surrogates for the rapists. Or maybe as practice for what she intends to do to the four rapists if they try to rape Susan or try to rape Megan again."

"You think Megan is waiting for the rapists to come back and try again?"

"Yes. Don't you?"

"I guess I do. That's why she watches Susan at work, isn't it? She thinks the rapists will come here first, then follow Megan home?"

"Yes. She saw Rod talking to Susan here in the restaurant, and she automatically identified him as a potential rapist."

"Didn't she also see you talking with Susan?"

"Yes," admitted Tim.

"Maybe you shouldn't be here, Tim. If she sees you in here again, she may think you're a potential rapist and she'll try to kill you."

"I'm not worried. I have you here to protect me."

"I'm worried. She may not attempt to kill you here in the restaurant, but she may follow you home and try to kill you there. She killed the other three men in their homes."

"They offered her a ride and invited her in. I won't do that."

"You better not. I don't want anything to happen to you, Tim. I've waited all of my life to find a man like you. Now that I've found you, I couldn't bear to lose you."

"Do you mean that?"

"Of course, I do. You're kind, sweet, gentle, brilliant, a good kisser, and you're a newspaperman like my father was and I wanted to be. What more could I ask for in a man?"

Tim leaned toward her and kissed her full on the mouth, a long and gentle kiss that told her she was everything he had always wanted in a woman.

"Are you ready for dessert?" Dottie asked, interrupting the kiss.

"Pie?" Tim asked Elsie.

"Pecan," she said.

"Make that two," said Tim.

While they were chatting over pie, Tim noticed a young man with acne scars all over his face take a seat at the coffee counter and order pie and coffee from Susan. The hairs on the back of Tim's neck had bristled as the man had passed by, and they were still bristling even though the man was facing the other way.

Tim hurriedly looked around. Was Megan watching him? Or was she watching the young man?

"See that guy at the coffee counter?" he asked Elsie. "I think he's the youngest of the four rapists."

"Why do you think that?"

"My neck for news told me. I felt it as he passed. I also felt Megan watching."

Elsie looked over her shoulder. "I don't see her."

"I know she's watching."

Elsie picked up her purse and placed it on her lap. She unzipped the purse and slipped her right hand inside.

Tim took out his cell phone. He selected camera from the menu and snapped several pictures of the man at the counter, capturing part of his profile.

"I'm going to get a better shot," he said, getting up and stepping out of the booth. He walked to the rear of the restaurant and pretended to take a picture of Susan (he even asked her to smile for the camera) that also captured the facial features of the young man.

"I'll run this in next week's edition of the *Gazette*, right next to the ad for Terri's" he explained to Susan. "I'll caption it 'the best pie in town served by the best waitresses.'" He turned to the young man. "May I have your name for the caption, sir?"

"I don't want my picture in the paper."

"Why not?" Tim said.

"I just don't."

"Okay," said Tim. "I'll crop you out of the photo."

Tim returned to his booth. "Gotcha!" he said.

"Are you sure he's one of the rapists?" asked Elsie.

"Positive," said Tim. "He refused to give me his name. Most people are glad to get their names and pictures in the paper. He's got something to hide."

The kid finished his pie and coffee. He got up to leave.

"We should follow him," Tim whispered. "Maybe we can get the license number on his car."

The kid gave Tim a dirty look as he walked to the cashier. He paid his bill and left.

"Come on," Tim said, reaching for his coat. He dropped two twenties on the table and didn't wait for Dottie to bring his bill.

"Next time I pay," Elsie said, carrying her coat and purse. She put her coat on as she followed Tim out the door.

CHAPTER TWENTY-SEVEN

I recognize your black Jeep Wagoneer as you park in front of the restaurant a minute or two before seven. I can see you clearly from the window inside the Metra station that looks out on Third Street.

Are your friends coming, too? Is this the night I'll get my revenge?

I patiently wait for the Dodge van to show up. I'm not worried about you while you're inside the restaurant. I'll wait for you to leave and I'll follow you as best I can. Maybe I'll shoot you on the sidewalk. Maybe I'll follow you home. Maybe your friends will arrive and I can shoot all five of you tonight. I can be patient. I'm nothing if not patient.

It's cold out tonight. I'm wearing a regular sweatshirt beneath my cotton hoodie. I don't own a coat. If it gets much colder, I'll simply add another layer to what I'm already wearing. Maybe a flannel shirt between the sweatshirt and the hoodie will be enough. It's not too cold inside the Metra station. But there's a raging wind outside that cuts through clothes like pinking shears, and I feel the cold every time someone opens the doors to enter or leave the Metra station.

I watch everyone who enters or leaves the restaurant across the street from the station. I see a red-haired woman enter at seven o'clock, an older couple leave at seven-ten, a few dozen local businessmen enter for the regular Tuesday night chamber of commerce meeting at seven-thirty that Terri herself hosts in a small banquet room. Tuesdays are relatively slow compared to weekends. It's a little after nine—all of the businessmen who attended the chamber meeting have already left— when I see the Dodge van park on the street and Pimples gets out.

My heart races. Tonight is the night I will have my revenge. I will not let any of those men leave here alive.

I walk out of the Metra station and turn left on Foster. I hurry west one block, walk north on Second Street one block, and east on Addison. I stop at the corner of Addison and Third where I can view the Dodge van half a block away. I see three men sitting inside the vehicle. I know they are three of the four men who raped me. The fourth is inside Terri's Restaurant drinking coffee.

I reach inside my purse and my thumb finds the safety on the Beretta and flips the safety lever up. There is already one nine-millimeter round in the chamber. The Beretta 92 is double action, and I don't need to cock the hammer. When I pull the trigger, the gun will discharge the round in the chamber, automatically eject the empty shell, and chamber another round.

How long does it take for a man to eat a slice of pie and drink a cup of coffee?

It's already nine-thirty. It feels good to know I'll have my revenge by ten. I have been patient so long that I've forgotten what it's like to feel excited. I feel my heart beat a mile a minute. Adrenalin courses through my bloodstream. I am ready to take my revenge on the men that raped me.

And then I see Pimples come out the door of Terri's Restaurant and walk toward the van. I turn right on Third Street and walk as fast as I can toward him. The Beretta is in my hand now. I pull the trigger.

My hand jerks as the weapon cycles. I fire again. Pimples now has two shattered kneecaps. He collapses to the sidewalk, screaming in pain.

I race to the driver's side of the van and shoot the leader through the window. I aimed down toward the driver's right leg, but I must have jerked the pistol in my excitement because the bullet hits the passenger's left leg instead.

The impact of the bullet shatters the safety glass in the window and I watch jagged glass fragments pelt the face and body of the driver. Blood oozes from his left eye and from cuts on his cheek and forehead. This time when I aim to shoot the driver in the leg, I hit what I'm aiming at. Both men in the front seat writhe in pain. The bearded man in the back seat has opened the rear door on the other side and is scrambling to get out of the car. When he stands up and takes two steps onto the sidewalk, I fire over the roof of the van and shoot the bearded man in the buttocks. He falls face forward onto the sidewalk, blood gushing from the hole in his butt.

I drop the gun into my purse and grab the butcher knife. I stab the driver in the groin so hard the knife gets stuck inside his body. I wiggle the knife, but it won't pull out. I must act fast because I know people inside the restaurant have heard gunshots and someone will call the police, if they haven't already. If I'm going to do all four men, I will have to forget the knife and switch to the box cutter and the pinking shears.

Who should I do next? The passenger? The bearded man I shot in the butt? Pimples still moaning and crying where he fell to the sidewalk and can't stand up because both knees are gone?

I decide the red-haired passenger should be next. I start around the rear of the van to reach the passenger in the passenger seat.

"Police officer," a woman's voice shouts. "Don't move or I'll shoot!"

I see the man I thought was the rapists' friend standing outside the door to the restaurant. Next to him is the petite red-headed woman. She holds a tiny pistol—it looks like a toy compared to my Beretta—in her right hand and a police badge in her left.

I won't shoot a woman. Will a woman shoot me?

I can't allow myself to die until my revenge is complete. I want to finish what I've started and castrate each and every one of the rapists. But I know if I try to cut them now, I'll be dead before I do even one.

So I don't try. I've been patient this long, I can be patient a little longer. I'm nothing if not patient.

Before the female police officer can shoot, I duck down behind the van and half-run, half-limp, toward Addison. I keep parked cars between me and the woman with the gun. I move as fast as my left leg will allow.

Neither the petite woman nor the man with her attempt to pursue me. The woman uses her cell phone to call for assistance, and the man kneels next to Pimples and tries to stanch the blood flowing from the two bullet holes where Pimples' knees used to be.

I'm dressed in all black tonight, and Addison Avenue is relatively dark, lit only with a single sodium vapor street light in the middle of the block. I disappear into the shadows as I hear approaching sirens in the distance.

All four of the rapists are in pain, but three of the four will likely survive. I buried the nine-inch butcher knife deep inside the leader's pelvis. His lap was covered in blood, and I'm fairly certain I cut some vital organs when I reached inside the open window with the butcher knife and rammed it in a downward arc toward his privates. Did I sever his penis? His scrotum? I only know I buried the knife so deep inside him, he'll bleed like a stuck pig if anyone tries to get it out. If I didn't kill him, he'll die before he reaches a hospital. He got off easy.

But I'll make certain none of the others get away that easy. I'll wait until hell freezes over to finish the job. I'm nothing if not patient.

Meanwhile, I can take care of their friend, the man with the eyeglasses I saw standing on the sidewalk next to the police woman. I know what kind of car he drives—a Jeep Wagoneer—and I know where it's parked. I have the license number. I'll learn where he lives, and I'll kill him in his own home.

I feel a cold wind cut through me despite two layers of heavy cotton, and I shiver. But the night is still young yet, and I have much to do before I can sleep. I need to find a place out of the wind where I can hide and also watch the rapists' friend, the man with the glasses. I intend to follow him when he leaves.

I walk north on Second Street four or five blocks, then east until I'm back on Third. I cross Third Street and duck into the recessed doorway of an office across from the Twin Rivers *Gazette*. From here, I can see all the way down Third Street to Terri's Restaurant six blocks away. I take the binoculars out of my purse. Now I can watch what's happening as police cars and an ambulance arrive.

More police cars, their sirens screaming and their flashing red and blue lights an epileptic's nightmare, come from all directions at once. I'm far enough away to be outside the blockade—stings of yellow crime scene tape tied to plastic saw horses—that diverts traffic from Third Street onto Fourth. I see the coroner's van. That means at least one of the rapists is dead.

I should feel elated, but suddenly I feel sick. I haven't eaten much today. I had a small bowl of Ramen soup this afternoon, but that's all

I've eaten in twenty-four hours. I haven't slept. When the adrenalin rush ended, my body wanted to collapse.

And now I can really feel the cold seep into my bones. My face hurts where my nose and cheekbones were broken, and pain radiates from my pelvis down my right leg. Fortunately, I can't feel the pain in my left leg. I still feel cold and pain in the rest of my body even if I can't feel much else.

I see uniformed policemen with flashlights combing the sidewalks for clues. There are a handful of detectives, too, looking at the bodies on the sidewalk and in the Dodge van. A tall detective talks with the petite policewoman and the rapists' friend. I may need to find another hiding place if the police decide to continue their search for the woman who fired the shots that killed at least one man and wounded the others.

I see lights on in the *Gazette* office across the street. Are they open this late at night? I use the binoculars to look into the windows. The bottoms of the windows are covered with the pages of last Wednesday's edition for passing pedestrians to view ads. Tomorrow someone will change those pages for the latest edition. I see no one inside, but I see plenty of places I could hide in the *Gazette* office.

I take a chance and hobble across the street. I turn the door handle and the door opens. I hear tiny jingling sounds as I push the door open enough to enter. I take the Beretta out of my purse. If there is anyone in the back rooms, they'll hear the door chimes and come to see who just came in. When no one appears from the back rooms, I open those doors and look. I see a mattress on the floor where someone sleeps, and I see a shower stall, a toilet, and a sink. There is a small refrigerator and a hot plate and a Mr. Coffee and a microwave. Someone obviously lives here, but they're not home at the moment.

It feels good to be out of the wind. I think I'll stay here until it's safe to wander the streets again. If anyone enters, I'll hear the door chimes.

I collapse on the mattress and close my eyes. I see the four rapists bleeding. I see the leader sitting in the front seat of the van with glass in his eye and a sharp knife rammed between his legs. I see Pimples on the sidewalk bleeding from the knees. I see the bearded man bleeding from the butt. I see the red-haired man with a hole in his left leg. A smile crosses my lips. Now they know pain.

I was impressed by how easily I handled the Beretta and how accurately I shot. Only once did I miss what I aimed at, and that stray bullet hit my next target as if I had aimed at the passenger's leg instead of the driver's. All those hours of dry-fire practice paid off. Now I know I can shoot as well as any man.

If a man enters the newspaper office, I will shoot him, too. Or maybe I will hold the gun on him while I wrap duct tape around his wrists, then herd him into the back room where I can give him pain.

I hold that thought in my head as I drift off to sleep.

CHAPTER TWENTY-EIGHT

"It was Megan Williams, I'm sure of it," Tim told Giffords.

"She had a gun?"

"A nine-millimeter," said Elsie. "I could tell by the sound. Larger than a .38 and smaller than a .45. Maybe a 9-mil Sig Sauer or a Beretta. It didn't sound like a Glock."

"You were in the restaurant when you heard the shots?"

"We were just leaving," said Tim. "We recognized the man she shot in both knees as one of the men who allegedly raped Megan Williams four years ago. We were following him to his car."

"It all happened so fast," said Elsie. "We came out the door and saw a woman limping toward him and then we heard the shots. She fired twice in rapid succession."

"Then she ran around to the driver's side of the van and fired again," said Tim. "We heard two more shots, then a third."

"That's when I drew my back-up gun and badge from my purse. I identified myself as a police officer."

"And then she just disappeared," said Tim. "Poof! Gone! She was wearing that damned black hoodie. I couldn't see her in the dark."

"I saw her run behind parked cars, but I couldn't get a clear shot," said Elsie. "I didn't realize a cripple could run that fast. I called dispatch for backup and an ambulance."

"We tried to stop the bleeding of the man who lost his knees. He was really bleeding bad. I asked Elsie to help stop the bleeding. Both knees were gushing bright red blood."

"He would have bled out if I had attempted to pursue the suspect instead of stopping to help," said Elsie.

"You did the right thing," said Giffords.

"The man in the driver's seat did die," said Elsie. "He was shot and stabbed and his face was cut by flying glass. His left eye was punctured. He was dead when the paramedics reached him."

"I'm sure they're the men who raped Megan Williams," Tim said. "All four of them. They match the descriptions Megan gave when she came out of her coma."

"If they're the same men," Giffords said, "we'll match their DNA with what we found at various crime scenes. Megan Williams may have done us a favor by getting them off the street. But now we have to find her. Any idea which way she might have gone?"

"East on Addison," said Elsie. "She moved like a shadow from behind the parked cars and dashed from Third to Addison."

Giffords keyed a hand-held radio and gave Megan's description and direction to patrol units. "We'll get her," he told Tim and Elsie. "It's only a matter of time. Now that we know who we're looking for, we'll find her. She can't get far on foot with a bad leg."

Ambulances had already removed the three injured men from the crime scene to the hospital, and the coroner was in the process of bagging the dead man still in the van. Tim had taken photographs with his cell phone, and he planned to run the pictures in next week's edition of the *Gazette*. It was too late to stop the presses on tomorrow's paper. By next Wednesday, he hoped Megan would be in custody and he could write a big fat final -30- to the violence that plagued Twin Rivers.

"That's all I need from the two of you," said Giffords. "Why don't you go home and get some sleep? All we have left to do is find all the spent brass. You said you heard five or six shots?"

"Five," said Tim.

"I heard six," said Elsie.

"I can't leave," said Tim. He pointed to the Wagoneer. "That's my car, and my car is boxed in"

"Mine, too," said Elsie.

"It may be a couple of hours yet before we get the van and all the emergency vehicles out of the way," said Giffords. "It's too cold for the two of you to stand around out here waiting. Why don't you go back inside the restaurant and warm up. Maybe have a cup of coffee. I'll let you know when the street's cleared."

Tim and Elsie agreed. They went back inside Terri's, found the same booth they had before was empty, and sat down where they had sat before.

"Lots of excitement," Dottie said as she brought them coffee. "Is it true a man was killed right outside our door?"

"Yes," said Tim. "The street's all blocked off. You probably won't have a lot of business until the barricades are removed."

Tim doctored his coffee with sugar and cream. He took a sip of the coffee and noticed Susan Williams standing idly behind an almost empty counter. It was the first time he hadn't seen her busy with customers. "How do we tell her Megan just shot four men?" Tim asked Elsie.

"Better we tell her than she hear about it on the news," said Elsie. "Let's go talk with her"

They carried their coffees to the counter in the back of the restaurant. When they were seated, Tim motioned to Susan to come over and talk.

"I'm afraid I have some bad news for you about Megan," Tim said.

"Oh, my God! What happened? Is she hurt? Is she dead?"

"No, she's very much alive. But she killed a man tonight and wounded three others right outside this restaurant."

"Not Megan! She wouldn't hurt a fly."

"She shot the four men who raped her four years ago," Tim said. "She killed one of them, and she sent the other three to the hospital."

"No! Megan wouldn't do that."

"We saw her," said Elsie. "It was definitely your sister. We also have multiple video recordings that show her getting into a car with Rodney Engleworth one hour before Engleworth was murdered last Thursday. We believe she killed Rodney Engleworth, Benjamin Willard, and William Murphy, as well as one of the men she shot tonight."

"Oh, my God!"

"Police are hunting for her all over town," said Tim. "If she tries to contact you, you must urge her to surrender to the police. She needs help, Susan. The police don't want to harm her, but they may have to if she doesn't surrender. Please try to convince her to give herself up. She'll get a fair trial, and she'll have a complete physical and psychiatric evaluation before she goes to trial. If she's found incompetent to stand trial, she'll be sent someplace where she'll get the help she needs."

"I haven't seen or talked to my sister in nearly a year. What makes you think she'll try to contact me?"

"She's been coming into Terri's Restaurant almost every day that you've worked," said Tim. Megan thinks she's protecting you."

"I haven't seen her."

"You have, but you didn't recognize her. She's the girl who hides her face under a hoodie."

"No. It isn't possible. Don't you think I'd know my own sister if I saw her?"

"Think about it, Susan. Megan had extensive plastic surgery, much of it completed after you last saw her. She also walks with a limp because the nerves to her left leg were severed and her left leg drags behind the right. So, even if you saw Megan's face, you probably wouldn't recognize it. But I don't think you've seen her face, have you? She's always kept it hidden beneath a hood or a scarf and dark glasses."

Susan collapsed against the counter behind her containing clean coffee cups and several Bunn burners, knocking three coffee cups to the floor where they shattered into pieces.

Elsie went around the front counter to steady Susan before Susan collapsed all the way to the floor. "Can I get you a glass of water?" Elsie asked Susan. "Why don't you go out there and sit down for a minute. I'll bring you a glass of water." Elsie led Susan around the front counter and seated her next to Tim. Tim put his arm around Susan to steady her on the stool.

"I'm sorry, Susan," he said. "I didn't want to believe it either. No one did. That's why Megan could keep on killing. Nobody suspected she was capable of murder."

"She…she…changed," Susan whispered. "What those men did to her changed her. They changed everything. It's not fair."

"No," Tim said. "It's not fair."

Elsie handed Susan a glass of water. "I worked as a waitress when I was in college," Elsie said. "When you've worked behind one diner counter, you can find your way around another easy enough. You just sit there, Susan. If any customers come, I'll take care of them. You get off at midnight, don't you?"

"Yes," Susan said.

"It's a quarter to twelve. When your relief comes, I'll see you get home safely. Where's your car?"

"In the Metra parking lot."

"If my car isn't available by then, I'll drive you home in yours. I know where I can get a ride back here."

"I'll follow you and give you a ride back to your car," offered Tim.

"If my car is still blocked in, so is yours," Elsie said. "I'll have the stake-out boys give me a lift back here. Why don't you go home, Tim? You can walk the six blocks. You look like you could use the sleep."

"I could," Tim admitted. "I've never witnessed a murder before. Or seen so much blood. I guess I'm a little shook up."

"You did great," Elsie said. "Where did you learn to apply pressure to the femoral artery to stop bleeding?" she asked. "You handled those gunshot wounds like a trained first responder. That kid would have bled out on the sidewalk if you hadn't intervened."

"Boy scouts," Tim said. "I earned a first aid merit badge."

"You were a boy scout?"

"Yeah. I was an Eagle Scout."

Elsie smiled. "Well, Mr. Boy Scout, you did good tonight. Now go home and get some sleep. I'll see Susan home, come back to pick up my car, and go home to get some sleep myself."

"All right," Tim agreed. "I'll have a busy day tomorrow delivering all the papers by myself. I don't have Rod to help me."

Tim wanted to kiss Elsie goodnight, but now was not the time nor place. "Why don't you stop by the *Gazette* office after you retrieve your car," Tim suggested. "I'd like to say goodnight before you go home. I'll wait up for you."

"We'll see," said Elsie. "If I'm not there in an hour, I'll stop by your office in the morning. Giffords will want both of us to sign written statements about tonight's events. I'll pick you up on my way to work. Is that okay?"

"Sure," said Tim, disappointed. He walked back to the booth and retrieved his overcoat. Then he walked out the door and began the six block walk back to his office.

CHAPTER TWENTY-NINE

I hear the door chimes jingle, and I'm instantly awake. I know someone has entered by the front door. I hear the chimes jingle again as that someone closes the door. I peek out from the back room and I see you standing there. I can't believe my luck. Tonight must be my lucky night.

Is this your home? Is this where you live? Or did you follow me?

If this is your home, then you live a lot like me. You don't have a lot of money to spend on clothes or furnishings. You live in a small two-room, and you sleep on a twin-sized mattress on the floor because you can't afford to buy a bed and you wouldn't have room for a bed even if you could afford one.

Should I shoot you now? No, there are too many cops close enough to come running as soon as they hear a gunshot. Besides, didn't I see you make Susan cry? Don't you deserve to suffer? I don't want to shoot you unless I have to. Shooting is much too good for you.

But I can use the gun to make you let me bind your wrists with duct tape. I can use the gun to order you into this back room and lie down on the mattress. Then I will put the gun away and take out my other tools.

You don't look surprised when you see me step out of the back room. You see the gun, and that doesn't surprise you either. I'm the one surprised when I hear you say, "Hello, Megan. I want to talk with you. You already hurt Susan with your actions tonight Do you want to hurt her even more?"

I hurt Susan? Never! I love my sister. I would never hurt her.

"Susan is worried about you. She wants you to give yourself up and get help. Why don't you put that gun down and come with me to see Susan? Let her tell you herself."

You lie. All men lie. You want to hurt Susan. You want to hurt me. I saw you make Susan cry. You're no better than that old man. All men are alike. I won't listen to you.

"I want to tell your story, Megan. I want people to know what happened to you and why you did what you did. I want Susan to know. I want everyone to know you're an innocent victim and not a cold-blooded killer. Susan doesn't want you to die, Megan. Susan saved you once. She wants to save you again. She loves you. She doesn't want her only sister to die after all you and she have been through together. If you die, Susan will be hurt. She'll never recover from the hurt your death would cause her. She'll live in pain for the rest of her life."

Shut up, damn you. I don't want to hear any more. It's your fault I am who I am. You, and men like you, made me a hateful person.

"I want to tell your story, Megan. Look. I'll show you. I've already started to tell your story. Just step over to that desk and move the mouse. Read what's on the computer screen. That's what will appear in tomorrow's paper. Even if you kill me, that story will appear. It's already at the printer. But the story isn't finished. It's not complete. It doesn't tell your side of the story. I want to print your side of the story in future editions, Megan. If you kill me, who will tell your side of the story?"

I keep the gun aimed at the man as I step behind the desk and move the mouse. The front page of the *Twin Rivers Gazette* appears on the screen. The headline reads, "Megan Missing" and below that are multiple subheads that read, "Megan Wanted for Murder" and "Is Megan Innocent or Guilty?" I see two pictures of me. One is me from my high school yearbook, before I was raped. The other is a picture of me after I changed.

I read the story written by Rodney Engleworth, the old man I killed. He quotes Susan telling him that she's worried about Megan. He tells about the men who raped me and alleges the same men may have also raped and murdered at least sixteen other women. He cites Sergeant Joel Giffords of the Twin Rivers Police Department and the regional task force saying police have DNA evidence linking the rapes and murders to the same four men. He implies the mutilations and murders of Benjamin Willard and William Murphy were done by a female copy-cat killer inspired by the rape of Megan Williams.

I skip past the ads to find where the story is continued. I find four pages in the middle of the paper dedicated to the memory of Rodney Engleworth. I see pictures of the old man and his wife looking happy together. I read about Helen's death and I read the final "Reminiscences of Helen" column Engleworth wrote after she died, telling about her pain and his. He ends the column by saying he looks forward to the day he's reunited with his wife in death. "I am seventy years old," he writes. "I can be patient. I won't have long to wait."

Now I know why the old man didn't struggle much. He didn't fear death but looked forward to seeing his wife again after he died. I feel tears creep from my eyes. I was wrong to kill the old man the way I did. He still loved his wife. He didn't want to rape Susan but only wanted to help Susan find her sister. That's why he talked to Susan every day. He didn't make Susan cry. Susan cried because of me.

I find the rest of the story in the back pages. I find a new column by Timothy Goodman, editor and publisher of the *Twin Rivers Gazette*. It's entitled "Megan's Story" and it ends with "To be continued."

The man in front of me, the man I wanted to kill, didn't lie. Was I so blinded by hate that I couldn't tell a lie from the truth? What's wrong with me?

My eyes fill with tears and I cry for the first time in a long time. I lower the gun because I can no longer see clearly enough to aim.

The man doesn't move. He knows better than to try to touch me. He just stands there while I sob uncontrollably.

I hear the chimes jingle as the front door opens. I can barely see through my tears. The red-haired policewoman stands in the open doorway with a surprised look on her face.

I hear her say, "Police officer, drop the gun or I'll shoot," but I'm still crying and the words don't mean much even when she repeats them again. I raise my hands to surrender, to give myself up, but I still have the Beretta in my right hand and the policewoman sees my right hand come up with the Beretta still in it and she doesn't notice my empty left hand also lifting.

I hear the man shout, "No! Don't shoot!"

I feel the bullet smash into my body but I cannot feel the pain. Suddenly, everything goes dark.

I disappear into the dark as if I never existed.

CHAPTER THIRTY

I awake in the hospital. I feel as if I have been here before because I have. Am I dead? Am I reliving past events as if they are happening now?

I see Susan sitting beside the bed. She came every day to visit me in the hospital while I was in a coma, and she never gave up on me. She was there when I awoke last time.

She knows the terrible things I have done, and yet she is here with me. It was I who turned away from her, drove her away from me. I couldn't bear to see the pain on her face each time she looked at me.

I love my sister. I would do anything for her, and she would do anything for me. I never meant to hurt her when I killed those men. I thought I was protecting Susan. I did protect her. If I hadn't been in that apartment when the four men came to rape her, they would have done her instead of me.

And they would have tried again to rape her if I hadn't been watching. I saved her when I shot the four rapists outside Terri's Restaurant. I am not sorry I shot those four men. They deserved to die.

But I am sorry I killed the old man. Rodney Engleworth didn't deserve to die the way he did.

Susan isn't the only one in the hospital room with me. I see Timothy Goodman, editor and publisher of the *Twin Rivers Gazette* standing next to Susan, and the red-haired police woman who shot me stands there, too, right next to Goodman. They hold hands.

I want to tell the policewoman that I don't blame her. She acted in self-defense. How could she know I would never shoot a woman?

"Don't try to talk," says Goodman when he sees my lips move but no words come out. "Elsie shot you in the chest and one of your lungs is collapsed. When you've had a chance to heal, I'll come back and let you tell me your story. I want to hear everything, and I promise to publish what you say word for word."

"You're going to be just fine," says the red-haired policewoman Goodman called Elsie. "My back-up gun is a .32, and I had it loaded with standard ball ammunition and not hollow-points. If I'd had a nine-millimeter or used hollow-points, you wouldn't have survived. Tim stopped the bleeding and I called an ambulance to rush you to surgery. Doctors expect you'll recover completely. You may be a little short of breath because of only one lung, but you'll learn to compensate with time."

"And Mr. Goodman and Miss Dorr—Tim and Elsie—hired a good defense attorney for you, Megan," says Susan. "Your lawyer plans to plead temporary insanity. He says no jury in the world will convict you after what you went through. Isn't that great? You may have to spend some time in a hospital—a mental hospital—but as soon as doctors certify you're well, he expects you'll be released."

That's wonderful, I want to tell Susan. I've spent time in hospitals before. I know how to be a patient and how to be patient. I'm nothing if not patient.

And when I get out of the hospital, I'll be waiting for the three men who raped me to get out of prison. I'll buy another gun and pinking shears and a box-cutter and a butcher knife. I can start all over again as I did the last time I got out of the hospital. I'll wait for however long it takes. I can be patient.

I'm nothing if not patient.

ABOUT THE AUTHOR

Paul Dale Anderson

has written more than 27 novels and hundreds of short stories, mostly in the thriller, mystery, horror, fantasy, and science fiction genres. Paul is the author of *Claw Hammer, Daddy's Home, Pickaxe, Icepick, Meat Cleaver, Axes to Grind, Pinking Shears, Deviants, Running Out of Time, Impossible, Abandoned, Winds, Darkness, Mysterious Ways, Light* and the critically-acclaimed Instruments of Death crime-suspense novels from Crossroad Press.

Visit Paul's web pages for more information:

www.pauldaleanderson.net

www.4windsnovels.com

amazon.com/author/pauldaleanderson

Paul has also written contemporary romances and westerns. Paul is an Active Member of SFWA and HWA, and he was elected Vice President and Trustee of Horror Writers Association in 1987. He is a current member of International Thriller Writers, Author's Guild, and a former Active Member of MWA.

Paul has taught creative writing at the University of Illinois at Chicago and for Writers Digest School. He has appeared on panels at Chicon4 and Chicon7, X-Con, Windy Con, Madcon, Odyssey Con, Minncon, the World Horror Convention, and the World Fantasy Convention. Paul was a guest of honor at Horror Fest in Estes Park, Colorado, in 1989. He is currently the chair of the 2015 HWA Stoker Awards Long Fiction Jury.

Paul is also an NGH Certified Hypnotist, an NGH Certified Hypnotism Instructor, a certified Past-Life Regression Therapist, and an IBRT certified professional member of the International Association for Regression Research and Therapies.

Be sure to read these other exciting novels by Paul Dale Anderson

Claw Hammer

Daddy's Home

Pickaxe

Icepick

Abandoned

Winds

Darkness

Light

Meat Cleaver

Axes to Grind

www.ingramcontent.com/pod-product-compliance
Lightning Source LLC
Chambersburg PA
CBHW020440270626
47155CB00022B/693